A MAN CALLED BOX

TINA CLOUGH

A MAN CALLED BOX

Copyright © Tina Clough 2025

PAPERBACK ISBN: 978-1-7386272-6-4

The author asserts her moral right to be identified as the author of this work.

All rights reserved. No part of this book may be reproduced, stored in a retrieval system, or transmitted in any form or by any electronic or mechanical means including photocopying, recording, information or retrieval systems, or otherwise, without prior permission in writing from the publisher, with the exception of book reviewers, who may quote short excerpts in reviews.

Disclaimer

The places in this book are real places in New Zealand, but the characters and businesses were created the author and are entirely fictional.

A catalogue record of this book is available from the National Library of New Zealand

Lightpool Publishing

www.lightpoolpublishing.com

Cover Photo: Tina Clough

1

Just before ten on a chilly Thursday night Sam turned the TV off and went to check that the kitchen door was locked before going to bed. She knew she had locked it, there was nobody else in the house, but just like every other night she did it again. And of course the door was locked, as it always was after dark. She knew that Dave was right, and she should move into town instead of living alone in this big house on the very outskirts of their suburb, the house that had been her mother's, with a long driveway from the street. Now that she had settled down after the shock of Dave leaving her she should get organised and do the sensible thing, sell this house and buy a unit in town. Looking back she could see that staying here after he left had been like hiding in a familiar environment, reluctant to face change.

She was heading to the bathroom when a knock on the front door made her jump. In the dark hall she stopped where the light from the outside lantern didn't spill in far enough through the window to reach her. On the front step stood a stranger supporting himself with one hand flat against the wall and the other raised as if to knock again. Cautiously she approached the window and peered out. Why had he come up her long, dark driveway? He looked exhausted, too tired to climb in the window, she decided, and opened it a crack with a firm grip on the latch.

'What do you want?' She studied his face and knew she was right. He was nearly spent, ready to drop to the ground.

'Please help me!' His hoarse whisper was desperate. 'Please! If they find me they'll kill me.'

'Who's going to kill you?'

'Please let me in!' His whispered plea was that of a man fearing for his life.

Should she? In undecisive turmoil she was silent for a few moments, but suddenly he sagged against the wall, nearly unable to stand and she knew she had to do something.

'I'll open the garage door, just to your left,' she said quickly. 'I'll open it from inside.'

She ran down the hallway, flung open the connecting door and raced to the button beside the folding door. The stranger stumbled in and leaned against the side of her car panting and coughing. God, the poor man, he looked ready to fall over. Quickly she pressed the button again and kept an eye on the driveway until the door was down, then she turned and looked properly at him. A middle-aged man, dressed in jeans and a casual jacket, a very ordinary looking man who would be hard to describe.

'OK, you can stay here,' she said. 'I'll get my phone and call the police. Sit down on that chair before you fall over.' She pointed at the kitchen chair she kept beside the washing machine.

'Please, no - don't call the police!' he said urgently. 'I'm not dangerous, I haven't done anything wrong, please don't call them!' He clutched his side and bent over coughing. 'I just need a place to hide for a few hours.'

'You need to sit down!' said Sam firmly. 'Of course I'll call the cops if someone's trying to kill you. Hiding here until morning isn't going to solve anything, is it?'

He stumbled towards the chair and sat down, leaned back for a moment with his eyes closed and Sam hoped he wasn't going to faint and fall to the floor.

'If you call them I'm dead,' he said, speaking more normally now and no longer panting. 'I think they've hacked my phone or how would they know I was ...'

Once again he stopped, then he took a deep breath. 'Listen!' he said after a long pause while Sam silently watched him, unsure of what to do. 'I'll tell you a bit, just the basics, so you know I'm innocent and why you absolutely can't call police.'

He's knocked his head in some accident, thought Sam, as he gingerly touched the side of his head. And now he's confused and scared at the same time. But I'll humour him for a while and let him calm down.

'OK,' she said and tried to sound casually interested instead of worried and doubtful. 'Tell me why I shouldn't call the police.'

'I was on my way to deliver evidence of something very serious – let's call it a network of corruption. I took a taxi because they've been following my car for a couple of days. I thought they'd put a tracking device on it.' His voice was growing stronger, and he sat up straight. 'But now I think they probably hacked my phone, or how would they have known I was in that taxi? I sent a text to my contact this morning and we agreed to meet at half past ten tonight. He flew up from Wellington after work to meet me.

'And then? Why did you come up this long, dark driveway and knock on my door? What happened out there?'

'They rammed the taxi a couple of hundred metres down the street, and we crashed into a tree. They would have got me then, but there was a party in a house just where we crashed, and a whole crowd came rushing outside.' He shook his head and winced, touched the side of his head again. 'The driver was injured, so I managed to get out and get away while they were all busy calling the ambulance and looking after him. I took off up the road and saw this driveway between other houses and thought it looked like a good place to hide.'

'OK,' said Sam slowly. 'So those guys that rammed your taxi – who are they?'

'Either police, or someone hired by them.' He took in her look of shocked surprise. 'Yeah, I know, it sounds crazy, but it's true. Will you let me stay here for a while?'

'All right. That little light that came on when I opened the door will go off soon, it's automatic. But you can turn on the ceiling lights if you want to.' She pointed at the switch by the door to the passage. 'You're safe here. I'm going to go back into the house now. Maybe you should sit in the car and be comfortable instead of sitting on that chair.'

'You won't call them, will you? I'll leave as soon as it's safe and I've had a rest, I promise.'

'That corruption network you mentioned – are cops involved in that?'

'They're all police – my friend and I say it's like a cabal of corruption.'

She was just about to leave when he said, 'And just so you know they won't come here – if they're tracking my phone, I mean. I turned it off as I ran from the accident and threw it into some bushes about halfway from the crash to your driveway. I'll find it when I leave.'

'You look as if you need a good rest - don't leave until you feel OK.'

He smiled weakly. 'If you really don't mind, I'll sit in the car for a while, and then I'll leave as soon as I feel rested.'

When she moved her arm as if to turn the ceiling light on, he shook his head. 'No, don't, leave it off, please. I need a rest, I think I might have as nap. I feel exhausted now.'

She left him there and closed the connecting door, slid the bolt home and stood still to listen for a moment. Well, at least he can see, she told herself, and if he didn't trust her not to call the police he could press the button on the wall and open the garage door again, it was his choice. She was relieved at how much he had improved in the last few minutes, so there was no need to check on him.

In the kitchen she turned the electric jug on and tried to make sense of what had just happened. A man on the run, with what he said was evidence of serious corruption – but could she believe him? He didn't seem dangerous, she thought, and then she nearly laughed at herself. How would she know if he was dangerous? He might have killed someone, or he could be a drug dealer on the run, or perhaps he had fallen out with criminals, maybe all he told her was lies. But she felt very strongly that his plea not to call the police was not based on lies, though what had given her this impression she couldn't say. She studied her reflection in the window above the bench while her teabag soaked and thought she looked calm, which was surprising and pleasing at the same time. There was no need to decide what to do right now, she had plenty of time. He couldn't get into the house, and if he changed his mind and was still there in the morning, she would make up her mind then about what to do. He might well leave quite soon, as he had said, because he had recovered remarkably quickly once he sat down.

On her way to the living room she made a detour to the hall and saw that there was no light showing in the crack under the door to the garage. He'll be OK in the car, much warmer, she told herself, and then he'll open the door and leave when he feels better.

Ten minutes later she was sitting in the living room with the curtains pulled across the windows and the untouched mug of tea beside her, carrying on an inner debate. Did it matter that she had more or less promised not to call the police? Her strong belief that he wasn't a criminal was only based on than the way he had come across, like a normal person nearly scared out of his wits. But he couldn't get into the house, so whoever he was he was not able to harm her.

She picked up her book, and failed to take in a single word, distracted by what she had just heard and wondered if his story was true. When the doorbell went half an hour later she was jolted out of her thoughts. This might be serious trouble, but until she knew who was at the door all she could do was stay calm and act as normal as possible. She slid the phone into her back pocket and walked down the hallway without turning the lights on. In the dark guest room she leaned out of the window and saw two men waiting by the front door.

'Yes? Can I help you?' she called. 'You'll have to come to the window if you want to talk to me, I'm not opening the door at this time of night.'

'Sorry to disturb you,' said one, 'but we saw the light was on in your garage, so we thought someone was up. We're police.'

'Have you heard anyone around the house in the last hour or so?' asked the other, a tall, skinny man. 'We're looking for a guy who might be injured. Is it all right for us to have a look around outside?'

They probably are who they say they are, she thought, but they're not in uniform. Maybe it would be a good idea to adopt a disguise. I'll be a timid woman, a bit nervous and uncertain, like that role I had in the Little Playhouse comedy a couple of years ago, Johanna, the silly woman, because I need time to think. Are these two genuinely trying to find that guy to help him, did someone in that crowd at the accident scene report him having taken off, or are they after him to kill him?

'I don't know,' she said indecisively and found herself slipping into the Johanna persona without consciously trying, even her voice took on a slightly higher note. 'It seems so odd. I'm not sure – I mean, how do I know you're really police when you're not in uniform? I mean, you could be … anyone.'

'Of course, I apologise, we should have shown you ID right away, particularly at this time of night. Are you alone in the house?' The tall man fished around inside his jacket and held up a little wallet, and the light from the lantern was just enough to show the blue and gold shield she recognised.

'What's he done?' she asked. 'Is he dangerous? Oh no! What if he gets into the house? I'm alone here, I wouldn't know what to do!'

'We have a warrant for his arrest. He crashed his car just down the road, but he managed to get away, so we're going around the houses here, he can't have got far on foot. If you're ok with it, we'll have a look around your property. But there's no need for you to worry, he's not a risk to you. If you want us to, we can come in and make sure he hasn't got into the house somehow, so you can relax, but we'll look around outside first.' He pulled a flashlight out of his pocket and nudged his colleague who did the same.

Any of it could be lies, she knew, either what the man in the garage had told her or what these two had just said. There was no way she could be sure who was telling the truth, but saying the man had crashed his car was probably a lie, when he had told her he was in a taxi. She stayed where she was and watched them disappear around the house towards the back garden, one in each direction, as if ready to cut off someone trying to make a run for it. A few minutes later they were back at the guest room widow.

'There's no sign of anyone in your garden,' said the taller man. 'Would you like us to check inside?'

Sam made a quick decision to let them in. It would be an opportunity to find out more, provided she did it right, to find out who was telling the truth. In her head she could nearly hear Dave saying, 'For God's sake, Sam! Have you lost your mind? It doesn't matter what they're about, just let them go. You don't want to be involved in this, whatever it is.'

'OK, I think I'd like you to come in,' she said in her hesitant Johanna voice. 'You know, just so I know I'm safe. I've been standing here waiting for you to come around from the back just in case he's somewhere inside. I had just turned the TV off when you rang the doorbell, so I might not have heard anything. Someone coming in, I mean. Like through the toilet window. You know?'

'Let's start at this end,' said the tall man. 'If he's got inside somehow he wouldn't hide where you'd come across him.'

'Oh, thank you!' She went to open the front door, turned the hall light on and cast a glance down the passage to the garage. There was a strip of light under the connecting door, and she heaved a sigh of relief. She knew now why they had said the light was on - he must have opened the garage door and left just before those two arrived, and the automatic light was still on. Very lucky for him that they didn't meet on the driveway, and lucky for her that she could relax and consign this whole strange event to the past.

'Here we are.' She pulled the bolt back and opened the door and took an instinctive step back in surprise. The ceiling light was on, and her nameless visitor lay on his back beside her car, as if he'd fallen without trying to catch himself, with one arm out to the side and a pool of blood under his head. His wide open eyes looked unseeing straight up at the bright fluorescent light. He was dead.

'Oh, no! How did he get in here? Is he dead? Oh, I can't look!' Even in her state of shock and surprise she noticed that the Johanna persona was still functioning, which seemed unreal. She took another couple of stumbling steps backwards and both men pushed past her and crouched beside the man on the floor.

2

For a moment Sam stood as if frozen to the spot and stared at the scene lit by the overhead light. One of the two men, who now crouched beside the dead man, said in a low voice, 'Listen, I'll have to go and talk to her. Check his pockets and have a good look around, search the car too – we know he had it with him.'

Before he got to his feet, Sam turned and walked quietly back along the passage to the front hall and waited, worried now and unwilling to let him see that she had heard his comment.

'I'm sergeant Brown, Gareth Brown,' said the tall man when he joined her. 'I'm so sorry this has happened in your home. Is there somewhere we can sit down for a moment and talk?'

'Come into the kitchen, so we can get away from ... all that.' She walked ahead of him turned the kitchen light on. 'I'll just get myself a glass of water. Do you want one?'

'No, thanks. I'm sorry you had to see that. How do you think he got into the garage?'

Sam took a sip of water and studied him over the edge of the glass. A middle-aged, thin man with a receding hairline, who seemed surprisingly unconcerned, though seeing dead bodies was probably part of his job.

'I don't know,' she said slowly, as if she was thinking back. 'I didn't go back to the garage after I got home, I don't think – oh, I might have - no, I'm sure I didn't, that was yesterday. So if the door didn't go down properly when I got home I wouldn't have known.' She paused. 'I usually just click the remote on my keyring to lower the outer door as I go into the house.' She gave a little shudder the way Johanna would when faced with something scary. 'He must have come in and closed the door, there's a switch on the wall beside the door. And then he turned the light on, I suppose. Or perhaps I pressed the remote button accidentally when I put my stuff down inside and the door opened again ... I might have; I had a lot of things to carry. I wouldn't have known if the door was closed or not. God, it makes me feel terrified, think what he could have done!'

'We'll take care of it now,' said Brown comfortingly. 'But in this isolated house it might be a good idea to make sure that door is closed, don't you think? And maybe don't leave the toilet window open at night? We'll probably be an hour or two. Will you be ok on your own?'

'I'll sit in the living room and read. I couldn't go to bed until you've finished. I feel really unsettled now. I've never seen a dead body before. You will take him away, won't you?'

'Of course we'll take him away. We'll organise everything, you mustn't worry. I'll come and tell you when we're done, we won't be long.'

She watched him walk down the passage to the garage and remained standing by the kitchen table, deep in thought. She knew now that Brown was lying, and that probably meant that what the man in the garage had told her was true. Those half-whispered comments from Brown as they crouched beside the body, they could only mean one thing. It fitted the dead man's story, that he had been on his way to hand over evidence, whatever that meant, which was what Brown and his off-sider were looking for. And quite apart from that, this whole scenario was too casual and simple. She thought of scenes from the TV news when someone had been killed and how there was always a whole team of people in white overalls, a little tent erected over the body and vehicles lined up, police vans and cars. This was too simplistic, just two officers taking a body away and he'd said they would soon be done in an hour or two, or what that just a reassuring phrase? Maybe his companion was calling in reinforcements and forensic people were on the way. She must wait and see what transpired, and she must be careful not to let her Johanna personality slip because the implication of danger for herself could not be ignored. She was a witness to something that seemed irregular and potentially dangerous. Somehow she felt very strongly that the arrival or non-arrival of a forensic team would be a defining factor. She would have to be very careful in her dealings with Brown.

After a few minutes' thought she went to the bathroom and opened the window a crack without turning the light on. By putting her cheek against the glass and looking sideways she could see along the front of the house to where the driveway emerged from the trees. There was a dark vehicle that looked like a utility truck parked halfway down the drive, and in her mind it added another fact that confirmed that those two were not really police. Or maybe they were police and part of what the dead man had called a cabal.

If a real crime scene team turned up she wanted to be aware of it right away, and from the living room she wouldn't hear them coming, so she would stay in the bathroom with the window open. She wasn't sure why this felt important, but a bit of advance warning would help her prepare for more questions. She sat on the edge of the bath, got up now and then to peer out the window until about an hour later she heard the garage door open. She leapt to her feet and took up her stance with her cheek against the glass looking along the house and saw bright light flooding the gravel forecourt. The shorter man came out and moved the car right up to the house, a utility truck just like Dave's, with a lid over the tray. He got out and said something to Brown, who must have come to stand just inside the door; his long shadow stretched out to the truck and over it. Sam pushed the window out a bit further and turned her head to a different angle so she could hear better.

'What do you think?' said the man who had moved the truck. 'Load him now before we search a bit more?'

'Let's have another look in here first.' Brown's voice was harder to hear. 'He wouldn't have left it in the taxi, so it's got to be some-where – we just haven't found it.'

'He was running though.' The other man sounded frustrated, as if he had already said this more than once. 'And as I said, he was panicking, so he could have hidden it on the way up here to avoid being caught with it.'

'But where?' Brown sounded impatient. 'He wouldn't have put I down somewhere outside to be picked up later, would he?'

'It's what I would have done,' said his companion stubbornly. 'Think about it. You're running from danger, you have damning evidence in your pocket, and you need to get rid of it fast. I'd put it some place I could go back and find later, like beside a gatepost or a fence post or something.' Then he laughed briefly. 'Even if I knew I'd never get back to pick it up because I'd be dead. Maybe he put the phone down in the same place. We know he had it with him, after all.'

He folded the truck lid up and got a bundle of something out before he went into the garage and she could no longer hear what they said. Quietly she pulled the window nearly shut again to continue looking out, then suddenly she thought of what would happen if one of them came back into the house and caught her watching. Quickly she ran down the hallway to the garage door and slid the bolt across, then returned silently to the bathroom. A timid woman might feel uncomfortable with strangers having access to the house, and she could keep talking about the body and how scary it was, to make bolting the door seem a natural thing to do. Thank God, she had suddenly been inspired to assume Johanna's personality because without that as camouflage things would be much harder to deal with.

Back at the bathroom window she tried to ignore how uncomfortable it was to lean against the window with her head at an angle and waited, and after what seemed like an eternity the men emerged from the garage carrying a long, heavy object, one at each end. A body bag, she thought, that's what he took from the truck. Two police officers in an unmarked truck with a body bag at the ready and looking not just for the dead man, but for something he had with him? Once again the thought that they might not be police at all appeared in her mind, but for the moment she must take them at their word and wait to hear what they said when they were ready to leave. She watched them load the body on the truck and fold the lid down, and suddenly aware that they might be about to leave, she silently shut the window and went back to the living room, pacing restlessly, unable to sit down, waiting for what would happen next. Then there was a knock on the door from the garage.

'Can I come in? I won't be long, just a couple of minutes,' said

Brown apologetically and followed her into the hall. 'I just want to tell you a bit more about this before I leave. My colleague is cleaning up the blood.'

'Thank you,' said Sam. 'You will take him away, won't you?'

'Don't worry, he's gone, there's no need to worry. You're not in any danger.' A slight smile curved his mouth, and she could imagine exactly why. Such a timid woman, so easily scared, he would be thinking, and how easy it would be to make her believe what he was about to tell her. Because in Sam's mind there was not the slightest doubt that he would somehow attempt to explain their hasty retrieval of the body, make it sound acceptable.

'Thanks for cleaning up – I'm not good with blood and things, so I was going to ask my boyfriend to do it for me.'

Brown hesitated briefly. 'This is a bit tricky and not how we usually do things, but I have to tell you something very confidential, so you understand what's going on. We're part of a big drug investigation, which involves several cities and nearly a year's worth of undercover work. And so far we've kept it quiet, very quiet, so getting a civilian involved was the last thing we wanted.'

He reached for her hand and held it in both his, and she had to make an effort not to twitch it out of his grip. 'So here's what I want you to promise me, so we can avoid potentially derailing the whole investigation. *Don't* ask your boyfriend to clean up what's left of the blood stain and don't mention what happened tonight to *anyone*, not to him or any of your friends. It's very important – crucial – and I need your help in this.'

His eyes were fixed on hers as if he was making sure she took him seriously, and his grip on her hand tightened. 'It's vital to keep this under wraps, and now you are part of our team. Can you do this for me?'

She looked up at him and tried to make her voice slightly unsteady, as if she was scared and excited at the same time. 'Oh, yes! Of course I'll do that now that I know what you're doing.' She tried a little smile, still looking straight into his eyes. 'I thought it must be something secret like what you read about in the paper sometimes. I mean, you're not here with a whole team of people and all that stuff you see on TV. I knew it had to be something special.'

He squeezed her hand and inside she cringed at how unsettling this felt, and how his concern felt like a façade hiding something he didn't want her to see.

'Thank you!' he said and smiled that kind smile again. 'I'll get someone to deliver a little bag of cement powder first thing tomorrow morning, he'll put it outside the garage. You just wet the stain, spread the powder over it and kind of pat it down, then sweep it up before it dries completely. And make sure you use rubber gloves, so you don't get cement powder on your skin.' His thumb stroked her hand. 'If you do that there will only be a dark grey patch left that won't look like blood.'

Sam nodded silently, and he continued without pausing, still holding her hand. 'And thank you for being so calm. I know this has been an awful experience, but you've handled it really well, better than most people would have.'

'It's been horrid! And I'm sorry I locked the door before, but I just didn't feel comfortable. I'm not used to dead bodies and blood and things.'

'Of course. We're very grateful for your cooperation. Will you please come down to the garage and close the door after me?' He smiled and finally let go of her hand. 'And this time, make sure it's down.'

Sam watched the truck disappear down the driveway, closed the door and stood for a long time staring at the blood stain trying to imagine why the unknown man had died. He must have had a head injury she didn't see, perhaps that's why he touched the side of his head a couple of times. And then his head split open when he hit the concrete floor. She wondered what they had used to mop up the blood and looked around. The roll of kitchen paper she kept on the shelf beside the washing machine was nearly empty and her green bucket was no longer on the shelf by the door where she kept the mop. They had mopped up the worst with paper towels, and rubbed it a bit, there were tiny fragments of paper stuck on the stain, and then they put all the bloodied paper in the bucket and took it with them. Either because they didn't want to leave anything that related to the dead man in her house, or they thought she would find it upsetting. She turned the light off, bolted the door and went back to the kitchen.

With a fresh mug of tea clasped in both hands she sat at the kitchen table mentally going through everything that had been said from the time that man had knocked on the door to her final conversation with Brown. Neither the dead man nor the two who came later had mentioned what that evidence was, but it must be something like a USB stick or an external hard drive, she imagined, something that could be left lying on the ground to be picked up later. Something waterproof and small, not papers. And while she sat there thinking the image of Brown holding her hand crouched like an uneasy presence in the back of her mind. There was something about him, a hint of threat at odds with the façade of concern and kindness. She wasn't normally fanciful, and he had said nothing in the least harsh or like a warning, but she still felt he was dangerous.

It was now half past one in the morning, but she knew she wouldn't be able to go to sleep. She must take some time to consider what, if anything, she should do next and what might follow on from this strange and unsettling evening. Before she finally went to bed she sent two text messages.

Barry, I'm sorry to give such short notice but I can't come to work today (Fri). As you can see I'm sending this after midnight after a tummy upset. I'll see you on Monday. Sam

Jill, I won't make it for that drink after work tomorrow. I've got a vomiting bug so will stay home and take it easy. Sxx

3

A few days later Sam still found herself looking at the stain on the garage floor every time she got out of the car, as if acknowledging it somehow honoured that poor man. The little bag of cement was outside the garage door the morning after that awful night, and she had done exactly what Brown had told her to do. Now the stain looked as it had been there for years, just a dark patch on the concrete floor with no indication it had recently been covered in red blood. She couldn't bring herself to walk on it, so tonight she reversed the car in and got out on the far side, but she still glanced at the stain as she made her way into the house.

An hour later she was back in the garage with a load of washing in her arms. She threw the tomato sauce stained tea towel in the sink and loaded the rest into the washing machine, before she turned the cold tap on to soak the towel. When she lifted the tub of laundry powder it slipped from her wet hands, and she just managed to catch it before it hit the floor, and something knocked hard against the inside of the tub, something heavier than the plastic scoop. When she prised the lid off and stirred the powder with the scoop it hit something hard, a grey plastic box, a little bigger than a match box with no markings. Instantly her mind played back the conversation she had heard from the bathroom window when the stubborn man argued with Brown about something the dead man could have hidden, the evidence he himself had told her he had.

She saw it in her mind like a little video: The man remains on the chair beside the washing machine, then after a few minutes the automatic door light goes out. He rests for a while in the dark, then he gets up and feels around for the switch beside the passage door and turns on the ceiling light to find a good hiding place before he gets into the car. He looks around, scans the shelves and sees the tub of laundry powder. He pushes the little grey box down into the powder, so it's well hidden, then he replaces the tub on the shelf. He takes a few steps towards the car, faints and falls backwards, and his head hits the concrete floor hard. He lies there in the bright overhead light in a pool of slowly spreading blood and dies.

She knew this was right, it fitted all the facts. She must have checked in the interval between the automatic light going off and him turning on the big light, when there was no light showing under the door. Perhaps the dead man had planned to get it out and take it with him when he left, or maybe he didn't want to leave with it on him in case they caught him. He could have planned to come back for it later; there was no knowing. And when those two police officer said there was a light on, she had instantly assumed the man had opened the door and left, the way he had said he would. Instead he had turned on the ceiling light to find a place to hide the evidence and then fallen, and the light stayed on.

Sam blew the remains of laundry powder off the box and turned it over in her hand, found a little notch and opened it. The black object inside had a mini USB port on one side that looked as if the cable she used to connect her phone to her laptop would fit it. This was what they were after, the evidence about what the man who died had called the corruption cabal, a tiny hard drive, smaller than any of the several Dave used to back up projects on. Quickly she pushed it into her pocket and felt an urge to look over her shoulder, as if someone might be watching her. She threw some washing powder into the machine, started it and headed for the kitchen where her laptop was always on the table by the window, unable to wait a second longer.

As soon as the little device was plugged in a list of file icons appeared on the screen: Database Auckland, Database Auckland south, Database Hamilton, Database Tauranga, Database Wellington, Video 1 carpark meeting, Video 2 interview room meeting, Video 3 Pete's place, Names, Contacts. She opened the first file and started reading.

Two hours later she looked up with a feeling of having been dislocated from reality and realised that it was now well into the evening, the washing machine had long since stopped and she was sitting in a totally dark house with only her laptop screen providing light. She got slowly to her feet and went through her normal after dark routine of turning on lights and pulling curtains across windows, but this time she went further and pulled the blinds down over the kitchen windows too.

She returned to the garage and transferred the load of washing to the dryer, then closed the door behind her and made sure the bolt was secure. Now she must come up with a plan of some kind, a way of safely dealing with this and the only person she knew who might know how to handle it was Dave, who had a whole network of contacts in the media world and knew far more useful people than she did. After thinking through the consequences of involving him and deciding she had no other options, she got a USB stick out of the kitchen odds-and-ends drawer, deleted the photos she had saved on it and copied a carefully considered selection of files from the dead man's hard drive to give to Dave. Giving him all the information might be taking a risk, both for him and whoever he found to help, but what she had copied would give him a good picture of what this was about.

'You overthink things', he used to say to her. 'The world isn't going to stop revolving if every single consequence hasn't been weighed up.'

But this time her cautious approach felt justified; she could not ignore the feeling of threat now that she realised how dangerous those files were. With the USB stick in one jeans pocket and the little hard drive in the other she picked up her phone and called Dave. Unless her schedule had changed, Sasha would not be home from the gym until at least half past nine or ten and it was safe to call him in the next half hour. Communicating with Dave was complicated by how suspicious Sasha was of Dave and Sam's continued friendship after the divorce, and how much she resented any contact between them.

'She's too young,' Sam had said to her best friend Jill when this problem first became obvious. 'She thinks all contacts between men and women mean something romantic or sexual. It's like she's never heard of friendships.'

And Jill had let out a snort of derision which was her usual reaction when Sasha was mentioned. 'With her it's nothing to do with being too young, I think she's probably as thick as a brick. Totally gorgeous, but probably not smart.'

The upshot was that Dave had sent Sasha's work schedule to Sam, so she could call or text without problems arising at his end.

'Hi,' she said now. 'Safe to talk? I need to talk through something tricky, and I don't know anyone else who might know what to do.'

'Yeah, we're fine to talk. Are you OK? You sound a bit stressed.'

'Stressed doesn't quite cover it but never mind. I've got involved in something very scary, and I need to talk through it with someone I can trust. Well, I'm not directly involved, but I know things.'

'What kind of scary?'

'Let's call it conspiracy scary, it's a network of corruption, criminal and far-reaching, and I don't know what to do about it. Can we meet somewhere quiet and talk it over? Not here, don't come here – I'm paranoid about this. Let's meet in the parking area at Coyle Park tomorrow, if that suits you. The far end where the walking track starts should be mostly empty at the end of the day. I don't want us seen together, and I'm not thinking of Sasha. You'll understand when I tell you the rest.'

They made a date for half past six the following evening and Sam thought that when he heard what she had to tell him he wouldn't think it was "way over the top" to meet at Coyle Park, which had been his first reaction. But it was reasonably handy for them both and the least noticeable place she had been able to think of, a quiet place at that time of the day and probably without cameras.

When Sam set out the next evening she felt she had taken all the precautions she could. The little hard drive was well hidden, and she had two USBs in her pocket - the one she had copied for Dave and another with the complete set of documents that she had copied as a safeguard.

As soon as she arrived at the car park and turned her lights off Dave appeared and got into the passenger seat and watched her click the button for the central locking.

'Hi there, agent 007.' He chuckled. 'This is a bit like Deep Throat or whatever that plot was called decades ago, people meeting in dark parking buildings to tell each other dangerous secrets.'

'Ha! You won't be joking about it when you see what I've got.' Sam reached down beside her seat and pulled up the laptop. 'I'll show you, but first you must promise me one thing. Never tell anyone you don't *totally* trust about this. Preferably only one person, someone who knows how to deal with it.'

She fished the two USBs from her pocket and plugged in the one with the X on it. 'This is my copy that I made from a hard drive I found, and I have another one for you to keep.' She handed the laptop to Dave and sat back to watch him read the files.

After a few minutes he turned and stared at her in the gloom. 'Where the hell did you get hold of this? It's dynamite, Sam! I didn't understand why you were so neurotic about safety, but holy shit, this is huge – and very dangerous. Where did you get the hard drive

from? And where is it now?'

It took half an hour to tell him the full story, and the more detail he heard, the more convinced was he that she was right; the two men, who came to the house that night and took the body of the dead man away, were police, but seriously corrupt police.

'I know,' she said when he agreed with her. 'It was obvious when I thought back and pulled all the details together into a whole. I think the guy who died was another cop, and he was originally part of it, or how would he have been able to film those meetings? They're so clearly filmed by stealth, so to speak, you can see his knee at the bottom of the screen in one of the videos, the one at someone's house where they're all sitting around a coffee table. So I guess he sat there holding his phone in his hand and just sneakily filmed it. But did he do it to blackmail them or to expose them? Was he undercover or an informer?'

'OK, I think you're right, but there's something I don't understand. How did he get to be in three meetings? Different guys in each meeting, so presumably they are groups in separate areas, maybe organised as units so everyone doesn't know about everyone else. You know, to limit the fallout if the proverbial hits the fan? It seems odd.'

'I know, I've wondered about that too, but perhaps he was some kind of trusted lieutenant – the person nominated by whoever the head guy is, to be the observer for some reason. And then he decided to become an informer, perhaps?' She waited while Dave processed this idea and nodded. 'And by the way, did I mention that he called them a corruption cabal when he explained why I shouldn't call the police? That's how I think of them now – a cabal.'

'I need to think about this. I agree with everything you say, but how to get it out there safely is the problem, I mean safely for us. I know a lot of mainstream journos in TV and print media, but who would handle this? God knows, maybe a blogger. Can I have a copy of this?'

She held out the USB with D on it. 'This one is yours, but don't for heaven's sake, save anything on your computer. I don't trust anything or anyone now. Well, apart from you, of course. There are a couple of files that aren't on yours, but only so whoever you approach doesn't get all of it at once. You know - that old principle of always holding something back.'

Then she remembered something he might not have noticed yet. 'And please check the tabs at the top of those Excel spreadsheets with lists of things, there's a lot of detail in other sheets in each file. Lists of gangs and individuals, with cryptic little abbreviations in the columns next to their names. I'm sure you'll get what they mean. Details of what they bought protection for, and what they paid and when, very organised and tidy.'

She paused and tried to think of what else he needed to know.

'That one who talked to me when they came to the house, he said his name was Brown, but that name isn't in the list.'

Dave held up the USB she had given him. 'This is unbelievable, Sam! This little thing has detailed evidence that would put them all away for years, ruin their careers, and maybe their relationships. I didn't think this kind of thing could happen here, blackmail and extortion. And that list of gangs and people paying big money in exchange for things not being reported or whatever. No wonder they were prepared to do nearly anything to get hold of it.'

She reached over and took the laptop from him. 'So now we've got to be very, very careful. The cops have access to the cameras at petrol stations and motorways and all kinds of places around the city, and probably facial recognition software in some places too. They could search by number plate or car model or a photo of someone's face. I've read up on it, and it basically means there is no way of not being tracked and seen if they try to check on you. So there mustn't be the slightest hint that we've got this or that we've met since that guy died.'

He turned in his seat and put his hand on the back of her neck and gave her a little squeeze. 'Of course, I won't tell anybody! I'll be very careful, and I'll let you know as soon as I find someone to ask for help with this. I would never do anything that might harm you.' Then he gave her an ironic smile. 'Well, apart from the harm I already did when I left you, but you're still my best friend.'

'I know, and thank you, but it's a compulsive habit now, this constant worrying, it's in the back of my mind the whole time. I've developed high grade paranoia since I found that damn hard drive. So you take the USB and make sure you keep it safe.'

A few minutes after they parted Dave called and she stopped on the side of the street to take the call. 'Hey, listen, I know this is a bit over the top, but please make sure you keep the original in a safe place, maybe hide the copy you made in a different place. I'd be happier if I knew I won't end up having the only evidence.'

She assured him it was all taken care of, but later that evening, just before she went to bed she thought about her hiding place and took their conversation one step further in her mind. She should take some extra precautions just in case someone came looking for the hard drive, find a better hiding place, and leave the USB in the car so it was always where she was. She decided to leave it for the morning, set her alarm for an hour earlier than usual and spent an unrestful night waking at intervals and refining her plans.

4

When Sam arrived home from work a couple of days later, she knew the moment the garage door swung up that Dave had been right when he told her to make sure she found a safe place to hide the hard drive, because this was the next step, the follow-on. She got out of the car and stared in dismay at the mess. Everything had been taken off the shelving units, boxes lay opened with their contents strewn about and the door to the passage was open. Slowly she reached into the car and turned the ignition off, picked up her phone and called 111. 'Yes, a burglary,' she said to the operator. 'OK, I won't go in. I'll just wait in my car.'

Sitting in the car with the central locking on she tried to form a plan. She must take care not to say anything that might make them suspicious, no references to anything out of the ordinary. She must give the impression she thought this was a regular burglary and say nothing that might raise suspicions. Should she try to come up with some explanation for this total devastation, some reason a burglar might have thought she had something hidden? Or just not mention it? The best way forward would probably be to once again don the protective mantle of Johanna, act a bit silly and maybe make some passing reference to drugs, lots of cash and mistaken identity, the kind of things you read about in the paper. Ignorance and innocent speculation initiated by herself was probably the safest option.

The morning after her meeting with Dave she had hidden the hard drive in a better place than the one she had first chosen, and then, just as she was about to open the garage door to leave for work she had impulsively turned around. 'Rather safe than sorry,' she told herself and ran back to the kitchen, picked up the laptop and the charging cord and put them in the boot of her car. The first thing she had Googled that morning was if copying directly from the hard drive to a USB would have left a trace on her laptop, and it seemed to be safe, but now she was making doubly sure.

That evening she left the laptop in the car. Her paranoia about having anything that could link her to the hard drive out in the open in the house was fixed in her mind, and even the slight risk of having left a trackable record on the laptop when she copied the material was a risk that couldn't be disregarded. Before she left for work the next day she moved the printer from the side table in the dining room where it had sat since her father died and put it on one of the shelves in the garage. And what else? she thought and removed all her USB sticks from the kitchen drawer and put them in the glovebox in the car, intent on removing anything that made it look as if she was in any way computer savvy, preferably creating the impression that she didn't even have a computer.

And I was right! she told herself triumphantly, when she entered the house with the police officers. They didn't get my laptop, because it's in the locked car outside, and I can claim I never had one.

While she waited for the police to finish their note taking she was itching to go and check the garden shed, but she couldn't do it until they went. It would be such an odd thing to do, and they would wonder what she kept there and maybe speculate and mention it to others.

'Not your usual domestic burglary,' said the woman officer as they stood outside talking before they got into their car. 'Normally they take stuff like small appliances, things that are easy to sell. It's usually about money to buy drugs or to pay off drug debts, and sometimes it's stealing to order, like someone's mate needs a new microwave oven or an air fryer. But upending the whole place like this, that's very unusual. Did you have cash lying around in a drawer somewhere, or something valuable you might have talked about at work?'

'God no, I just have ordinary things, nothing particularly valuable,' said Sam dismissively. 'Perhaps they got the wrong address - you know, like mistaken identity.' She even managed a little laugh. 'Maybe they thought I was a drug dealer instead of a librarian and had bundles of cash hidden somewhere, like you read about sometimes.'

'And remember not to touch that window frame until forensics have been to get fingerprints off it,' the officer said before she closed the car door. 'You can nail it shut in the meantime, but don't touch it with your hands. And if you claim on insurance for those things they stole, quote the incident number on that docket I gave you.'

As soon as they left Sam sat down at the kitchen table, surrounded by chaos, checked Sasha's work schedule on her phone and called Dave.

'For fuck's sake!' he exclaimed when she told him what had

happened. 'They must have known that guy had it on a USB or on a portable hard drive or whatever. I bet they chased him that night because they'd found out what he'd downloaded, or they were on to it that he had video of those meetings. And then, when it wasn't in his pockets or in that taxi they rammed ... I bet they searched that too. And then they went to where he lived and looked there, don't you think? And still failed to find it.'

'Exactly what went through my mind when I lay awake at two in the morning the night after we met at the park. They might still be working on the idea that he hid it when he ran from the crash to my place. And that call from you when I was on the way home made me think, so I made some plans. The hard drive is well hidden now, and I decided not to keep the USB copy I made for me, I printed the lot instead. Spreadsheets, list of names, every page of every document on that drive, quite a stack of paper. It seemed like something nobody would suspect, just a bunch of papers. I snipped a few stills from those videos and printed those too.'

Dave chuckled. 'I didn't know you knew how to do that. Very clever! And where are those prints now?'

'Same place as the hard drive, in the catcher of that rusty old lawn mower in the back of the shed that nobody's used for decades. I put the prints in one of those zip lock bags and put it in the bottom of the catcher along with the hard drive in its little box and sprinkled some very dry grass clippings over them. And they're still there.' She smiled to herself. 'And they didn't get my laptop because I've been taking it with me to work every day, I just leave it in the car.'

'Brilliant! I've got to go, talk later. No, wait - how did they get in? Did they break a lock or a window?'

'They jemmied the hall window open, broke the latch. I'll go and get a hammer and nail the window shut from outside right now and get someone to come and fix it after the fingerprint people have been.'

'Make sure you do! Have you told anyone else about this?'

For a moment she couldn't think why he asked. 'No, you're the first person I've told, the police have only just left. And of course I won't tell anyone that it was really a search! I'll just say I was burgled, which is actually true - they took my microwave and the air fryer and maybe other things that I haven't noticed yet. Thanks! See you soon.'

Where to start? she wondered tiredly as she walked around the house again, looking at the mess while thoughts of how to keep herself safe revolved in her mind. All evening, occasionally stopping for a drink of water, she continued working. Having started with the kitchen made her feel that a nearly normal evening might be possible, but by half past ten it was clear that nothing would be remotely normal that night. With the kitchen and her bedroom sorted out, she tackled the garage and moved the car inside. But the persistent feeling of danger was like a constant background noise in her mind that. Was this the end of their interest in her or would they come back? What if they came back to pressure her to tell them if she had found the hard drive, force her to hand it over? She didn't know how good she would be at lying or being evasive in the face of real danger, but what could she do? And you can't prove a negative, she thought despondently, there is nothing I can do to resolve this.

Leaving the rest of the house as it was, she heated a can of soup and sat down at the kitchen table with a sheet of paper from the printer and tried to sort out what was a priority and what could wait. As ideas came to her she jotted down things that might keep her safe: get the window latch fixed, get an alarm system and a security camera outside, maybe spend the nights in a motel, put a lock on her bedroom door - and then she stopped with a groan of frustration. None of those things would protect her from harm. Determined men would smash a window and nowhere in the house was safe, her only hope was that they would presume the evidence had never been in her house. They had searched the house and found nothing, so hopefully they thought that the man who died in the garage had hidden or dropped the hard drive when he ran from the crash. But it was useless speculation, and all she could do was wait.

5

On Saturday morning Sam did some housework, which was badly needed after the mess the searchers had made, when little bundles of dust turned up everywhere once everything was picked up from the floor. She was in the garage emptying the vacuum cleaner when the doorbell went, and instantly the sense of danger that was constantly in the back of her mind ramped up a few notches; she wasn't expecting anyone. What would she do if someone forced their way inside? Briefly the idea of pretending she wasn't home popped into her mind, instantly followed by the realisation that whoever it was could just wait or even break in. Calm down, she told herself and tried to shake off the feeling of apprehension, don't be so neurotic, it's probably someone collecting for a charity.

Through the window beside the front door she saw Brown and quickly pulled the Johanna personality into the front of her mind, hoping it would once again serve as a protective shield, because she was frightened of this bland looking man, who somehow managed to give the impression he was kind and dangerous at the same time.

'Good morning! I'm sorry to come uninvited, but I was in the neighbourhood, and I thought I'd pop in and check you're OK and not too traumatised.' Brown smiled his nice, comforting smile. 'I heard you'd been burgled, and I knew how worried you would be.'

'Oh, that's so kind, come in,' said Sam and stood to one side. 'You were so nice and calming the other night, I was very grateful afterwards when the shock wore off and I could think straight. Come through to the kitchen. Would you like a cup of coffee?'

Surely the last thing she would have said if she had anything to hide, she thought and led the way to the kitchen, he wouldn't have expected that if he was suspicious. They sat at the kitchen table with the morning sun streaming in the window, and Brown looked around and smiled again. 'What a nice kitchen this is! I didn't think of it that night. These large old-fashioned kitchens with room for a table are great, aren't they? But listen, how have you been? Are you able to sleep?'

Sam pushed the packet of biscuits in his direction and shook her head. 'I'm reasonably OK, but I'm still a bit shaken up. It's hard to believe I got burgled too, isn't it? But luckily they didn't destroy anything, they just took a few things to sell.'

He nodded in sympathy, and Sam thought of the laptop and the charging cord still in the car, where she kept them all the time now apart from when she actually needed a computer.

'As I said, I worried about you when I heard about the burglary.' Brown took another biscuit. 'Women living alone must feel particularly scared when these things happen. And I see in the notes that you thought it might be a mistaken address.' He noticed her unspoken question and added, 'I'm not only involved in that undercover drug investigation - but I hold down my normal job as well, so when your address popped up in the system I thought I'd better come and check you're OK.'

'It's so kind of you to worry about me,' said Sam and tried to look grateful despite her inner tension. 'When I was talking to the officers, who came, I had this idea - just a silly thought, but it could be right. You know how you read about shots fired at houses or cars set on fire or whatever. And then it turns out some gang people got the address wrong. Because what else could it be? Who in their right mind would search a house belonging to a librarian for whatever it was they looked for – drugs or money perhaps. Or weapons.' She gave him a wry smile. 'Particularly a rather dull librarian like me.'

He shook his head. 'You're a lovely woman, and you don't deserve having all these random things upsetting your life. What did they take? I hope it wasn't anything irreplaceable.'

'Oh, nothing much that I've discovered so far, you know, a couple of small appliances and the little flatscreen TV in my bedroom. I haven't got a lot of valuable stuff. This house was my parents' - it's just a funny mix of new and old things, but not antiques or anything they could sell quickly, I don't think.'

'We see a lot of heartbreak,' said Brown and sounded genuinely sympathetic. 'People lose laptops they've saved all the family photos on and things that matter like jewellery.'

'I don't have a laptop, I just use my phone,' said Sam and sent a regretful smile across the table. 'And no expensive jewellery either. I'm very undesirable as a burglary subject. All our family photos are in the albums in the sideboard in the dining room.'

'But wasn't there a laptop here the night it happened? I seem to remember one just where you're sitting now.'

'Oh dear! Was that here the night you came? You're very obser- vant!' Sam tried to make her voice convey admiration, but inside she shivered at the implications of this comment. 'It's your training, I suppose. But please don't tell anyone I had it, *please* don't! I sometimes borrow one from work, and I never leave it in the house, of course – I take it back to work the next morning. I go in early, so nobody sees me with it. I borrow it to read all the reviews we download for new books, which I never have time to do at work. You won't tell them, will you? We're not supposed to take them home, they're City Council property and if they find out I'll get into trouble.'

He smiled his comforting smile. 'Of course I won't tell anyone. You'll keep the secret about the man we found in your garage, and I'll keep the secret about your illegal use of the library laptop. Deal?'

'Deal!' said Sam and smiled her friendliest smile. 'And you can trust me - I truly haven't mentioned what happened that night to anyone. It's quite hard not to, but I'm getting used to it. I kind of push it aside when I suddenly remember it and try not to let it take over.'

When Brown was leaving, he put his hands on her shoulders and said comfortingly, 'That awful memory will fade over time, my dear. Believe me, I know all about things like that from when I started in the police. You're doing a great job and remember you're on my team now.'

Sam watched until his car disappeared under the trees lining the drive and returned inside deep in thought. Sasha worked every second Saturday, so she checked the schedule and called Dave. 'Yes, it's fine,' he said. 'Sasha's at work, and I'm just coming out of the supermarket. Do we need to meet?'

'No, just get to your car and put the shopping down, so we can talk undisturbed. Call me back!'

When he heard what she had to tell him he was stunned. 'Shit! I hope to God you managed to convince him, because he was obviously checking up. And great idea to say the laptop was one that belongs to the library.'

'He regards me as a slightly ditzy, easily scared woman without excessive amounts of brain power.' Sam laughed. 'I couldn't really have come up with a better disguise that night, you know. It was pure inspiration, I just switched to the role I had in that play at the Little Playhouse, remember the one where I played the crazy woman who kept losing things. Being silly and harmless seemed like a good idea.'

'Yeah, right!' said Dave sarcastically. 'Harmless little woman? You? Don't make me laugh. But I'm glad it worked.'

Sam put the phone down and thought of the rather strange impulse that had stopped her telling Dave how Brown had put his hands on her shoulder and left them there just a few seconds too long. How his thumbs had stroked her as if she was someone who belonged to him, a sister or a child. It made her shudder with distaste and fear, but that gesture confirmed her conviction that she had managed to dupe him, that he thought of her as someone he could manipulate and control.

6

Two weeks later nothing had changed. Dave had texted a couple of times and called once.

'Any luck?' asked Sam, hoping it would be good news. Not that finding someone to deal with the issue would make her feel any safer, but at least things would be moving forward. As soon as she had looked at those files on the hard drive she had known that reporting it was out of the question. There was no way of knowing if the file called "Names" was the total list of corrupt police officers, or if they were just the ones the unknown man had known about. And as she said to Dave in that phone call a week ago, 'What if we reported it to someone who's involved or who mentioned it to someone who's involved? Catastrophic! You must find someone who can take it on, make it public!'

Dave was making what he called "general-sounding, casual inquiries" to find someone who was known for in-depth, solid reporting on sensitive subjects, someone whom others trusted. 'It's not that there aren't a whole bunch of people who do the sort of writing we want, but I think this needs a bit extra caution, and I want to make sure we give it to someone who's gone deep with dangerous material before and managed to get away with it. We've only got one chance to get this out there in the public arena, so taking the time is worth it, I think.'

Going to work and trying to appear calm and content was a struggle some days when she had woken in the night after unsettling dreams about the night Brown and his sidekick came to the house. Having real and dangerous men in her threatening dreams, men with real faces, was far worse than dreaming of unknown men conjured up by her mind.

Tonight she was having dinner at Jill's place, something she looked forward to because they had been friends since high school, and quite apart from knowing that the meal would be delicious and possibly exotic, she also loved being in Jill's house. At Jill's, tidiness was an unknown concept, there were always discarded jumpers draped over chairs, sneakers left all over the floor inside the front door, and the danger of stepping on randomly scattered Lego blocks. She had known the children since they were born and was godmother to Bindy, the oldest girl. All she had to do tonight was keep cheerful, chat to the kids and listen to Jill's gossip from her job at the supermarket, and all would be well.

But within half an hour Jill had picked up on the background tension. She put down the knife she was slicing tomatoes with and turned to face Sam. 'Is something wrong? You're not quite yourself. Anything you want to talk about?'

'No, it's just a minor problem, but Dave's helping me with it. He'll get it sorted.'

'God, you're so lucky that you and Dave are still such great friends! Very unusual.'

'It's bit like we're brother and sister now, we look out for each other and we're always in touch.'

Jill gave her a narrow-eyed look, worried and suspicious at the same time. 'OK, so long as that's enough, and so long as Sasha doesn't throw a tantrum again. But remember I'm here if you need me.'

'There's no need to worry about her. Dave and I only talk while she's at work, he sent me her work schedule, so I don't text or call when she's home. And please don't look so worried. When this problem is sorted out I'll tell you about it. At the moment it's pretty sensitive, but it's not about me, it's something kind of public, something I came across by accident.'

Jill studied her face for a minute before she replied, clearly intrigued but respecting Sam's reticence. 'You've had something dire on your mind lately. The last couple of times we've talked on the phone I've had the feeling your attention is only half on what we're talking about. But I'll wait until you can tell me more.' She turned back to the tomatoes, and they talked of other things.

When Dave called a few days later he was upbeat and confident. 'I think I've found the right person. You've probably heard about her or read her articles – Liz McCarroll. She's done some amazing work on complex and sensitive issues, very in-depth with lots of good research. I've talked to her a couple of times now, and she's very intrigued by what I've told her so far. She's going to call me in half an hour, so we can set up a time for a meeting – I hope for tomorrow or the next day. I'll let you know later. Sasha will be home by the time I've talked to Liz, and I don't want any more fuss if she hears me talking to you.'

He called the next morning, and Sam excused herself from the front desk where she was helping out and retreated to the staff lunchroom. 'Is she going to take it on? How much did you tell her?'

'I told her we have proof that medium and some high ranking police officers in several districts are involved in extortion and something like a protection racket, and I said it's about payments demanded for what I chose to call "actions not taken". I put it like that just to give her an example, and I said it involves gangs too. She's written about gangs in the past, very good stuff that must have taken a lot of research, so she's thorough. And I Googled some of the names from that list, I went to an internet café to be safe.' He chuckled. 'I think your paranoia is catching. So I know their ranks now, and everyone on that list is a cop, which I told Liz.'

'Did you give her any names or details? I hope she understands enough not to start stirring things up before you sit down and go through the lot. Gossip about this would be the worst thing, wouldn't it?'

'I was pretty careful and refused to go into details, because I think she should make up her own mind when she deciphers the abbreviations in the databases and figures out what they mean. I've given her a rough outline of what it's about, and I had to tell her we have definitive evidence of who's involved, or she might not have taken it on. I still don't know which one on the list is the guy who told you his name's Brown, but it doesn't matter.'

Sam knew what he meant about actions not taken, and it was exactly what she thought herself. It could mean evidence had been suppressed or destroyed, perhaps mislaid on purpose, so someone wouldn't be charged. Or it might mean that threats of arrests for drug trafficking had been invented and used to extort money. She voiced this thought and Dave said, 'Ah, yes – there's all that, of course. But you left out the most obvious reason why money's being paid so frequently. I think it's what the Americans call protection money, an ongoing thing, and the gang pays like an insurance premium per month. But there's got to be more important things than those too, bigger issues.'

'You're right, that sounds very likely, far more reasonable than ad hoc little interventions. A few big payments now and then for taking care of things that involve a bit more risk, perhaps.'

'Exactly what I was thinking. Or maybe just advance warnings, a text message from a burner phone to say, "raid coming up in two days"? Who knows? But listen, I've been thinking of that hidden row in the spreadsheet with the names. That Box guy. What do you think? Any ideas?'

'I never saw that! In among the names?'

'Not visible when you open that file, but if you look closely you'll see that the numbered rows jump from sixteen to eighteen. You know how rows in spreadsheets are numbered, and someone's done that thing you can do in Excel and hidden row seventeen. The name on that row is Box, the only name in the list that isn't a real name, and there's a phone number for him. And when I watched those videos of meetings I noticed that there's always a phone in the middle of the table. So I played them slowly and you can see everyone's eyes fixed on that phone now and then, which I think is when the person at the other end speaks, the same voice in all three meetings. Maybe there's a head guy somewhere, who stays anonymous, calls himself Box and takes part remotely? Maybe he's called Box because his voice comes out of a "box" – like he's likening the phone to a little box.'

'How weird! But what would be the point?' And then she had an idea and laughed. 'Maybe he's a top cop who found out what they're doing and they're having to pay him a percentage, like protection money, so he won't report them! Oh my God, that's hilarious.' She heard noises and someone talking loudly. 'Where are you?'

'I'm sitting in the car outside the supermarket. It's just some noisy girls walking past. I had to drive mum over, so she could do her shopping, she's lost her distance glasses and can't drive. Oh, here she comes now, I'll tell you more when I've given Liz the USB. I'm driving over to her place tomorrow. Bye!'

7

Sam stopped outside Jill's house to let her eleven-year-old goddaughter out after two hours in the West City mall where she had taken Bindy after a rash promise that she could choose her own birthday present.

'Exhausted?' called Jill from the doorstep as Bindy dashed inside with two shopping bags, and Sam made a sweat-wiping gesture across her forehead, wound up the window and drove away.

Hoping to do some gardening she had a quick lunch, but clouds were coming in from the east and the prospect of gardening seemed less inviting. While she stood undecided by the living room window watching her Saturday afternoon taken over by the elements, her phone beeped in the kitchen. She ran for it, saw Dave's name on the screen and took the call.

'Sam! They're going to get me! Listen!' He was shouting. Sam had no idea what was going on, terrifying scenarios played out in her mind. 'They're trying to push me off the road, they've hit me twice. Listen! It's a black SUV with bull bars on the front. I can't see the plates, two guys inside. Shit, here they come again.' Another pause that she didn't dare interrupt, then Dave's frantic voice, louder still. 'It's pissing down and ...' Another pause and a hard bang, then Dave was back. 'I'm driving as fast as I can. I just wanted to tell you that I ...Fuck! They got me again ...' Chaotic sounds filled Sam's ears, then a scream. 'Nooo!' Then nothing.

She couldn't move, just stood there paralysed with shock with no idea what to do while disjointed thoughts swirled in her head. Had they managed to push him off the road? Where had this happened? She had no idea where Liz lived and couldn't think of her surname. Mc-something, she thought. Should she call the cops first or call Sasha? Maybe she knew the road Dave had been on, so at least she could tell the police something definite. After a few moments her mind settled down and she called Dave's number, but the only reply was an automated voice saying, "this number is unavailable, please leave a message after the beep."

Sasha first, she decided, because finding out which road it was must be the first priority, and if she called the police there would be even more attention on herself and Brown would get suspicious. And if Sasha didn't know, then at least she would have been told that something was wrong, and it was up to her to alert the emergency services. She had Sasha's number from that time last year when she called to abuse Sam for "trying to hang on to Dave", a call that had tested Sam's patience to the very limit, but she had manged to keep her cool.

'Sasha, it's Sam,' she said a moment later. 'Listen, I just had a very strange call from Dave. Do you know where he is?'

'He's out somewhere. What did he say? Why are you calling me?' She was irritated and a bit confused and Sam couldn't blame her. She steadied her voice and made an effort to speak slower. 'I don't know where he was, but he was in the car, and he screamed that someone was trying to ram his car and push him off the road.

And then the call cut out and when I tried to call him back I got a message that his phone isn't available.'

She tried to find the right way to put this without making it sound strange, but it was important, and she must do it without Sasha reverting to old grievances. 'He thought he was talking to you - he must have pushed the button for the wrong name and got me instead of you, both our names start with Sa.'

Sasha started to cry, and her voice broke on sobs. 'Oh God, please, no! What should I do? I don't know what to do!'

'Listen! I know this is awful, but you must call the police.' Sam tried to sound calm despite the urgency in her head mounting to a crescendo. 'Say that he called you, no need to mention me, because I truly don't know anything that would help - he only said half a dozen words. It will be much better for you if nobody finds out he called me by mistake. You know what they would do, speculate about why and say nasty things. I mean, he thought he was talking to you, so it's the same as if he had.'

A long silence and the occasional sob then Sasha said. 'OK, I think you're right. They *would* talk and wonder why he called you instead of me. I'll call the cops right away, but you have to tell me what to say. I can't think straight.'

'Just dial iii and say you need to talk to the police, tell them that your partner called, he was in his car somewhere, but you don't know where, and he shouted half a dozen words, and said he was being pushed off the road. That's all he said, and you don't need to add anything, because we don't know anything more. They'll find him, I'm sure. Someone's probably reported it already.'

After a few seconds, still sounding hesitant and scared, Sasha said slowly, 'OK, I think I can do that. I'll do it right away, so they can find him. Can I call you back after?'

'Of course. And I'd like to know what they say too, find out how badly injured he is,' said Sam, feeling strangely touched by this unexpected request. That Sasha, who was possessive and jealous for no reason and had once screamed that she hated Sam, should now ask for her support felt very odd.

She remained at the kitchen table, unable to move, and tried to imagine the consequences of this conversation. Whether Dave was injured or dead, problems might arise. The thought of Dave dying made her stomach clench; he was her best friend and there was nobody else in her life to fill the place he had occupied for fourteen years. She pushed the feeling aside and tried to concentrate on the immediate situation. Probably Sasha would do what she had suggested, but what about the next step at Sasha's end? Someone coming to sit with her, maybe her mother or someone from Victim Support arriving, talking about it repeatedly. Would she stick to the version they had agreed on, that Dave had called her? Impossible to tell, but one thing was certain. If the police linked herself to Dave via this ghastly event it could mean serious trouble down the line, whatever the outcome. Out west, he had said, Liz lived somewhere out west, whatever that meant, but she hadn't mentioned it to Sasha because how would she have explained how she knew? Perhaps I should have told her anyway, she thought, then at least they would have some clue as to where it happened. The thought of Dave injured in a crumpled car down some steep bank filled her with horror. She got up and got a glass of water, but she didn't drink it, just stood there with the glass in her hand and stared vacantly at the raindrops on the window, tense with worry. Hopefully he was alive, or would they have stopped to make sure he was dead, not just injured? It was strange that she had been able to talk so calmly to Sasha when her mind was in turmoil, but for the moment her emotions still seemed frozen. Then her phone beeped, and she jumped.

'It's me,' said Sasha, her voice a notch higher than usual and only the occasional sniff betraying that she had recently cried again. 'They asked if I knew where he was going, and I said didn't know he was going anywhere, and I said I only just got home from work at the gym when that call came.'

'Did they say what they can do?'

'They said accidents are usually reported quickly, but no serious crashes have been logged in the last hour. And they asked me to tell them exactly what he said, so I just repeated what you told me. That he shouted someone was trying to push his car off the road and then nothing, the call just cut out.'

'I'm so sorry, Sasha! I hope they find him soon and that he's not badly injured.'

'Me too, I'm so worried I feel sick. We had another road rage thing a couple of weeks ago. Someone braked hard right in front of us because Dave had tried to filter in from a merge lane, and we nearly hit them when they closed the gap. I told the cops about that too, and they said it's quite common. Oh no, I've got another call coming, I'll call you back.'

Sam stared at the phone in her hand and wondered how this rather immature girl had snapped out of her resentment and was now suddenly on speaking terms with her. The call came half an hour later, and Sam knew the moment she heard Sasha's voice. No tears now, just quiet desolation. 'Sam, it's me. He's dead. They found him. Someone reported his car down a steep bank some-where out near Waitakere.' She started to cry again, and Sam could hear how hard it had been for her to say that word - dead.

'Oh Sasha, I'm sorry! You shouldn't be alone, darling – is someone coming to be with you?'

'My mum's coming, I just called her, and she said she'll be

right over. I just thought you should know straight away. And I'm sorry I was so horrid to you that time – I didn't really hate you, I was just jealous.' She was sobbing again.

Sam felt tears pool in her eyes and tried to keep her voice steady. 'I know. Let's not think about that now. If there's anything I can do, just let me know. And I hope we'll be able to keep it to just the two of us that he called the wrong number, so you won't have to deal with gossip. That's the last thing you need now.'

'True,' said Sasha sadly and Sam could hear the effort it took for her to stop sobbing so she could talk. 'I'm so glad we talked about that. I don't know if I would be able to cope if people started saying he was still in love with you. I mean, that might be what they'd say if they thought he called you rather than me.'

'Exactly - it would be horrible for you. Look after yourself, you poor girl.'

She put the phone down and sat there thinking that what she had said to Sasha was all genuine, she had meant every word. Her initial suggestions that Sasha should say Dave had called her had been based on self-protective instinct, but now she was genuinely glad that this version was also better for Sasha. It would make her life slightly easier, but it felt very odd. She sat looking vacantly out at the rain for a long time before she got up, and then she couldn't think of single thing to do. Now she had nobody in her life like Dave, nobody who understood her so well.

8

Over the next few days trying to appear reasonably normal at work was nearly more than Sam could cope with, a constant struggle that now and then nearly overwhelmed her. The physical act of smiling felt like lifting a heavy weight and keeping her voice under control required constant awareness. It was obvious from the first morning after Dave died that her voice gave her away; the others gave her concerned looks and spoke softly to her, but it was hard work. It's just acting, she told herself, no different from being in a play, but of course it was different, this was real.

'It's so tiring,' said Sam to Jill in a late night call. 'It sucks all the energy out of me. It's like acting a part I haven't learnt yet. I can't let go of my self-control, but they can sense how upset I am. Not that they know how close Dave and I have continued to be since he left me, but I know they want to give me sympathy and hugs, and I just can't cope with it.'

'I know it's no comfort now, but it will get easier over time. When is the funeral? Have you heard?'

Sam shook her head in disbelief, though she was alone and there was nobody to see it. 'It's on Saturday at twelve. Sasha's in constant touch, would you believe? She calls me whenever some decision needs to be made. I had her on the phone just a few minutes ago, the second time today. It's like I've become her go-to person for support and advice. Last night she called and asked if I'd come and sit with her and Dave's families at the front at the funeral, and when I said both her and his families might be uncomfortable with it, she said she'd already talked to them, and they thought it was a nice idea!'

'Good heavens, how weird! But why does she turn to you? Doesn't she resent you now?'

'Oh, didn't I tell you?' Sam couldn't believe she hadn't thought of this question, it was such an obvious one, and now she must quickly come up with something that sounded credible. 'I think she's feeling overwhelmed. I called her as soon as I heard, and she was grateful, and I gave her some advice about how to deal with all the questions the cops might ask. I knew Dave was going to see some woman, who's a big deal in the media world, he told me a couple of days before he died.'

Jill's voice sounded impatient as it always did when things were vague or poorly expressed. 'I still don't get it, you'll have to explain. Did you think Sasha was going to go ballistic if the cops told her where he'd been? And how would they know who he'd been to see, anyway?'

'I was worried that they might spring something on her. The worst thing would be if that woman was in the car with him when he crashed – imagine how Sasha would feel. So I called her, and we talked through it, and she cried, and then she said she didn't really hate me that time she called and screamed at me, she was just jealous. And now she treats me like a favourite aunt.'

'Don't be ridiculous, you're too young to be her aunt, you'll have to be her cousin.' Jill chuckled. 'You're too good to be true, you know. Not many women would be concerned about how their ex-husband's new partner would react in a case like this. Particularly not one who'd been so antagonistic and rude.'

Sam put the phone down and thought that Jill had no idea how this weird friendship with Sasha had come about and she never would. But she was gradually understanding what it was Dave had seen in her that had attracted him at the start. Not just her gorgeous body or her pretty face, but the combination of naiveté and simplistic approach. Not to mention her kindness and the upfront way she apologised for being rude. The way she said that, when she'd just been told that Dave might be injured or dead, was a very kind and endearing thing to do.

On the way to the funeral Sam thought of the phone call from Jill the previous evening and her offer to pick Sam up, so they could go together.

'It will be better for you than turning up alone,' she had said. 'We can turn to each other if people stare, you know what some people are like, the vulture types who'll want to study your reactions.'

But Sam had turned down the offer of going together, though she wasn't sure why. She just knew she needed to turn up on her own, face any curious glances and act the way she would at the funeral of any close friend.

'Thank you,' she said to Jill. 'I do appreciate the thought, and I know what you mean about some people looking at me, but for some reason I feel that I need to do this on my own. Please don't be offended. We can go and have lunch or a drink afterwards.'

It was predictably agonising. Sam arrived early, greeted people she knew and took a seat at the back of the church, where she could sit unnoticed when the families arrived. But Sasha's mother saw her and caused even more looks when she walked back down the aisle and asked Sam to come and sit with them, so she followed the woman up the aisle and took a seat next to a man who turned out to be Sasha's great-uncle. When she joined the procession out of the church behind the coffin, she waited and filtered in toward the end, wanting to make sure that though she had sat with the families at the front, she made no claims on having a right to be close behind the coffin.

Outside she stood quietly to one side and watched people approach Sasha and Dave's families. She noticed some of her friends on the far side of the forecourt with Jill, but she stayed where she was and just nodded without making a move to join them. When the hearse was ready to drive away, Sasha turned and instead of getting into the waiting car to follow the hearse she came over to Sam.

'I want to say thank you for being so kind to me, just lovely. And you've lost him too, so we're both sad.'

Before Sam could think of a reply Sasha took a step closer and pulled her into a tight hug. By this time people had noticed and were staring at them, so to avoid the hug seeming one-sided, Sam put her arms around Sasha and hugged her back and said quietly, 'Any time, darling, don't hesitate to call me if you need to talk.'

Sasha took a step back and gave her a watery smile before she turned back to the waiting cars.

Out of the corner of her eye Sam noticed Jill looking across at them and could just imagine the expression of stunned surprise on her face. Unable to cope with any kind of conversation right then, particularly not one that might involve a lot of questions, she abandoned her plan for lunch with Jill and slunk quietly away to her car. On the way home she came apart, suddenly and unex-pectedly. She pulled over and cried for several minutes with her forehead resting on the steering wheel before she could control her tears and continue home. But she knew that pulling herself together was vital, because now she must plan how to protect herself.

There was no doubt in her mind that sooner or later those men would realise that Dave was linked to her despite their different surnames and despite how she had avoided it being known that Dave had called her from the car. But as soon as that link was discovered she would be under threat too.

9

On Sunday night Sam was at Jill's place for dinner and to stay the night, which she had only done once before, the day after Jill's husband had left her with three young children and in dire financial straits. But Jill had suggested a little "holiday from trauma" as she put it, a change of scene.

'Let's face it,' she said in a phone call a few hours after Dave's funeral. 'You've had more hard stuff to deal with in a month than most people have in a year, first the burglary and now this. Come for dinner and stay over, so we can sit down with a bottle of wine after dinner. You can go straight to work from here in the morning. The kids would love to see you.'

'Hey, listen!' said Jill after dinner, when the children were in bed and the kitchen tidied up. 'I don't know if I told you about the new guy we just hired. I don't see him very much. You know how my office is just a little room behind the scenes, so I'm close to the produce deliveries and the chillers – being the produce buyer is no glamour job. The new man is upstairs in the big office, something to do with security and the in-store cameras. But I came across him the other day, and I asked if he knew the best thing to have for home security – thinking about your burglary and how isolated your house is. He said, a camera or two on the outside and one inside. Plus a sign on the gate saying there's surveillance gear installed and monitored. So very much like what I have here.'

'I'll think about it. Dave and I talked about it when we took over mum's house, but we never did anything about it and then he left shortly after, so I never got around to doing it. But the risk of being burgled twice can't be very big – probably about the same odds as being struck by lightning twice.'

At half past ten Jill got up and picked up their wine glasses and the now empty bottle. 'I'll empty the dishwasher, so it's done. Have a shower now if you like and avoid the chaos in the morning. There's a towel for you on the edge of the bath.'

Sam went back downstairs in her PJs after her shower to see what Jill was doing because all the lights were still on, and she could hear someone talking.

'I just turned on the repeat of the news – trying to listen to the news in the morning is doomed. The kids make too much noise.' Jill was curled up in her favourite chair and the introduction to the news had just started.

Sam sat down on the sofa and watched rather than listened, her mind endlessly circling back to Dave's phone call and that horrible scream before the connection was broken, which she seemed to be unable to relegate to the back of her mind, but suddenly a name caught her attention. A reporter was standing in front of a house with crime scene tape across the driveway, and she had just mentioned "Liz McCarroll, a respected journalist with many credits to her name".

Stunned Sam listened to the account of how a neighbour had found Liz stabbed to death early that morning when he took his dog for a walk. 'She was just lying on the side lawn – between our houses,' said the man with barely suppressed excitement. 'I only just spotted her from the street, she was right up by the fence so I couldn't see her from my place. I rushed over, but she was dead, her skin was cold and there was a lot of blood dried up all over her front, it looked as if she'd been stabbed. So I just raced back to my place and called the cops. It must have happened hours earlier, maybe more. Her back door was open - I could see it from my kitchen window.'

To get her feelings under control Sam turned slightly away from the TV and when she looked back Jill had snoozed off. Now she must keep a cool head and remember that nobody knew there was anything to link her to the murdered journalist. There was no doubt in her mind that Liz had been killed by the same men who killed Dave. After a few minutes she got to her feet and lightly touched Jill's shoulder. 'I'm going to bed now. Don't sit here all night!'

Lying in the second bed in Bindy's room listening to her nearly inaudible breathing Sam felt a shift in her thinking and realised that wondering if the men had found or not found the USB she had given Dave was not the point. What they were doing was making sure nobody, who might have seen those files, was alive to talk about them. And with that thought her mind switched gears, and she was flooded with a compulsive urge to escape, to disappear fast, simply vanish and somehow leave no traces for those people to find her. But how? And was it even possible to disappear in today's world with cameras everywhere, everything noted online and facial recognition software in places like supermarkets? Worry and tiredness, mixed with grief and regret came together into a solid certainty that it couldn't be done; disappearing into some safe place where she couldn't be found would be impossible. And along with that thought came a deep feeling of sadness. Not fear, she realised with surprise, but sadness that her life might end with nothing much left behind. Dave and she had shared precious memories of special occasions, personal triumphs and disappointments, but now she was the only one who knew those things. Her sister in Australia was the last person left who mattered in that special way of family and those you are very close to; the ones tied to you by invisible threads that can't be broken whether they are close by or far away.

At work the next day her thoughts constantly reverted to her impossible situation until, in the middle of a conversation with two colleagues, she remembered a book she had read years ago, prompted by a stray comment.

'I do like books that include nature,' said one. 'If the book is set in New Zealand, I mean. Descriptions of native bush and rivers, places I recognise, it makes me feel I'm nearly part of the story, and it seems more real somehow than some city in another country.'

And Sam remembered a novel about a woman, who fled from threats, and how she worked out how to do it without leaving any clues, a book where a Hawke's Bay river played a crucial part. It must be several years since she read the book, but that character's escape was surprisingly clear in her mind. The way she had planned each step towards total anonymity, a life out of sight of cameras, leaving no trace. She immediately started thinking about what she herself would need to do to simply vanish and stopped listening to the others. Could she duplicate the plan from that book, whose title she couldn't remember?

By small increments during the rest of the day something that resembled a plan began to form. On the way home she realised that she had compiled a mental list, and she was impatient to get home, to write it down and start elaborating on it, improving it.

But when she turned into the long driveway between the trees, apprehension suddenly gripped her, and she stopped just where the drive emerged into the yard in front of the house. What if they were already there, waiting silently for her to drive into the garage and go inside? She clicked on the central locking and got her phone out just in case and sat for a couple of minutes studying the house, but there was no sign of anyone and if someone was in the house they must have walked up. Or was their vehicle in the garage right now? Commons sense kicked in after a moment and she realised she wasn't thinking straight. If she came home and opened the garage door and saw a strange car there, she wouldn't go in, and they'd never do anything as stupid as that. When she opened the door from the garage to the hallway she stood for a long moment listening for sounds, but there was only silence.

Full of nervous energy she found herself unable to think of dinner or anything domestic. Instead she checked all doors and windows, pushed home the bolt on the door to the garage and started planning. Later she would marvel at this instant response, how she hadn't hesitated or delayed for a moment but simply started putting things in place. It no longer mattered how serious the threat was, or how extreme the measures she planned. The only thing that mattered now was constructing a plan and acting on it. She felt as if pursuers were only a few steps behind her and there was no time to lose. The moment they discovered that Dave had been her ex-husband they would connect the dots between him, her and the man in the garage, and come for her. Fear ran a cold finger down her spine when she recalled the scene Liz McCarroll's neighbour had described, and in her mind she pictured herself lying on the ground, her skin cold and grey, covered in dried blood.

She wrote, pondered, looked things up on the internet, added to the list, jotted down names and phone numbers and only looked up when she realised that hours had passed since she last got up. Stretching her arms over her head, she groaned at how stiff she was and got up to turn on lights and pull the curtains across the windows. All the while she talked out loud to herself, argued a point, reminded herself to write down something that had just occurred to her, and returned to the planning with a glass of water and an energy drink beside her.

Last thing before going to bed she read the news online and came across Liz McCarroll's name in a headline, and the article brought home how acute and possible close danger was now. Liz had not been killed the day before her neighbour saw her body on the lawn, she had been dead for several days but lain unnoticed. Police were asking for witnesses or dashcam footage from the street where Liz lived for the day after Dave was killed. And Sam knew without a doubt that she must get away and simply disappear. It was only a question of time before they were on her doorstep.

10

After a few hours' sleep Sam got up at five the next morning. The intense feeling that danger was only one step behind her was so powerful that there was nothing she could do other than make a plan to disappear as fast as she possibly could. She could neither ignore the compulsion to flee nor reason it away, and the urgency fuelled her even as her body protested at not enough sleep. She knew what she was planning to do was extreme, but then, so is being killed, she told herself, it's one extreme or the other.

The email she sent to the library manager was minimal, which she hoped would seem natural in the situation she used as an excuse. She wrote that due to a serious medical emergency involving her sister in Australia she must leave for Melbourne immediately, she would be away for an indefinite time and apologised for resigning without giving notice. Sitting at the kitchen table she composed a text message to be sent later to half a dozen close friends and to a few women in the two book clubs she belonged to, leaving the question of what to tell those closest to her until she had worked through the consequences and decided on how much to tell them. She was spinning a web of lies, but it was crucial that she created a smoke screen. She must avoid probing questions or emotional conversations until she was safe, and lying in text messages was easier than lying in a conversation would be. Right now she needed all her energy to do what had to be done, and wasting time on long and difficult conversations was more than she could cope with.

In the back of her mind she blessed her parents for the way they had kept her and Emily away from what they referred to as "computer culture" with the result that Sam had never owned a smartphone until she was twenty-three and never had a presence on social media. For the first time she realised what a bonus this was in her present situation, because there was no history online that could be used to link her and Dave.

Finally she drafted an email to her sister, saying that something dreadful had happened, she was in serious danger and would have to disappear for a time. Somehow, she must make Emily understand that people might call to ask about her and not to trust them, whoever they said they were. Later in the day she would go through the message very carefully before she sent it, weigh up how it would come across to Emily and maybe edit it. The worry it would cause was uppermost in her mind, but there was little she could do to lessen the impact. If she made the threat sound less dire Emily might not be alert enough if someone called to ask for her and fall for some phony reason why she must be found. And if she made it too terrifying she would cause constant worry for Emily and Neil.

"...Please help me in this when people call or text you. Say there's nothing wrong with you and you don't know where I am or why I left.

They're bound to call you or Neil but plead ignorance whoever they say they are – believe <u>nobody</u> apart from me or Jill. If you contact Jill do not text or email, make a phone call, she will explain why. I won't tell you any more now, but sometime in the future you will have the full story, I promise. I am in real fear for my life. I know who killed Dave, and they will come for me as soon as they realise the link between Dave and me. Neither of us did anything wrong, we were innocent bystanders who got involved by chance, found out about serious crimes and now on the wrong side of very dangerous people with far reaching powers. Please don't call when you get this, I have no time to talk, wait until I call you, which I will do in a couple of days. It will be a call from a number you don't recognise, an anonymous phone I'm going to buy. And please don't save that number in your contacts list and don't text to the new number, just <u>wait for me to call you</u>. Sam xx"

Jill answered against a background of children talking and dishes clattering. 'Sorry, I know it's a busy time of day,' said Sam quickly. 'I just want you to tell me a time when I can call you at work without disrupting your routine. I need to share something that's quite urgent, but I won't tell you now when you're trying to get the kids ready for school.'

'Any time between nine and half past ten. I'll take my morning break when you call. See you!' Sam could picture Jill briskly dismissing the call from her mind, putting the phone down and reverting to organising the children.

For the next few hours Sam consulted her list from the previous night, added things and crossed out others. She made phone calls, pleaded and cajoled and mostly achieved what she wanted. And all the time thoughts about how much she would tell Jill revolved in the back of her mind. She had to know enough to understand why Sam was taking such desperate action, but she would not tell her what was on the hard drive, nobody else needed to know. The most important thing would be to prepare Jill for a possible visit from someone trying to find out where Sam had disappeared to, but hot on the heels of that thought came another: they might find her first and kill her, and then nobody would turn up and ask awkward questions of Jill. She shook her head to dismiss the feeling of doom this created and continued her frantic preparations.

With a mug of tea beside her and the pen and pad in front of her Sam called Jill just after ten. She had to force herself to sit down and concentrate on the conversation instead of doing other things at the same time, but how she put things was important, so she must focus to avoid being drawn into details.

'OK! Tell me what's wrong,' said Jill, and Sam heard the concern in her voice. 'I'm outside, so we can be away from all the noise, and my team can look after things for a while, so don't rush it. What's happened?'

Telling the story in verbal bullet points didn't take long but answering the questions Jill fired at her took time and involved long pauses while Sam considered how to reply. 'Listen,' she said after a particularly long silence on her part. 'There are so many details I can't tell you that it's hard to draw a line between keeping you safe and still explaining things. It's not that I don't trust you, you know that, but this is so dangerous - I just can't risk anyone else being killed.'

'How much does Sasha know?' asked Jill suddenly. 'You said you told her to say Dave made that call to her, but did you tell her what it was about?'

'God no! At that stage I didn't know if I could trust her to even be able to keep the lie about the phone call to herself, so I told her nothing. I pretended I didn't know where Dave had been or why, nothing! But now, of course, I know she can be trusted, so I'll tell her a bit, but not as much as I've told you. She's a very surprising girl. But I must make sure you're both prepared in case people come asking about me, someone from that group of corrupt cops I mean.'

She considered for a moment, tried to imagine Jill opening the door to someone who could identify themselves as police and had some genuine sounding reason to ask for information about herself. 'They could turn up with proper police ID, say they're investigating something, and they must find me and put me in witness protection or something. So you can't trust anyone whatever reason they give you. You can only trust me in this.'

'OK, of course I'll do that. But I need to know how to let you know if someone asked about you, won't I? And you said I mustn't text, so I'd have to call you.'

'I'd rather you didn't, just to be safe - wait for me to call you. Listen, I know you've got a camera outside the front door. Does it still work? If someone turns up would you be able to see their car on the street, or someone standing around waiting for them?'

'It works fine, and it picks up movement from a wide area out the front, so if someone triggers the sensor when they enter the path to the front door or the driveway it films a big area. Right across the street and wide out to the sides. I had it set up like that when it was installed after the neighbours were burgled.'

Sam tried to think of the ramifications of how much to tell Sasha and if there would be any point of telling her that Jill also knew the basics. 'Hey, do you think it might be good if I tell Sasha that she can talk to you if something happens? I'm hoping to find somewhere to live with no cell phone reception, but I'll call you every so often – go somewhere with reception and call you and Emily and maybe Sasha.'

'Why do you want to be out of cell phone cover?'

'I want to find somewhere to live that's a dead zone – safer all round, I think. So don't call me, because I don't want text messages or voice messages. Those are the kind of things that can be traced after the event, so to speak, they can see what you wrote or hear what was said in a message, but conversations don't get recorded.'

Jill didn't need to think. 'Tell Sasha whatever you think she can cope with and give her my number and tell her to only call, no messages of any kind. Tell her to put a fake name on my number – oh, and give me her number right now, I'll get my pen out and write it on my arm.'

The relief Sam felt after this call was like a tonic. It made her feel that she had a back-stop, someone she could trust, who could tell her what was going on, and best of all, someone who could be Sasha's support person as well. She went back to her sorting and tidying with renewed energy and a sense of having achieved something constructive.

11

Punctually at half past one the woman from the property management company arrived, after rather grumpily agreeing to come at short notice.

'My diary is full,' she said when Sam called at eight that morning. 'I can come on Wednesday afternoon.'

'It's a genuine emergency, my sister is very seriously ill in Australia, and I might have to stay there for some time, so I'm leaving very soon. But never mind, I'll call someone else.'

'OK, then – I'll make an exception, I'll be there at half past one. Text me the address.'

No goodbye, no I'm sorry to hear that – very brisk, thought Sam, but she's coming, so I don't care what she's like.

'Hi, I'm Veronica,' said the property woman when Sam opened the front door. She was surprisingly young and pretty compared to how serious and severe she had sounded on the phone. 'This a very nice house!'

Brisk and efficient she rapidly scanned the hall, taking in the details, then moved to the open door of the guest room, cast a glance inside and turned back to Sam. This was a woman who wasted no time on casual chatter, which was exactly what Sam needed.

'You're welcome to look around, and please excuse the mess, but I've been working very fast today, no time to tidy as I go.'

'How is your sister getting on? Have you heard anything more?'

'No improvement,' lied Sam. 'Not yet, but I hope to hear more tonight. Please feel free to check everything. I imagine you need to have a full picture before you can find tenants. I must continue what I'm doing but come and find me when you need me.'

Veronica didn't seem to mind being left to her own devices, just fished a pen out of her bag and said, 'OK, I'll make some notes, and we'll talk when I'm done.'

It took no time, fifteen minutes later Sam spotted her in the garden, then she reappeared inside and asked to see the garage and that was that. 'Excellent! Let's sit down and sign the agreement. First your bank account details, of course.'

The form filling took a while, but it had to be done and Sam reined in her impatience. 'Right,' said Veronica and turned a page. 'So, if something minor goes wrong you authorise us to arrange repairs? Good! Please sign here. And you will set up direct debits for rates and insurance? Don't forget to change your contents insurance from this address to the storage company.' And a moment later, 'Are you leaving the shelving units in the garage? And what about the things in the garden shed?'

When she was leaving Veronica stopped before she got into her car. 'Don't forget to leave your key under that rock when you leave, so I can have one and give the tenants two. I'll organise for the commercial cleaners to come in before I show the place to anyone.' And with a brisk 'Bye!' she got into her car and disappeared down the drive.

Mentally and physically exhausted after her fraught night,

Sam texted the removal company to confirm that their agent was coming, decided she had time for a cup of coffee and sat down to study her list. She had told everyone the same story to explain why she was acting in such a hurry, and now everyone she was engaging with believed that she was leaving for a family emergency and that she would stay and get a job in Melbourne. Nobody had asked any further questions. My personal affairs are of no interest, she thought, and gulped down some hot coffee too fast and nearly choked. They don't care, it's just another business transaction, thank goodness! She had barely finished her coffee before the doorbell went again.

'You want all this taken away tomorrow or the next day? That's an awful lot of packing to do,' said the man from the removal firm thoughtfully as he looked around at the untidy living room. 'Are you going to do most of it yourself or do you want us to come in with an extra couple of people to do it? We can do it, but it will cost you.'

She could hear that he didn't believe she would get it done in time and hold them up, disrupt their schedules. She had considered what to get rid of during wakeful hours in the night, but now she changed her mind on the spur of the moment and decided that the Salvation Army truck would have to make an extra trip or two.

'Oh no, it's not all going to the storage unit. The Salvation Army is taking more than half of the furniture, probably two thirds plus all of the kitchen stuff, and a lot is going to the dump. I haven't organised that yet, but maybe you know someone who can come with a truck to take the rubbish away?'

'I'll give you a name before I go, I've got it in the car. He'll charge per hour plus the dump fees. And remember to get the contents of the fridge taken to the dump too, if you're not giving it away.'

Forty-eight hours later, as a third frantic day drew to a close, Sam stood at the front door watching the second-hand shop's truck disappear down the driveway for the second time and tried to think of what she might have forgotten. That something had been left out of her panicky plans was probably a given, but just then she couldn't think of anything. She thought back to her desperate call to the Salvation Army shop, pleading with them to make an exception to their rule about booking their pick-up service a week in advance. How she had heard her own voice breaking on a sob of exhaustion when she begged them to come sooner, and how it had softened the heart of the woman she spoke to.

After minimal sleep and with worried thoughts constantly revolving in her head she knew some of her decisions were probably irrational, and at some point in the future she might regret getting rid of so much furniture. But the haunting thought constantly in the back of her mind, that she might only be days or even hours away from being killed, could not be ignored.

To start with she had wondered how the connection between Dave and Liz had been discovered, but it could only be that Liz had started asking questions based on what Dave had told her in their phone calls before the meeting. He had said he told her quite a bit to make sure she'd be interested in taking the job on, so if she discussed it with someone else and that person decided to make further enquiries of their own, then it could have spread much further. Maybe someone contacted a police officer they knew and asked careless questions, and the rumour spread from there, that would be enough for someone with the right contacts to track it back to first Liz and then Dave. And they were bound to continue probing into Liz and Dave's connections. This was it, she knew without a doubt that this is how it had happened. All her previous theories had flaws, but not this one.

Walking through the empty house in the grey light of dusk she felt dislocated from reality by the speed at which everything had happened. Over a few short weeks her life had changed from being mundane and contented to one infused with fear and grief. Her whole existence had been disrupted by violence and death and might never return to its normal state, and now she was about the leave her home, her friends and her job, possibly for a very long time, perhaps forever. The devastating thought of possibly never being able to come back nearly overwhelmed her. Who would she be without background or history or old friends? Blinking back tears she picked up her suitcase and bag, swallowed hard and locked the front door before she put the key under the rock beside the front step. A minute later she drove away without closing the gate behind her.

Two blocks away she pulled over to the side and picked up her phone. After a short moment of doubt she sent the draft emails and text messages she had composed three days ago, which had been revised and finetuned several times since. She knew some would respond instantly, but she would delay reacting until she had gone through the final two steps of leaving, until she was truly on her way. The inevitable call to Emily would be hard to deal with. Making her understand that the decision to disappear was based on solid reasoning without giving too much away would be a balancing act. How she wished she could discuss all this with Dave! But there was nobody she could confide in, and knowing she had caused Dave's death by asking for advice made her determined to keep things to herself. She would never again burden anyone with the details of what she had discovered.

She glanced at the time, turned off her phone and set out for the supermarket car park where she would hand over the car to

Simon, the man who was paying cash for the privilege of getting it so cheap. They had agreed that she would park in the corner closest to the loading bay, which he suggested would be a safe place to hand over so much cash and he was right. Sam looked around and realised this was the perfect spot, far from the entrance and therefore not popular with shoppers. Only seconds after she parked there was a knock on her window.

'I got dropped off a bit early,' Simon said when she got out. 'If you get into the passenger seat we'll do the formalities, and I'll take you wherever you want to go.'

'Thank God for smart phones!' Sam smiled in the dim light inside the car when they had finished. 'This was easier than I'd though it would be – transferring the ownership, I mean.'

Standing on the dark side of the car she put the twenty-one of little oblong plastic bags of banknotes he gave her into her suitcase, tucked one into her shoulder bag and turned down his offer of a ride with the excuse that she needed a couple of things from the supermarket. Once he had driven off she hitched her bag over her shoulder and walked away trailing the suitcase. She would walk the five blocks to the motel she had selected and take a taxi to the nearest bus station in the morning.

12

Two days later Sam was in Tauranga, heading for a charity shop a woman she met at the bus stop had told her how to find. She had taken the SIM card out of her phone when she caught the first bus, so asking for direction rather than using Google maps was already a habit. At every stop she changed her appearance in some way, and now she needed a non-descript jacket and a cap. The racks in the shop were crammed with clothing of all kinds, not always logically sorted, and working her way through it all took time, but after a frustrating half hour she found exactly what she needed; a dark grey rainproof jacket with four inside pockets and a hood concealed in the collar. She paid twenty-eight dollars in cash for the jacket, a black cap, a little plastic bag of safety pins and a large carry bag.

In the little lane beside the shop she opened her suitcase and crammed everything in before she made her way to the public toilets she had noticed on her way from the bus stop. The suitcase was now full to overflowing, and as she wheeled it along she smiled at how lucky it was that she had found that large vinyl carry bag hanging on a rack just inside the door. Before she donned the jacket and the cap she must do something to coordinate her luggage with her appearance. The suitcase was far too distinctive, so finding the carry bag was a stroke of luck. Her careful plan had been wrong in one aspect, and in the last couple of days she had worried that going into a sports shop to buy a backpack while pulling an expensive looking wheeled suitcase would not only look strange but worse, memorable. But now, with the large carry bag, she would be able to nearly instantly transform herself into an anonymous and plain woman with luggage to fit her clothes, before she caught the next bus. But before the transformation she must deal with her bundles of cash.

Blessing how spacious the self-cleaning public toilet was, she sat fully dressed on the lid-less stainless steel bowl and started organising herself. With the plastic bags of banknotes laid out on the open suitcase at her feet she considered the options and after a couple of failed experiments the bags of money were evenly distributed in the grey jacket. Most of them in the inside pockets, the last two in a front pocket, all secured with safety pins and the pocket zips done up. She got to her feet and tried the jacket on. Bulkier than she normally looked, she decided, but nothing out of the way. The jacket and cap went back into the suitcase, and she left the toilet looking exactly the same as when she went in.

In a park that seemed to have no cameras Sam sat on a bench under a large pin oak with a paper mug of coffee and a sandwich in a paper bag beside her, ready to burn yet another bridge behind her. She got the very basic cell phone she had bought the previous day out of her shoulder bag and started entering the eleven phone numbers she had decided she must have on the new phone. When she had finished she ripped the page she had written the numbers on into pieces and put them in the bin beside the bench. Am I paranoid, she asked herself, or am I just very careful? The plan to remove herself from risk according to her step-by-step escape list was always uppermost in her mind, an obsession unlike anything she had experienced before, impossible to ignore as it endlessly revolved in her head. There could be no ad-hoc decisions, everything had to fit the plan.

Since she arrived in the park the sunshine had disappeared, and clouds were scudding in from the east. She drank the coffee, ate the sandwich and got to her feet. After looking around to see nobody could see what she was doing she put the suitcase on the bench and opened it. Quickly she changed her pink jacket for the second-hand grey one, put the cap on and sat down again. It was a moment's work to put the card back in her smartphone, then she fished around for the little bag of safety pins and poked one hard into the hole in the side of the phone. A quick check proved that the factory reset had removed her contacts, text messages and photos. The SIM card went into the bin beside the bench, but she would dispose of the phone separately, and some lucky person might find it and use it. She walked away dressed in grey and black, with most of what had been in the suitcase now in the bag she had bought in the charity shop, the kind of bag she hadn't know existed, a huge box-shaped vinyl bag with a zip and two handles.

She turned and looked back at the bench under the tree and nearly laughed at the sight of her smart blue suitcase sitting abandoned beside the rubbish bin. Someone would take it and find a few clothes including the pink jacket inside and count themselves lucky. Hopefully someone who would simply take the case and keep it and not report having found it. But on that thought she stopped abruptly and reconsidered. Maybe it would be better to remove the pink jacket, which had been another charity shop purchase the previous day and dispose of it somewhere else and break that link too? She retraced her steps, got the jacket out along with the light blue jumper she had worn on the very first bus ride and put them into the big bag to throw into separate rubbish bins along the way.

Now she was unremarkable, dressed in dull colours and with the option of wearing a cap or pulling out the concealed hood, the perfect camouflage for someone travelling by bus from one random location to another, dull and unremarkable.

Before she returned to the bus station by a long, round-about route, she sat on another bench, this time at a bus stop, and called Jill, who answered nearly immediately which was lucky; she was often unavailable to take calls during work hours.

'Listen,' said Sam quickly before Jill started asking questions. 'I know you're at work and busy, but I just want to check nobody's been around asking questions before I go completely underground. I'll try to call every second Friday morning. If I can't call, you mustn't assume the worst, just wait, OK?'

'Thank God you called! A man came last night and asked for you and said he'd been told you were staying with me, and when I said you weren't with me he asked where you are. So I said, "she's in Australia with her sister who's in hospital, but you could ask at the library, they might have a forwarding address". He didn't say he was a cop, very casual, soft-spoken.'

Fear ran a cold finger down Sam's spine. 'What did he look like?'

'Middle-aged, tall, quite thin, not much hair. He said his name is Johnson. Who is he?'

'He's not called Johnson, his told me his name is Brown, but that's not his real name either. He's very dangerous - I think he organised Dave's murder. Did he believe you?'

Jill snorted. 'He wanted to know where your sister lives and what her name is, but I said I only know her first name, and I've never heard her married name, so he left. I tried to sound casual and a bit snippy, as if he'd just interrupted something, which he had actually.' She laughed. 'I was just about to pour myself a glass of wine after a very busy day and finally having got the kids to bed. Strange time of the day to call, I must say. I've saved the recording of him from the security camera, but he appeared on foot, and no car and no companion that I could see.'

Then Sam remembered what she had forgotten to tell Jill. 'Hey, don't hang up! I've just remembered that I gave the rental manager your name – sorry! I didn't even have time to ask if you're ok with it.'

'That's fine – what do I need to do? And what's her name?'

'She's Veronica somebody, and she's got you down as my nominated contact person for anything she wants someone to make decisions about, like repairs, unless they're minor – all those things that might crop up over time. The payments for insurance and rates are all set up to happen automatically, so it's just having someone with common sense she can talk to if she needs to.'

Jill's voice changed by a couple of degrees. 'God, I'm going to miss you. I'll worry about you all the time! Look after yourself!'

Now it was urgent to call Sasha. The thought of Brown locating her too and putting pressure on her and maybe asking her to let him in conjured up unthinkable consequences. The thought of how frightening he could be, and how Sasha might panic at his strange mixture of kindness and underlying threat gave Sam goose bumps. She must warn her and tell her more than she had planned to, but first she must decide exactly how much to say.

After five minutes of considering potential pitfalls, she had made up her mind and called her. 'I'm glad I caught you at home, Sasha, because this is important, very important. I've left Auckland now and I'm going into hiding. I'll go to some place where I can't be found, as I said in that message I sent a couple of days ago. No, please don't interrupt, just listen for a minute, so I can explain.'

She took a deep breath and hoped this would work out and not scare Sasha to tears. 'Dave and I both knew something very dangerous that involves corruption among police officers, and I think that's why he was pushed off the road. I hate to tell you this, but I think I must - he was murdered, I'm sure of it. But I can't tell police that's what I think because I don't know which cops are involved. When I left they still hadn't discovered that Dave used to be married to me, but that is the reason I have to go into hiding.'

There was a long silence, but when Sasha replied she sounded surprisingly calm, no tears. 'I thought there was something you didn't tell me,' she said slowly. 'But I knew I could trust you, so I did what you said. I did wonder if it was something from Dave's past, but I thought you'd tell me later, probably, when everything had settled down a bit.'

Sam had to swallow hard before she could reply. 'Thank you for trusting me – you're very generous. I could have told you about this, but I thought it might be too much for you that dreadful day. I decided you needed comfort, not scary surprises.'

'But what was it that he knew that's so dangerous that you have to leave like this? Oh, please don't! I wish I wasn't moving in with dad, because you could live in the guest room in my flat. But I didn't want to stay there alone, and I've already moved quite a few of my things. But, yes, of course I can change it - we can live in the flat together, and I won't tell anyone you're there, you can just stay inside and nobody would know.'

Thinking fast Sam said, 'Listen, Sasha! I *can't* change this, and I would put you in danger too if I stayed with you, which I refuse to do. I want to keep you safe – it's what Dave would want me to do.' She took a deep breath to suppress how emotional this made her feel. 'Please move in with your dad right away, today, and leave the flat as it is. Just take your most precious things. I'll feel a lot happier if you don't stay there any longer than you have to, in case they work out where Dave was living and come asking questions. They've already tried to find out where I've gone from my friend Jill, and I don't want them anywhere near you. They're very dangerous, and it would be easy to say too much if they started asking questions.'

'Ah yes, of course they might, but ...' Sasha was clearly thinking as she spoke. 'No, I don't think they'd be able to find out. It would be very unlikely, I think. I lived here before Dave moved in, ever since I was seventeen. My dad organised it for me when I left my mum's house because we argued all the time. But the lease is in dad's name. He pays the rent, and I pay him, then later Dave and I paid dad half each, you know?'

Better, thought Sam, less direct connection, but still a potential risk. 'Let me think for a moment. So you're giving up the flat?"

'Dad says I'll probably want to move back after a while, so we'll just leave it as it is because the lease has a couple of years to run, and it's a very nice flat. He says I can sub-let it until I decide what I want to do.'

Sam knew that now she must tell her more, because things seemed to become more urgent by the minute, and it was important that Sasha got out of harm's way. 'Listen, darling – I don't want to scare you, but you need to understand how urgent it is that you move out right away. My house was searched just after Dave died. A few things were taken, but that was just to make it look like a burglary. It was a very thorough search.'

'But why? What were they looking for?'

'I don't know for sure, but they probably think either I or Dave had something in writing or something saved on a laptop or on a

USB, and they're trying to make sure none of the evidence is left anywhere. They're making absolutely sure nobody's got any evidence against them – and they are completely ruthless.'

Increasingly worried about where this conversation was going Sam hoped that Sasha wouldn't start asking questions she would rather not answer but removing her from risk was important.

'Ah, of course,' she said after another pause. 'I see why you asked all those questions about the flat. OK then, I'll move today, right now and just go back and get stuff now and then if I need something. I don't have to sub-let it right away. God, I wish you weren't leaving! I'll miss you so much! I thought we would meet for a drink now and then and talk about Dave perhaps.'

'I'm sorry, but I must disappear, I really do. I'm a liability now, too dangerous for anyone to have in the house, and as I said, I'm not prepared to put you at risk. I don't think I'll be safe until I'm somewhere they'd never think of, with no traces of where I went. And the number I'm on now is a cheap phone I bought. I've got rid of the smart phone. Please don't save this new number with my name attached, don't even have me in your contacts list. You mustn't call me or send text messages, because they can be traced. Just wait for me to call you, even if it's not very often. I'll try to call you every second Friday, OK?'

What else could she tell her to make this less traumatic? 'My friend Jill will be in touch, I've given her your number, and you can trust her just like you trust me. I've only told you and Jill the truth about why I'm leaving, so meet up with her now and then if you need someone to talk to who knows about this. And she knew Dave well, of course. She was very fond of him, so talk to her if you need a bit of extra support. And look after yourself!'

· · ·

Three days later Sam sat on yet another bench, this time at the Wellington central railway station, waiting for the shuttle to take her to the South Island ferry and suddenly realised the dangerous situation she might unwittingly have put prospective tenants in. She called Jill and prayed she would take the call, because she didn't want to risk calling from the South Island until she was in a safe place, but to her relief Jill took the call on the first attempt. 'Hi, are you OK?'

'I'm fine, but I've just realised that I might have put someone else in danger! What if Brown or his men come to find me after Veronica's found tenants for the house? It could be a disaster.'

Surprisingly Jill laughed. 'Relax - that worry's out of date already. Veronica called the day before yesterday and said she went up to let the commercial cleaners in and the place had been broken into again. She'd already organised someone to replace a broken window, she just thought I should know. So they'll have found the place completely empty and drawn their own conclusions.'

'Oh, thank God! The moment I realised, I was terrified. I knew I was bound to forget something when I left in such a hurry. Here's the bus, I must go.'

PART 2

13

When Carter called and left a message saying it was urgent, and we must talk as soon as possible I just put the phone back down. The report I was just finishing was so close to completion I couldn't bear to be interrupted. My phone had been on "do not disturb" for a couple of days, though I checked now and then to see who had left messages. But half an hour later I changed my mind. Carter had never before left a message about urgency, and normally he never called at all, he just texted. He'd never like talking on the phone, so something must be wrong.

'Hey,' I said a few moments later. 'I just checked my phone. What's wrong? Are you in some kind of trouble?'

'You won't believe this!'

Carter was panting hard, and I got seriously worried. 'What's wrong with your breathing? You sound terrible - are you ill?'

'Climbing a hill in the Nelson Lakes district, very steep! I'm fine, but Thomas, listen - I think I saw Tilda yesterday. I've called you several times, but your damn phone's been on DND, and I was just about to send an email instead when you called. Or I would have once I got to the top of this hill. I only tried calling just now because I was finally getting a couple of bars on my phone. There's a lot of places down here where you don't get a single bar.'

'You saw Tilda? Where?'

'Hang on. Let me sit down and I'll tell you. I'm as hot as hell and I need a drink. So, I was in this little village on the west coast, a bit inland from Reefton, up in the hills as they say down there – more like mountains. There's an old track to a little lake there I wanted to do, lots of bird life, and I'd just arrived back in the village. I was driving down the main street, well, it's the main road actually, and I saw this woman come out of a shop. I'm sure it was her. I stopped and ran back, but she'd gone. I went into the shop and the guy there said he didn't know who she was. But this is interesting - I think he was lying. He said she was a tourist who'd just come in for a bottle of water. And she did have big backpack, but I think he does know her and for some reason he wasn't telling. I only saw the side of her face, but you know how Tilda's body language was always a bit different from other girls?'

'No, I didn't know that. Explain about the body language please.'

'Tilda walked like a boy, I always thought. Or like some boys. She used to stride around, as if she was on her way somewhere and knew exactly what she was about. Not blokeish, just focused, like purposeful. And this woman walked just like that. It's quite unusual.'

I was simultaneously trying to picture what Tilda had looked like walking and taking in Carter's information. 'OK, I'll take your word for it, but don't forget it's twenty-four years since she disappeared – no, it's twenty-five now. And I was nine at the time, while you were both sixteen. We probably didn't notice the same things.'

'I'm certain it was her. I'll send you the name of the place and maybe draw a little map of where she was heading. I really think you should take a week off and go down there. Have a look around and try to talk to the guy in the shop - his name's Vijay. I'm certain he knows something, and he might tell you if you explain about Tilda.'

That evening I sat for a long time in the dimly lit living room and gazed unseeingly through the glass barrier on the balcony. Below me lay the sweep of Wellington's inner harbour with the glittering lights on the other side of the dark water, but in my mind scenes from long ago played out. I stayed up late, unable to escape my memories until I thought I was finally tired enough to go to bed, still with my mind on the past. Lying on my back I watched the stars through the skylight above the bed, but for once the sight didn't put me to sleep. Instead I re-lived the last time I saw Matilda, that cataclysmic day two weeks after my ninth birthday. I could remember every word and every touch, feel her breath on the side of my head as her arms clasped me from behind, and she whispered, first words of comfort and then her farewell message.

Over dinner that night I had said something long forgotten, and my father erupted into one of his fits of instant rage, dragged me into the passage and beat me with the broken broom handle he kept in the corner by the door. The only thought in my head was the vain hope that this punishment session wouldn't end with a hard punch to the middle of my chest, but of course it did. I tore lose and ran out the open back door, squeezed through the narrow gap in the fence where a plank was missing and crawled into my safe space under the large hydrangea bush in the corner of the neighbour's garden.

A bit later Matilda crawled into my hiding place and wrapped her arms around me, held me tight and whispered, 'I can't protect you, Thomas. I'm sorry! He does things to me too, different things that don't show. Please, darling, try not to answer back, don't scowl and *don't* interrupt him. If you're careful you can avoid most of these beatings.'

And I sobbed, 'I'll try, I will, but it's so hard. Nearly everything I do makes him angry now. I have to learn to fight back.' And then a few minutes later, still holding me tight, Matilda said very quietly, 'I'm going to leave tonight, after everyone's asleep. I've hidden a bag of clothes behind the bus shelter down the road, and I'll hitch a ride to some other place and get a job. But I'll come for you as soon as I can, and we'll live together far away from here, in some place where he can't find us.'

In the morning she was gone, and I never saw her again. Over the years I tried to find her in every way I could think of. I've Googled her name, then her name and our mother's maiden name, then various combinations with her middle name, I searched social media and contacted her friends from high school and checked police records. I asked questions of everyone I could think of, but I never found her.

'Hi Linley,' I said to my adopted mother two days after Carter called. 'I won't be in town for Dion's birthday unfortunately, but please use my house as planned. I know Robert and Lisa are staying at Dion's, but you and Martin should still stay here, or turn it around and you stay with Dion, and they take my house, so they have lots of space for the kids. You all have the security app for the alarm system on your phones, and you know where everything is.'

'But what's happened? Where are you going to be? I was just saying yesterday how nice it's going to be to have the whole family together.'

'I know – I was looking forward to it too, but an old friend thinks he saw Matilda in a little town in the South Island and I'm going down there to see if I can find her.'

'Good Lord, after all this time! Of course, you must go. But how could he see her and not talk to her?'

As usual Linley put her finger on the exact thing you hadn't told her, so I explained, but we cut the call short when someone came into her office. Next I called Dion and had nearly the exact same conversation, promised to keep the family informed and went back to my packing, reminding myself to have a present for Dion delivered.

Three days after Carter's call I drove off the Cook Straight ferry in Picton and headed for the West Coast. I had emailed Carter the previous night and told him I was going to the South Island and would keep him informed. Carter had been Tilda's boyfriend on and off for a couple of years, and he was devastated when she left without a word. He called back as soon as he got the message. 'Keep me informed, please. Where are you staying?'

'I've rented a house, the only one for rent in that little village, and I'll work from there for a while. I can work from anywhere that has an internet connection. I'll start with that chap in the grocery store and let you know if I find her, of course.'

'Perfect for what I need,' I said that afternoon to the woman who stood beside me in the little house I had rented. 'I presume there's linen and things in a cupboard somewhere?'

She laughed. 'Oh yes, it's fully equipped. I put some sheets out to air on the bed, and I turned the fridge and the hot water on this morning, opened all the windows for an hour or so. Marina asked me to do that seeing it's a while since anyone rented it.' She pointed at the potbellied stove. 'That little thing throws out a lot of heat and there's firewood out the back, but you've got the heat pump too, of course. And if you need me, just call! I work at the sawmill down the road, in the office, and if you can't get me, try Bess in the café, she's like the local intelligence service, knows everyone and everything.'

When she left I unloaded a mountain of stuff from the car and didn't know where to start. I had loaded the car the evening before with a mental list of what I would take, but then I kept adding things. Even while I packed everything from the fridge into the chilly bin that morning, my mind constructed a new list of things I might need. More warm clothes, rubber boots, hiking boots, a couple of comfortable pillows, my backpack and a lot more, determined to be prepared for anything. When I drove out of the garage at half past five to get on the early ferry the far back was full. In the last minute I thought of half a dozen things and just chucked them on the back seat. I was laughing at myself and how unlike me this was, as I drove downhill towards Oriental Bay. I'm not an impulsive type, but this time I had an urge to cover all bases, just in case. With every possible contingency catered for I could comfortably live away from home for months, which was definitely not part of the plan. The very last impulsive addition was wine, two unopened boxes of six bottles that had arrived by courier only days earlier and a bottle of whisky from the drink cabinet. 'Bring it on!' I said to myself. 'I'm prepared for everything.'

By the time dusk turned to night it was done, everything was put away and the small bedroom had been turned into a storage space with all my gear spread out on the bunks. I made four pieces of toast, heated a can of chicken soup and poured a glass of wine before I sat down at the little table and tried to decide how to approach that shopkeeper in the morning. On the four hour drive from Picton I had thought about it on and off and reached no conclusion, but somehow I must persuade him to tell me what he knew. And now I realised that my planning was too inflexible; I had rented the house for two weeks, but I might need to stay longer. My plan had been based on Carter's mention of the woman's backpack, a large one, which indicated either someone who was moving around and not likely to still be found in the area, or someone who had hitched a ride up here and was living somewhere locally. And if she was living here and simply went hiking sometimes, it might take time to catch up with her. Having the cottage for longer would mean I could it as a base for a wider search, if that turned out to be necessary.

I could think of many reasons why someone would live quietly here, like an author or someone writing a thesis, or someone doing family history research. Lots of peace and quiet with nature and hiking on the doorstep. The guidebook I bought on the ferry mentioned "basic tracks" with splendid views right down to the coast from some locations. It sounded pretty rough, not like the tracks with huts for overnight stays I was used to, but if that woman was fit and independent she might prefer solitary trekking and not sleeping in crowded huts.

Tomorrow I would start with Vijay in the store and then find someone to tell me more about those tracks I'd just read about. I put the wineglass to one side, picked up the phone and emailed Marina in Christchurch to ask if I could have the house for a couple of months. Even if I didn't discover anything useful here I could use this as a base and travel around asking questions. Marina replied straight away: "Certainly! I don't have another booking until the summer tourist season starts in November. I hope the house is OK. The nights are probably still chilly up there, but there's firewood in the little shed at the back and the heat pump in the living area warms up the main bedroom too if you leave to door open."

Chilly was an understatement, freezing was more like it; up here in the mountains it was still winter. But the cottage was perfectly adequate. One biggish room with the kitchen at one end, two bedrooms, one with two sets of bunks, a rather antiquated bathroom with a shower over a big clawfoot bath, and a veranda equipped with four chairs and a table.

The next morning I walked down the steep lane to the shops on the main road and was pleasantly surprised. When I drove in the previous day my focus had been on finding the cottage and now I stopped on the corner to look around. A café on the corner and an old villa converted to a backpacker lodge, a pub with a sign advertising "hot evening meals by pre-order" and Vijay's store directly across the road from the café. The main road in the westerly direction was lined with houses, some of them tiny old cottages, perhaps from gold mining days. To the east the road climbed a steep hillside covered with native forest and disappeared out of sight. A little microcosmos way up here in the hills with everything you need for a quiet life. I crossed the road to the store and picked up a basket on my way in.

14

Shopping first seemed like a good introduction and a reason to have a chat, so I walked slowly around and picked up an item here and there. I was the only customer, and the man behind the counter was talking on the phone, laughing at something. 'No way!' he exclaimed suddenly. 'I'd never do that.' He sounded friendly and relaxed which was promising. When I reached the counter the call had ended. I unloaded the basket and returned his smile. 'I'm impressed – you've got a very well-stocked shop here. It's nice to have good cheeses and seed crackers just around the corner.'

'We do our best. If there's something you want that I don't have I can get it. Are you the guy who hired Marina's place up the lane?'

'Yeah, I've rented it for a while. I'm looking for my lost sister.' I saw him instantly make the connection between someone asking about a woman a couple of weeks ago and me turning up. His expression remained friendly and calm, but I heard the slight caution in his voice when he replied.

'I don't think you'll find her here. This is a small village, only a few hundred people live here, and we all know each other. What made you think you'd find her here?'

'A friend of hers from high school told me he thought he saw her here, quite recently. She's been missing for twenty-five years.'

'I'm sorry, that's very sad,' said Vijay. 'I remember the guy who came in and asked, but the woman he saw was just a tourist I'd never seen before.'

I left without asking anything else and decided to return the next day. I was certain that Carter was right, and Vijay knew more than he was letting on, but maybe I could convince him to talk by taking it slowly. I returned to the cottage and spent the rest of the day working. The next morning there was thick frost on the grass, but by mid-morning the sun had appeared over the hills, the frost had melted, and I set out on stage two of my search.

The woman in the backpacker's lodge said she hadn't had any women staying in the last couple of months, only a few men. 'It's not the tourist season for us yet – we're more of a summer hiking place than a winter place. There's no skiing around here and we're not on the way to anywhere interesting. But in summer we get a lot of people now, ever since that British influencer couple were here two years ago.' She grinned. 'They did us a lot of good! Raved about the scenery and the bush walks and praised both this place and the pub – particularly the pub dinners.'

Disappointed I thanked her and went to the café, hoping for better news. 'I'm renting a cottage up the lane. I'm sure you'd heard I was coming,' I said. 'I was talking to Vijay yesterday and I didn't need to introduce myself, he knew who I was already – must have seen me coming down the lane and crossing the road.'

'It's a bit like that around here, unavoidable,' said the middle-aged woman behind the counter. 'It's still winter, or nearly, so we don't get a lot of people coming through. Are you going hiking? Do you want something to eat?'

'I'll have one of those date scones, please. I'm here to check on a sighting of a woman who might be my sister. A mate of hers from long ago swears he saw her coming out of the grocery store a couple of weeks ago – a woman with a big backpack. Tilda ran away twenty-five years ago, and I've been looking for her ever since.'

The woman, who I presumed was the famous Bess, handed me a plate with the scone and a little packet of butter. 'I'll bring your coffee in a minute. I know who you mean, but she's never been in here.'

This was a surprise. 'Do you know who she is?'

'It'll be the one who turns up now and then, not very often. She only ever goes into Vijay's, does her shopping and walks away.' She frowned. 'You know, I never thought of it before, but why doesn't she just park outside the shop?' Another pause. 'But that's why she has the backpack, of course, she walks from wherever she lives, but I can't imagine where that would be.' She thought for a moment with the creases deepening between her eyebrows. 'You know what? There *isn't* anywhere she could stay, not that I know of - and I know most things around here. Maybe she's camping. But in the winter?'

After eating the scone at a little table where I could sit facing the window and see the grocery store, I called out a thank you to Bess and crossed the road to Vijay's. He looked up when I entered the shop, and it was easy to see that he was not in a mood to answer any questions.

'I just came in to show you a photo,' I said when the only other customer had left. 'This is Matilda when she was thirteen or fourteen. Does it ring any bells?'

Vijay studied the photo for a moment and shook his head. 'Very hard to tell from a photo of someone that age. This could be a lot of different women. I can't say it looks like anyone in particular.'

'OK, thanks.' I put the old school photo back in my pocket, paid for the chocolate biscuits I'd picked up and left, more convinced than ever that Vijay knew her, but for some reason he wasn't going to tell me anything.

The next day I changed my approach and sat for over an hour at the little table by the window in the café with my laptop. I had two coffees and another date scone while I recorded video of the shop across the street on my phone, which was propped up behind the laptop, so Bess wouldn't wonder what I was doing. The thought that the backpack woman would come and go from the store while I was looking down and I'd miss her had struck me as soon as I sat down. I was well aware that catching sight of her by sitting there for an hour or two each day would be an incredible coincidence, but I did it anyway, just on the off chance. Before I walked back up the lane, I went across to Vijay's and bought milk and a bag of bread rolls, said nothing about Matilda and imagined I felt Vijay's eyes on my back as I crossed the road. On the fifth day Vijay said briefly and surprisingly, 'She's called Anne, so she's not your sister.'

'Ah, so you do know who she is. I thought you probably did, but for some reason you said you didn't.'

'She asked me not to, when she first came. She said someone's after her and she's terrified of him. And it's no point asking me anything else, because that's all I know. I've never asked her to tell me more - it's not my business.' An admirable attitude for someone living in a small community.

15

A week after first asking Vijay about the woman he called Anne, I picked up the packet of pasta I'd just paid for and was halfway to the door when Vijay said, 'That guy over there, who just got out of the orange SUV, heading for the café, that's Boris. Go and talk to him. She hitched a ride with him once, just outside here, but it was ages ago.'

I waited beside the orange SUV until Boris reappeared with a take-way coffee in one hand and a paper bag in the other. A burly, grizzled man in his mid-fifties, definitely not a man who would put up with any nonsense, I thought, and met his penetrating gaze.

'Hi, I'm Thomas. Have you got time to talk to me for a couple of minutes?' Sound casual, I thought, don't make any demands of this guy, take it slowly.

'OK,' was all Boris said and took a sip of his coffee, his eyes steady on mine.

'I'm here looking for my sister. She disappeared twenty-five years ago and a mate of mine thinks he saw her here a few weeks ago.' No change of expression on Boris's face, so I carried on. 'Vijay said you might have given the woman my mate saw a lift once.'

'I might have.' Boris drank some more coffee, didn't smile.

I sighed. 'I'm running out of ideas, and if you did pick up this woman I'd like to know where you dropped her off. Nobody can tell me anything. Bess knows who I mean, but she's never talked to her, and Vijay says she calls herself Anne and she's scared of someone and doesn't want to be found. She's never been in the pub and there's nobody left to ask. I'm running out of options. But it seems reasonable to assume she lives somewhere not too far away if she walks in regularly.' Boris continued drinking his coffee and contributed nothing.

'This is how it seems to me,' I said, increasingly frustrated at this man who stood there like a block of granite, solid and unmoving, the one person who might be able to help me. 'She walks into the village every couple of weeks, buys provisions, puts them in her backpack and walks away towards the hills. Nobody knows where she lives, or so they say, which is weird in a small place like this where everyone seems to know everyone else. If I could only see her I'd know if she's my sister. She ran away when I was nine and I've been actively searching for her ever since, or ever since I had access to a computer. I've tried the police, social media, googling different versions of her name, everything I could think of.'

I ran out of things to say. Nothing seemed to make an impression on Boris, who just listened and said nothing. Just as I decided I was wasting my time and turned to walk away, he nodded. 'OK. Get in the car. Let's go to your place and talk. You can make me another coffee – if you've got a proper coffee maker.'

I made coffee, and we sat in the sun on the front veranda, Boris opened his paper bag, got out a ham and cheese sandwich and said, 'Tell me why she left.'

'Our father abused us. He was very violent and regularly beat me black and blue - and though Tilda didn't say it, I'm sure now when I look back as an adult, that my father sexually abused her. Our mum was incapable of protecting us, she drank, and she was scared of him too. Tilda was like a mother to me, she was seven years older, but she couldn't protect me from the beatings. She left in the middle of the night, but she said she'd come back as soon as she could and take me away, and if she hadn't come back when I was in my early teens I should just leave, steal money, do whatever it took, and go far away.'

'I don't know if Anne's your sister, and I don't know where she lives. I've given her a ride several times now, but all she's told me is that she's in danger, serious danger. She got involved in something really bad, just by chance, and she's convinced these people will kill her if they find her.'

This was interesting. Vijay had said she was scared of a dangerous man, Boris said she was scared of people, plural.

'Who are they, those people? Did she give you any clues?'

'No, she's very cautious. All she said is that she knows too much. She won't tell me where she lives, and I don't know where she's from. She's got to be camping - there's nowhere around here where she could shelter, no empty houses or anything. Camping up here in the winter would be a real ordeal, but where else could she be living? I thought about her many times these last cold months.' He shook his head, disturbed by the thought, 'I've helped her a couple of times, got some stuff for her that she couldn't get in the village. She pays me in cash. How old would your sister be now?'

'Forty-one on her next birthday, which is next month, fourteenth of September. I've checked the Birth, Deaths and Marriages database, and she's not listed as either dead or married, and she hasn't legally changed her name - that's why I say she's disappeared. I hope she's still alive somewhere. How long is it since you first came across her?'

Boris took a bite of his sandwich and chewed thoughtfully with his gaze in the middle distance, without focus. Finally he said, 'It was probably about October last year, maybe November. It was a fine day, and she was in a sweatshirt, no jacket. Once we got into proper summer she always wore a T-shirt even if it was raining.' He thought some more. 'I guess she got hot walking with that backpack, so even if it rained she would stay warm – in the summer, I mean. She'd have a jacket in her pack, of course, she's a very careful person. But I don't think she's as old as forty-one. More like early thirties.'

'Hang on, I've got an old photo. I'll show you.' But when I handed Boris the photo, he shook his head just like Vijay had. 'I couldn't say, mate. That could be anyone. But I'll show you where I drop her off, I've got a map in the truck.' He made to get up, but I stopped him with a gesture. 'I'll get my map, just a moment.'

'Here,' said Boris and made a mark with the pen I put beside him. 'Right here where the road is straight for a bit before those twisting turns before the bridge, a kilometre or so from the village. And this is another thing that might help. I'd dropped her there a couple of times, and then one day I came around the bend at the end of that straight and she'd got out of a car that was just driving off, and she crossed the road. When I dropped her off she told me to stop by that old track to the lake, but no, she disappeared into the bush on the other side of the road. Very cagey, as I said. Even though she trusts me now.'

A few minutes later Boris drove off. I stayed on the veranda and watched the orange SUV turn right at the bottom of the lane while my mind constructed the first real plan since I left Wellington. I would do some more work on the analysis I was doing for the Department of Internal Affairs and get ready to explore the area across the road from the old track to the lake.

16

Despite the plan to start a real search the next day I went to Greymouth instead. I had woken to pouring rain and a strong wind, so after laying out my tramping gear I decided to have a day away from the village and the rather limited opportunities it offered. Have lunch somewhere nice down on the coast, perhaps, and have a look around.

Halfway there I suddenly thought how ironic it would be if the woman who called herself Anne came to the village that day, but obviously she wouldn't walk in on a day like today, and anyway, I could miss her on any given day if I wasn't in the café or in Vijay's store when she came. This was becoming an obsession, I thought, and slowed behind a truck turning into the mill with a load of logs. To be so close and still not be able to confirm who she was; it was impossible to ignore, particularly after my chat with Boris.

Lunch in a bistro overlooking the river was pleasant, but the wind from the Tasman Sea swept in unhindered, and rain lashed the big windows.

'It won't last,' said the waiter confidently. 'Changing to a southeasterly tomorrow which means the rainclouds get caught in the mountains and all the rain falls up there.' The logic of it was indisputable, but it was hard to believe, as I battled through driving rain across the street towards a sports shop I had spotted on the way in, where I might find something useful.

I returned to the village at the end of the afternoon with two self-heating army ration packs, a new pair of wool socks and some frozen meals from the supermarket. I put my purchases on the table and read the back of the self-heating meal packets and wondered if I was ever going to use them. It wasn't as if I would spend days in the bush, but perhaps they would be good for lunch while I searched for any signs of the woman, who called herself Anne. Tomorrow would be the first day of the search and I wanted to start early, so I packed the backpack, filled two water bottles and went to bed early.

By mid-afternoon the following day I realised that I was lost, which felt exciting and terrifying at the same time. I had set out straight into the bush across the road from where the nearly overgrown track to the lake was. There was something that might have been a track a long time ago on this side too, but the vegetation had taken over to such an extent that I kept going off it and had to backtrack to find it again. But after a while I began to wonder if it had ever been a track, and perhaps I was just following gaps in the forest. When I admitted to myself that I had no idea where I was, I climbed to the top of a ridge and looked for a landmark that I could pinpoint on the map and then navigate back to the road from there, but the map had no contour lines, and it was far too small. What I thought of as hiking bore no relationship to navigating through thick native bush with no tracks. As dusk set in I gave up on trying to orientate myself and concentrated on the simpler task of finding a dry place to sleep.

At lunch time, two days after I set out, I was finally back at the car thanks to a large portion of luck and a little stream I followed downhill in what seemed to be the right direction. Now a complete re-think was needed and a session of internet research. On an impulse I stopped outside the café in the village because a hot cup of real coffee and a scone suddenly seemed like the most desirable things in the world.

'Well, look at you!' Bess grinned. 'I haven't seen you for a couple of days. Did you get lost?'

'What on earth gave you that idea? Is it the stubble, or the filthy clothes or just the general look of exhaustion?'

She laughed. 'I wasn't sure you'd got lost, but I must say I wondered if I'd have to start a rescue mission. Boris saw your car parked up the road and came in to check if I knew anything.' Her forefinger was aimed straight at my chest. 'So next time you go off, you tell me first, and then you report back when you return. I'm the unofficial safety officer here.' She pointed at the blackboard by the door. 'You write the date and time and your name over there, and where you're going – there's chalk on the windowsill – and of course how long you think you'll be away. And if you don't come back I do something about it. They have another blackboard down at the backpacker's lodge – we keep each other informed. Do you want the last two date scones with your coffee?'

Having a long, hot shower had never been so enjoyable, not to mention the pleasure of clean clothes. I turned on the washing machine, lit a fire in the pot-bellied stove and sat down with the laptop and something to eat while I made a shopping list. I knew I only found my way back to the car by luck and could have been lost for much longer, so good planning was a must. I would make another trip to Greymouth, get better equipped and buy more army ration packs, and then set out again.

17

The next day I entered the sports shop in Greymouth for the second time with an extensive list and a raft of questions in my head and hoped there would be someone there, who was older than sixteen and competent to give me the kind of advice obviously needed.

'Tell me what your plans are,' said the middle-aged man whose name tag said Marcus. 'I can't give you any advice unless I know what you're going to do. What you call hiking in the bush could mean anything. Is it walking on tracks, or going cross-country without tracks, or hunting? Looking for gold?'

I wasn't going to mention I was searching for a woman, who might or might not be my missing sister and decided on a halfway true explanation. 'A mate of mine was here a while ago and he mentioned he'd done some great hiking in the high hills inland from Reefton. There's an old track to a lake up there - a nice six hour hike there and back. I'm keen to have a go, but I want to have the right gear. I might spend a night or two in the bush and walk around the lake. He said it's full of wildlife.'

'Well, here's basic checklist. Why don't you cross out what you have and then we'll have look.' He handed me a sheet of paper and a pen and went back to sorting socks into boxes. The list was long and divided into sections according to the type of activity, so I went for the most demanding, which was headed "multi-day trek in rough terrain, no tracks" and handed the paper back with a few things crossed off. 'I'd better be prepared, I think.'

'Very wise,' said Marcus after a glance at the list. 'You're going to need a lot of gear.'

'I've got some gear, but I've only been on tracks before, and I must have topographical map. The map I have is rubbish, no contour lines and the scale is useless.'

With more all-weather clothing, another pair of wool socks and a merino base layer piled on the counter we turned to what Marcus called survival essentials and added twenty army ration packs and a topographical map in a clear waterproof bag and gaiters.

'Stops rain and most of the water from getting into your boots if you wade through a creek, mate. Keeps your feet warm and reasonably dry, the wool socks do the rest.' Marcus glanced at the list. 'Torch, binoculars, water bottles?'

'I've got those, but let's add one of those little folding solar panels in case I need to charge something.'

'And a personal locator beacon, or something a bit more sophisticated?'

I left with three large carrier bags after paying a surprising amount of money, but I was happy to do it. Having the right gear made me feel I could cope with a few mishaps like a week lost in the bush.

Another lunch in the bistro, this time with perfect views of the river and more good food, and then I drove back deep in thought about the next day, and how I would map out my search plan.

Having a good map and a compass felt good, not to mention the comfort of now having a self-inflating sleeping mat and the nylon fly I had chosen rather than a tunnel tent. It would be luxury compared to the two miserable nights I had spent outside the first time, lying on the ground under trees, colder by the minute and not getting much sleep.

With everything spread out on the sofa and the table I decided what I would wear the next day and what would go into the back-pack and decided to pack it right away, see how it fitted and how much it weighed. The pack was nearly full when I suddenly realised my mistake and took everything out again. Things that would only be needed in a dire emergency would go in the bottom, then the rest either in the top or in the outside pockets. The sleeping mat in its waterproof bag would be strapped on one side and the nylon fly on the other. I considered the pack, took the sleeping mat off and turned it around so the drawstring opening was down instead of up and lifted the pack. Not as heavy as I had expected, and quite a bit of that weight was food and water.

Over dinner I sent identical text messages to everyone in the family and to Carter, saying I had a good lead now and was continuing the search, but I made no mention of exactly what I was doing. Linley would worry if I told her about possibly spending in a week in the mountains, and Martin would call me with advice, all of which I was trying to avoid right then.

With the topographic map beside my plate I ate dinner without noticing what I was eating and studied the elevation lines. The best approach would be to get as high as possible, identify hilltops where I might be able to scan a wide area and use the binoculars to do a kind of visual grid search. Apart from her actual camp site there might be some trace of her considering that she had been there for a year, and presumably she walked the same route to and from the road on her way to get supplies every couple of weeks. A tent would be hard to spot under the tree canopy, but maybe I'd get lucky and see some sign of where she lived.

Somehow this search had become a mission without an end date, and I no longer considered anything in the light of "when I'm back in town". It didn't matter how long I spent here; I would work interspersed with searching for her, and in between I'd continue the habit of spending an hour or two nearly every day in the café.

The following morning I set out early, after first leaving a note under the café door for Bess, and once again I parked off the road just beyond the old track to the lake. Who would have thought I'd have to resurrect my high school orienteering skills all these years later, I thought, as I hefted the backpack and crossed the road. The new map was folded in its waterproof transparent bag with the four possible high points I had identified marked with an X. I started walking, map in one hand and the compass in the other.

18

Sitting in the shade of a manuka tree I lifted the binoculars, did a slow sweep across the landscape and wondered how many times I had done this in the last two days. It was the third hill of the four I had marked and still not the slightest sign of anyone, no tracks, no tent, no movement - nothing. I was now further from the road, up in the higher hills, which was probably not a realistic place to look for the woman called Anne, a very long commute to the village for supplies. This morning it was warmer, which was a nice change, and the sunshine made it easier to make out shapes in the distance from this hill, which was higher and had a wider view then the previous two. After finding it and climbing to the top at dusk the previous evening I spent the night quite comfortably under the trees at the very crest. I stretched the fly between three manuka trees, quite low to the ground this time and discovered that not getting covered in stray seeds and dew made a real difference to how I slept, like having a very low tent without side walls.

I reached the end of yet another two hundred degree scan and had just started the slow sweep back when I spotted movement, and my heart missed a beat. A figure dressed in grey and dull green working her way up a steep slope on a hill to my left, not very far away. I kept my eyes on her as she moved among the trees, just clear of an open area until she got to the very highest point where the narrow clearing opened into a wide open space in bright sunlight. Fascinated I watched her stop just inside the tree-line at the top and take her backpack off. It was hard to see her movements among the tree shadows, but she seemed to be unpacking things and stacking them on the ground, then she lifted something and emerged into the sunlight with a load carried in both hands.

One at a time she laid out four large rectangular sheets that glinted in the sunlight as she shook them out. Folding solar panels, I said quietly to myself, that's why she's on that open hilltop that faces nearly straight north – perfect light from mid-morning until late in the day. Next she picked up a bag, took things out one by one and connected them to the solar panels. I couldn't take my eyes off the scene; it was like watching a movie. It looked like a well-established routine, something she did without hesitation. Each item she connected was put down on the ground, and I had to guess what they were, but probably things like a cell phone, a power bank and perhaps a lamp. But at no time did I get a clear view of her face. When I saw her profile her face was shadowed by the cap, and most of the time she looked down at what she was doing. She sat down under the trees at the top of the open area, higher than the solar panels, and I felt as if we were connected by an invisible thread. I on my higher hilltop sitting in the shade of trees watching her, and she slightly lower and a couple of hundred meters away, sitting just like me, leaning back against a tree trunk. The feeling that she might be Matilda, but that I couldn't confirm it, created a nearly unbearable tension.

A couple of hours later I realised that eating lunch was out of the question. I would have to get up to reach the backpack a couple of metres away, and if she happened to glance my way she might catch the movement. I could see the solar panels were still there, so if I kept my eyes on them I'd know when she was ready to leave, but for the moment she was so well camouflaged in the shade that she was invisible to the naked eye. If she spotted me she might take flight and go into hiding in her camp, so I would stay where I was and try to track her when she left, see it I could work out which direction she went. My map was on the ground beside me where I had put it when I sat down, and by glancing down at it I identified the location of her hill and mentally marked it, because my pen was also in the backpack. Sitting still and waiting for her to leave was vital, so I could observe her descent and get a clue in which direction she went.

By mid-afternoon the sun had disappeared from my observation post, but I stayed and watched until the woman on her distant hilltop was getting ready to leave. She picked up the devices, folded the solar panels into flat, square bundles and packed everything into her backpack. As soon as she entered the now darker tree line along the slope of the clearing she became invisible. The colours she wore blended with the environment, and I wasn't able to follow her line of descent. Disappointed I unfolded the fly and stretched it between three trees in the same place as last night, unrolled the sleeping mat and decided on an early dinner and hopefully a good night's sleep, so I would be ready to set out at dawn.

19

After another two unsuccessful days of searching a wide area and finding nothing, I spent the night under trees east of the hill where the woman had spread her solar panels. Again I rigged the nylon fly between trees, unrolled the self-inflating sleeping mat, sat down and tried to think where I could search next. Two days with no results and I was nearly out of ideas. The next morning I woke to a fine day, which meant an easier day with better prospects of spotting things in the distance after two days of low cloud and drizzle. Today I would explore a long, narrow valley between steep hills slightly further inland, a sheltered spot it would seem from the map, and one of the last logical search areas I had identified. I had soon realised that walking around at random and checking the landscape from hilltops was unlikely to yield results, and now I was concentrating on places that seemed to offer shelter from prevailing winds or winter storms.

A few hours later I stood at the mouth of the valley I had been looking for. A very narrow valley with steep sides, as straight as a die and progressively narrower until it was no more than a sharp

V-shape in the distance. At my feet a stream trickled silently downhill, easy to get across at the moment, but I imagined it would turn into an impassable torrent after heavy rain came down the sides of this valley. But the valley was a perfect place to camp long term, protected from the bitter winds of the high mountain ranges from one direction and from the storms coming inland from the Tasman Sea from the other, and with water easily accessible. But I needed a better observation spot than standing there on the valley floor and decided to climb up one side to get an overall view, to see things from above and maybe be able to spot a tent.

Halfway up I stopped to catch my breath, looked out over the view - and saw her. My breath caught in my throat, and I froze. She was standing with her back turned towards me on a small flat area facing a vertical rock wall, a lot higher than where I was, but nearly straight across the valley. I got the binoculars out and got her in sharp focus as she stood there with the bright sunlight on her back, as if she was warming up after a chilly night. She was looking down at something, perhaps she was reading. I lowered the binoculars for a second to sit down and when I looked up again she had disappeared. But where? The vegetation on that side was mainly scrubby bushes and small trees with only occasional taller ones lower on the slope. How could she have vanished so quickly? I scanned every inch in both directions and saw no movement. I must make my way down to the floor of the valley and up on the other, steeper side to the spot where she had stood when I saw her. It took longer than I had thought it would with obstacles and rocky outcrops to negotiate, but about halfway up I found a narrow track that she must have made over time. Stopping to catch my breath, I studied the opposite side of the valley until I identified the tall tree where I had been when I saw her. I must get a lot higher and a bit further along, and I must do it quietly or I might scare her off if she was still there.

Finally I stood on the little shelf with the exposed rock wall behind me, this was where she had stood, exactly here. I walked along the narrowing shelf, looking down to see if there was any sign of a track going downhill, continued past a vertical edge like a fold in the cliff, and there she was – a slim figure sitting on an inflatable cushion leaning against the rock wall. She was reading on a Kindle and hadn't heard me. After a moment she looked up, alerted by my presence, though I hadn't made a sound as I stood mesmerised, waiting for her to raise her head, so I could see her face.

The only thing I could think of saying was, 'Sorry! I thought you were my sister.'

She leapt to her feet and stared at me, terrified, her eyes darted from one side to the other as if she was going to run, and I said quickly, 'Please, don't run! I'm no threat to you, whoever you are. I heard a woman was living in the bush, and I was hoping it was my sister.'

Her shoulders dropped, and though she was still tense she was no longer in flight mode. 'How did you find me?'

'I've been trekking around these mountains for days looking for some trace of someone living here.'

'But how did you know where to look? Who told you?'

'It's a long story,' I said. 'Do you mind if I take my pack off and sit down? I'm hot and thirsty, and my water bottle is in the pack.'

'You might as well come inside. At this time of the day in winter the sun disappears early from this shelf,' she said after studying me for a long moment, an intense silent scrutiny, as if she could read my character. She picked up the cushion and turned, and I followed her around a second deep fold in the cliff wall and into a narrow cleft, which surprisingly opened up into a deep cave. She gestured towards an inflatable mattress against one side wall where the ceiling sloped down to no more than shoulder height.

'Sit down and tell me how you found me. And mind your head.' She put her cushion on the floor and sat down on the opposite side.

I got out my last bottle that still had water in it and shook it; no more than half full now. 'I should have filled it from that little stream down in the valley. Never mind, I'll do it when I leave.'

'I have lots of water here, but you can't drink directly from the stream, it's not safe. I bring up water from the stream every time I return, but I filter it with a special filter. There could be dead animals rotting further up and you don't know what's in the water, it could be contaminated with E-coli or salmonella from the birds. Now, would you please tell me how you found me.'

I had been thinking about how to tell her since the moment I discovered she was not Tilda, to start at the very beginning and possibly be able to reassure her that I was no threat and would tell nobody where she was. There had to be a compelling reason for her to live like this, so carefully covering any traces of where she was. I would tell her the whole story, hoping she would realise I was genuine and no threat.

'My sister disappeared, left home very suddenly twenty-five years ago, when I was nine and she was sixteen. We grew up in a family where abuse and heavy drinking were everyday events, and she couldn't take it any longer. She used to protect me from beatings – when she could. And she comforted me when I was covered in bruises and cuts after my father beat me. A little while ago an old friend of ours was driving through the village where you shop and thought he saw Tilda. He was certain it was her. He didn't see her whole face, just one side under a cap, but it was the body language that made him so certain, the stance. He said very few women walk like Tilda did. He parked and ran back, but he couldn't see her.'

I shook my head. 'I mean, he couldn't see *you* - so he went into the Vijay's shop and said he thought he'd seen someone he'd known twenty years ago just leave, and did Vijay know where she lived, and got nowhere. He was baffled, but he was sure that Vijay lied, that he knew more than he was willing to say. So I came down here from Wellington, rented a house and started searching.'

Surprising me, she said quietly, 'You must have loved your sister.'

'I did, she was my protector, the best thing in my life - no, the only good thing in my life. Before she left, she said I must remember what she was about to tell me because it was very important. I had been hiding outside after a terrible beating and she came to find me, sat down with her arms around me and said I must put up with it for now and then leave when I was old enough, plan my escape, steal some money if I had to, and leave. She said I had to have a map in my head of how I would do it, work it out in advance. She would come back when I was thirteen or fourteen and get me if I hadn't left already.'

I felt a need to tell her everything, so she understood how important it had been to find out if she was Tilda. 'My mother was too scared to interfere when dad beat me. usually when he was drunk or when I annoyed him, which seemed to happen more and more often as I got older. She drank a lot too, and she wasn't much use as a mother, not with a father like ours. Matilda knew our mum wouldn't help me, and she never told me what dad did to her, she just said it was "something different". As I got older I understood what she meant, but at the time it just puzzled me.'

'How old were you when you got away?'

Tell her everything, I told myself, privacy has nothing to do with this, she needs reassurance.

'I had just started high school. One of the teachers had noticed the bruises now and then and a black eye a couple of times, and then one day he took me to the headmaster and said, "call the cops, this kid's being abused and now he's got finger mark bruises around his neck". And that was it, the cops came and took me with them, alerted the right authorities and I was put in a foster home. And from that day I never saw my parents again, it was my choice.' I heard how that sounded and added, 'I would probably have done it differently if I'd been older. I might have got in touch with my mother, but at the time all I wanted to do was forget the past and have a normal life in a normal family, and the thought of coming face to face with my dad made it impossible. The authorities asked her if she wanted a safe place to live with me, if she needed help to leave my father, but she said no, she wouldn't leave – abandoned me, in fact.'

She made no comment, so I carried on. 'And I was lucky, very lucky. The family who took me in were marvellous and they're still my family now. They saw to it I got a good education just like their own two sons, encouraged me and turned me into who I am today, and showed me what normal family life is like. About a year after I moved in with them, I was told my mother had died of pneumonia.'

'Let's have coffee,' she said suddenly, breaking the spell of the past. 'We'll have to drink it cold, though. I haven't had anything to eat today, and I was just going inside to have coffee when you turned up.'

'I've got lots of food in my pack.' I pulled it towards me. 'Self-heating army rations - we can have one of those each.' I fished around in the pack and pulled a couple of packs out. 'Do you want beef and onion stew or spicy chicken casserole?'

20

We ate our late lunch directly from the packs, and the woman, who might be called Anne, sighed with pleasure when she took her first mouthful and looked dreamily into the pack. 'I haven't eaten a hot meal for a year. This is bliss. Thank you! I don't dare make a fire, because outside it would show from far away, and in here the smoke would just hang around and maybe make me sick, but I'm used to cold food now.'

I had a hundred questions I wanted to ask, but she asked first. 'How did you know where to look for me? Who told you?'

I drank the last of the water in my bottle, hoped I wouldn't get either Vijay or Boris into trouble and tried to find a good way of telling her. 'I went into the general store and talked to Vijay, and he pretended he had no idea who I was talking about. I went back the next day and showed him a photo of Matilda, a school photo from when she was thirteen that I've kept all these years. I told him the basics of my story and said I was prepared to stay in my rented house until I found out where she was. He remembered the guy who came in and asked him about you a couple of weeks earlier, but all he would tell me was that your name is Anne, he said he doesn't know your surname and he doesn't know where you live.'

'And?'

She wasn't giving up, so I had to tell her. 'I talked to him every day for a week. I said if it's my sister she must have a reason for living so secretly, and I must find her and help her, she might just say her name's Anne, but she's really called Matilda. Then one day he pointed out the window and said, go and ask Boris, the guy with the orange car. He gave her a lift from here once.'

'*Boris* told you! I don't believe it, and I trusted him!' She was devastated, looked down at her clenched hands and visibly tried to control herself. 'Oh God! Where am I going to get supplies now? I can't go back there if he's told people about me.'

'He hasn't told anyone but me, I promise, please don't panic, you're perfectly safe.' I tried to sound calm, as if my tone of voice could convince her that this was beyond doubt. 'Let me tell you how it was.' Her despair was nearly palpable, she felt I had ruined her secure existence. 'He's *not* going to tell anyone else, and neither am I. I said I was looking for my sister, told him the basics of how long it was since she left and how worried I was about her, how I had moved into that rented house and that I was prepared to stay and search and keep looking. I said Vijay told me to talk to him.'

I thought for a moment. What else could I add that might lessen her fear, make her realise that Boris had only told me because he believed my story and decided to help me. 'And I told him how I've spent a lot of time in the café across from the shop, sitting with my laptop at the table facing the window, pretending to work but really filming everyone who comes and goes at the store, hoping to spot you, scared I'd miss you if I didn't look up often enough. And he believed me, he said he didn't think I was one of the people who were a threat to you, he knew that someone was, but he said it couldn't be me.'

'Why did he believe you?'

I could only shake my head; I had no idea. 'I don't know. He told me that you trust him, and he knows the spot where you go off the road, but he doesn't know where you live or how far you walk, or any details of why you're living way out here.'

'I've never told him where this cave is, there's no need for him to know. He picked me up once and I said to drop me at the track to the lake, and then a few weeks later – this was a long time ago, last spring, he was driving down the road, and he saw me get out of a car I'd got a ride in. So he slowed and watched me walk across the road into the bush on the other side from where I'd told him I was going when he picked me up. He told me about it later. He wasn't asking where I lived, he just said it was good someone knew at least which side of the road. That was right at the beginning, and then a little while later he saw me walking towards the village – I mostly have to walk there and back.'

She stopped and reached for a bottle of water I hadn't noticed among the things lined up along the wall beside her. 'And that second time he saw me I had a bandage on my hand, so he stopped a bit ahead of me and got out and asked what had happened to my hand. I told him I'd cut myself a couple of days earlier and he just took charge. My hand was red and swollen and he said it was dangerous - he really told me off.'

She smiled at the memory. 'He was a paramedic in the army for several years when he was younger, and he's got a great first aid kit in the car, a big metal box full of stuff. He cleaned the cut and sprinkled some kind of antibiotic powder on it and wrapped it up properly. When I came out of the store that day he was waiting in his car a bit down the road, and when I went to walk past him, he just leaned over and opened the passenger door and said to get in, we needed to talk.'

'You were very lucky he noticed your hand. Just think what that cut could have turned into.' I studied her face across the gloomy interior where little daylight was now coming in after the sun's angle had moved and no longer funnelled light along the cleft in the cliff.

'I know, my hand was a real mess and very painful. Anyway we sat in his truck down a little sideroad for ages, and I told him I was in serious danger, that I had escaped powerful people with lots of contacts, like a whole network, who have access to nearly everything. I wouldn't tell him why, only that it wasn't my fault. I was the classic bystander who got drawn into something dreadful. I don't know why, but he believed me, and he said he'd like to help me. Now he puts more credit into my burner phone when it runs low, and I've got his number in case I would need help sometime, like a ride somewhere or even a place to hide. And I have a real smartphone now that's registered in his name for emergencies – he got it for me a few months ago. I took a lot of cash when I fled, so I pay him when he buys me things. But he told you the truth, he doesn't know where I live or any details of why I'm here.'

'So you get cell phone reception here?'

'Oh no, not in the valley or anywhere near, but I follow the little stream downhill for half an hour and climb to the top of the brown hill and get two bars on my phone if I move around up there until I find the exact spot. I had to try a lot of hills before I found it. I've called him a few times and asked him to get me things from Greymouth, and once or twice he bought things for me on the internet. And then we organise to meet on the road to the village, and I pay him in cash.'

'What do you need right now? Have you got antibiotic cream and enough first aid things? There's no pharmacy in the village, but I can get things for you in Greymouth, like batteries or what-ever you need.'

'I don't need anything at the moment. I buy food for a couple of weeks in the village, mostly packets and sachets of things I can eat cold, cans of soup or baked beans, crispbread, peanut butter, bananas. Stuff that keeps well and is nourishing. And as you know, I drink cold coffee. Not much worse than iced coffee that's lost some of its chill.'

'Bet you miss things like warm coffee and hot food.'

She shrugged. 'You get used to it, and I don't have a choice. I should have got myself one of those little camping stoves, but I didn't have much time to prepare when I ran away, and I didn't know enough to plan properly for this kind of life, so there were a few things I didn't think of. Sometimes I think I should ask Boris to get me one of those little single-burner stoves that run on gas.'

'I can get one for you and a few gas canisters. But tell me more. You said dangerous and powerful people are after you, so how did you get away and manage to set yourself up here?' And then I realised how long I had been there, and how long it would take to get down to the bottom of the valley. 'Sorry, I'd better head off, but I'll come back tomorrow, so we can talk some more. I don't want to climb down that steep slope after dusk sets in, it's tricky going even in proper daylight, like an obstacle course. I did find your little path after a while, but I'm not trying it after dusk.'

'Where are you going? It's a long way to the road, you'll never make it before dark. It's a good two or three hour trek depending on the weather and how high the streams are.'

'I'm not going anywhere in particular, but I need to get down to flat ground and find a place to sleep.'

'Don't be an idiot!' She said it the way you say it to someone you like when they come out with something silly, and it nearly made me laugh, it was so unexpected and spontaneous, the first thing she had said that sounded like she might in her normal life. 'Why would you do that rather than stay here? Is that one of those self-inflating mats strapped to your pack, like a thinner version of mine?'

'If you don't mind me being here, I'd like to stay. But now I've got to go outside and pee. Any particular place?'

'I'll show you. There's one place to pee and another place to poo, this is a very organised camp. We don't tolerate people randomly fouling the environment.' It was heart-warming to hear her sounding relaxed. Her tension earlier had been very obvious, and I hadn't been able to think of any way to make her feel safer apart from just trying to sound calm and confident myself.

We walked a short distance back the way I had come, and she gestured to a patch of bare ground just below the little track. 'This is the pee place. I just squat and that stick is lying there so I don't step on the soggy place, so please aim on the far side of the stick. Now follow me a bit further.'

Her outdoor toilet arrangement was a few metres down, just where narrow rock shelf started. In among low trees she had laid a short ponga log between a rock and a bump in the slope, so it formed a seat with a deep hole dug under it.

'How on earth did you dig that hole? The ground here must be full of roots and rocks – you certainly didn't do that with a spoon.'

'With a great deal of hard work.' She looked proudly at her latrine. 'I have one of those folding spades, whatever they're called. Boris got it for me because I hadn't thought of needing to dig a hole before I got here. It took a couple of weeks of digging a bit more every day - I had to prise rocks out of the ground and dig around roots, *very* hard work. But if you sit on the log you've got to be careful because it wobbles a bit. I've tried to fix it, but it never stays put, so I usually hold on to that branch on the right hand side, it's very sturdy.'

She left me there and I watched her walk back to the cave and considered this extraordinary woman. The way she was so organised, the isolation of how she lived, and how self-contained she had to be to cope with this lonely existence for so long. Whatever she was frightened of must be deadly serious or she'd never go to these lengths and stay here for so long. And how did she think she'd ever resolve her problem from this location with no resources? How would she know when it was safe to come out of isolation? It seemed to me that she was in a lose-lose situation, and I must find a way to resolve it.

21

Dusk was setting in now and when I entered the cave a lantern had been lit and a soft yellow glow made it look more like a room than a cave.

'Nice! I didn't see any light from outside as I came along the path.'

'It's those little angles in the passage.' She gestured at the entrance. 'You hardly notice as you walk in, but if you have a closer look you'll see that it angles first to the right and then to the left, so there's no direct line for the light to follow and the lantern isn't very bright. I keep it here in this corner as far away from the opening as possible. I haven't checked, but I doubt the light shows at all from the other side of the valley or from below.'

I shook my head, once again with questions lining up in my mind. 'How did you find the cave in the first place? It's the perfect place to hide, but it's so well hidden - I can't imagine anyone finding it by chance. I never spotted that cleft from the other side, it just looked like a shadow.'

'I read about this cave in a very old book of my dad's that I came across then I packed up my house before I ... escaped. He had several books about surviving in the South Island bush, so I took it and two others and read them on my bus trips and in back-packer hostels I stayed at. My dad was a keen trekker, as he called it, and he had lots of books like that. I was planning to hide out somewhere in the South Island, and I took that book, because it was described on the back as a story about someone who survived against the odds in the South Island bush well over a hundred years ago. And it turned out to be written just for me.'

She smiled at the thought of how lucky this was. 'So until I read it I had no idea that it had a description of this cave and where it was, it was just an interesting book. The author and his mate camped in this cave for a week about a hundred and twenty years ago after one of them twisted his ankle badly when they climbed down into the valley to get out of a blizzard. It was just chance they found it, but he described the environment around here in great detail. Those early explorers were tough nuts.'

'So are you – I'm very impressed. And you managed to locate the cave from his description?'

'I can show you the passage in the book if you like. I'll never throw that book away, it's part of my life now. And I bought a good topographical map and a compass on the way down here after reading that book. I came here to search for this long, very narrow valley between the hills with one side where the rock face is exposed like a wall with vertical folds in the rock like it's pleated. His description is bang on, like he turned at the bottom of the valley when they finally left and memorised every detail of the scene. Maybe he thought someone else would need to find it sometime in the future, and I did.'

She smiled again and her pleasure in telling me about this was written on her face. 'In the book he mentions that the valley runs northeast to southwest with a stream at the bottom. I spent ages looking for it, but it seemed worth it. The description of how safe and protected from the weather this cave is just stuck in my mind.'

She pointed at a pile of things in the corner. 'I slept in a tiny tunnel tent all the time I was searching for the right valley, because at first I wasn't very good at reading the map, but I learnt. I knew about that kind of map, of course, but I'd never used one before. When I found the cave it felt like a miracle after nearly three weeks of searching. You know, the relief of knowing I had a safe place where I'd be protected from bad weather. Oh, and I found a couple of things those guys had left behind, probably by mistake, an enamelled tin plate and a spoon were sitting on that little ledge to your left. I use the plate sometimes, a little link to the past.'

She noticed me taking in things I hadn't noticed earlier and chuckled. 'It's funny, isn't it? With the lantern lit you see things in a different way – I notice it too. I think it's because in the daytime the light is so diffuse in here and it's never very bright, of course, and the lantern gives it a different perspective.' She pointed further in. 'Those plastic bags over there are my spare supplies in big zip lock bags. Food and emergency stuff – all kinds of things I hoard that I want to keep safe from moisture, and things I brought with me or that Boris got for me. In the winter I sometimes don't even try to make it out to the road, so during the coldest periods when we got snow I was stuck here for ages once or twice, dressed like an arctic explorer, when I would normally have gone into the village. And see the toilet paper roll by the entrance? You have to remember to take it when you go to the poo place.'

I could sit there for days listening to her; everything she said was interesting or intriguing. 'Tell me how you managed to get here. You said the people you were getting away from have access to nearly everything, so how did you get here without getting tracked down when there are cameras everywhere.' I wasn't going to say it, but I was certain that those people she talked about were police, thought the context seemed weird.

She nodded. 'Particularly if you're on the run from the people I was getting away from, because as I said, they've got access to everything, literally everything.' She shook her head. 'I got my escape plan from another book, believe it or not. When I was desperate and trying to work out how to disappear, I remembered a book we had in the library that I read several years ago. I was a librarian in a suburban library in Auckland, by the way. I couldn't remember the name of the book at the time, but it's come back to me since. It's called Running Towards Danger, and in it an inno-cent woman is trying to escape from drug dealers, I can't remember why, but she's got to get away fast and become invisible. So she sets up a whole timeline of what she must do, step by step, and at each step she cuts off one strand of the string that links her to the previous step. And much to my surprise, I found I could kind of re-create it in my mind.'

She shook her head at how strange this coincidence was. 'It had interested me when I read the book - how the timeline and the logic were so important. That she had to do things in exactly the right order to sever all links effectively and make it impossible for anyone to trace her. So you change one thing at a time, sever that link – you change how you dress, what you carry, your mode of transport, hair colour – one thing at a time in different places. You become a cash only person, and you don't go into supermar-kets or anywhere with a camera. And the order of how you do it is very important. The more I listed things, the more that story came back to me. Amazing how your memory works, isn't it? Some of what I did was different, like I had to go on the ferry for example, but in the main it was very similar, and I stuck to the principle of never changing more than one thing at a time.'

'I wish I'd brought a bottle of wine. This is riveting and feels like an evening of storytelling. A glass of red would be perfect.'

She laughed then. 'I'd probably fall flat on my face after one glass. I haven't had alcohol in a year. But I can tell you more if you really want to know. How I organised how to leave my life behind.'

'I'm fascinated,' I said. 'This is the best story I've ever heard.'

'OK, then. I'm ... widowed and I have no children. I booked a removal company to shift things from the house to a storage unit I rented, hired a guy with a truck to take a big load to the dump, gave loads of stuff to the Salvation Army - they took away two loads of furniture and all the household equipment, and then I sold my car for cash on TradeMe. I put a ridiculously low price on it and said it would only be for sale for two days, like first in, first served, but it had to be a cash sale. The guy who bought it couldn't believe his luck. When I met him to hand over the car he said he'd gone online and checked it wasn't stolen and that it had no hire purchase debt on it. He was dying to find out why I was selling it for at least five thousand less that it was worth, so I said the same as I said to everyone, that I was going to Australia for an indefinite time due to a family emergency, and I was in a hurry, and I was going to stay there.'

'The list you made must have been as long as your arm, so much to think about.'

'Longer than my arm! Pages of stuff.' She drank some water from her bottle, and I knew I'd been right earlier. She was enjoying telling someone how she had done it after keeping it to herself for so long, the careful planning and all the decisions that had gone into it, proud of what she had achieved, and rightly so.

'Anyway, I transferred my savings to my current account, withdrew some of that too, and set up the payments to the storage facility as a monthly automatic payment. I can exist a long time on the cash from the car, now that I'm living here, so I needn't have withdrawn some of my savings, but at the time I thought I'd be paying rent for some little place, possibly for a long time. It was a safety thing, to make sure I wouldn't need to withdraw cash at some later stage where my location could be tracked. I haven't accessed my bank account or been near a petrol station or a super-market in more than a year. I was caught by cameras of course – at the bus terminals, for example, but there I changed my appear-ance from one place to the next. And on the ferry, but I had my cap and sunglasses on all the time. But when I think of it now, it's amazing how cheap it is to live like this. I've used very little of that money since I stopped paying for bus tickets and backpacker hostels.'

I thought about it for a moment and counted things off on my fingers. 'No rent, no power or broadband bills, no car registration, no car insurance – good God! You just pay for a few items here and there plus food. I mean now, after you made it here. But you still have expenses for the house you left behind, don't you?'

'That's right. The house insurance and the council rates are paid by direct debit from my bank account. But there's more to it, you know - you just haven't had time to think it through. I organ-ised for a rental firm to let my house and do any maintenance that might be needed over time, and the rent money goes into my bank account. I left my job without notice and said I had to leave imme-diately because of a serious family emergency in Australia, everyone knows my sister lives there. I lied and lied, without hesi-tation and according to the plan in my head.'

'Incredible, and all this when you were under pressure.'

'I bought bus tickets with that cash, shopped for various items in different towns where I stopped for a few hours or a day, caught another bus to another place, did a long zigzag journey south, and

I often got off a bus before the destination I'd bought the ticket for - just to make it even harder to track where I'd gone, another trick I remembered from that book. I stayed in back packer places and bought the big items in Greymouth, got rid of my suitcase and bough a backpack and gave away a lot of clothes. After reading about the cave I changed my plan, and I needed to equip myself differently. I bought the kind of clothes I needed in second-hand shops, and some in that outdoor place in Greymouth.'

'And then?' I was fascinated by the process, followed each step and mentally added it to the long row of actions before it. A perfect and very logical sequence of actions to disconnect from the past and go forward into anonymity.

'In the second town where I spent a night I got a short haircut and bought a beanie, then I had my hair coloured blond in another town. All according to the plan in that book. Isn't it amazing how things come back in such detail even after years? Oh, and I bought the burner phone, entered some phone numbers and took the SIM card out of my old phone after cancelling the phone contract.'

'But what about your sister, what have you told her? She must be worried.'

'I told her a sketchy outline of why I had to leave, including the fact that two people had been murdered, but not everything, no dangerous details that she might be tempted or pressured to share. We're very different – she's artistic and less focused than I am. Now we talk once every couple of weeks, when I can make it. I climb the brown hill and call her every second Friday, but she can't call me because I don't live on top of the brown hill. Sometimes when the creeks are running high or there's snow I can't get there. Every now and then I call a couple of friends, too, tell them I'm all right and that I'm safe. Apart from those two and my sister everyone thinks I'm in Australia.'

'It's an intriguing name - the Brown Hill.'

'Oh, it isn't a real name, it's just how I think of it. It's a convenient spot to go to from here and there are burnt trees and shrubs at the top, so from a distance it looks brown. There must have been a lightning strike there and it burnt the vegetation at the top, but for some reason it didn't spread.'

'I've just realised I never introduced myself, I'm sorry!' It made me laugh how crazy this was. 'I'm Thomas.'

'My real name is Sam, well Samantha really, but please don't tell anyone.'

'I promise you can trust me,' I said after a while. 'I know you've told me things because I've found you and there was nothing you could do about it, but I'd never say or do anything that could put you in danger. I'll give you my phone number in case you need to find me. I hope you do trust me now.'

'Oh, yes, of course I trust you.' She sounded quite casual. 'I don't know why. It might be because of how you've spent so many years trying to find you sister. It seems unusual.'

Over dinner of spaghetti with meatballs, once again out of survival packs, I thought of something else. 'How on earth do you find your way back here? How do you avoid getting lost? The bush is like a jungle, and you're a long way from the road, in the middle of nowhere. I didn't notice any markers like yellow discs nailed to trees or anything.'

'Guess! It's so simple it's stupid, really. But I remembered reading about those tags – you know, the ones people use to track misplaced things from their phone. I can't get on the internet from my burner phone, and this was before Boris got me a smart phone, so I asked him, and he did a lot of research for me, he's been marvellous.'

She gazed unseeingly just to one side of me, and I watched her face without speaking; she was remembering something that upset her.

'I got lost a couple of times,' she said finally. 'Once I spent three days wandering around. I had my map, I always have it in my pack, but I still couldn't find my way back. It was cloudy and the lack of sunlight and shadows made things harder. For some reason I couldn't find the compass in my pack, but it had got tangled in my spare jumper and I didn't find it until I was back here. It was very cold ... very hard.' Then her expression brightened. 'But I did have food, because I was on my way back from the village, so I didn't starve.' Another pause while she looked down. 'After the first two nights I was really scared. You read about people lost in the bush and never found. It wasn't as if anybody would have known I was missing or where to look.'

Still traumatised by the memory of those days, I thought, and nobody to talk to about what it had been like. A lot of traumatic memories that have coagulated in her mind.

'I'd like to know more about how you use the tags, if you don't mind telling me. I never heard of using them as markers before.'

'Oh, Boris worked it out, he loves that kind of stuff, delving into science and learning how things work. He ordered them, seven packs of four, and then he got me the smart phone and set it up. The phone is in his name, so there's nothing to link it to me. And I paid him, of course. I needed a better phone because I don't have GPS or Google maps on the burner phone, but now if I'm lost I just turn on the other phone and use the app and the GPS shows me where I am, and where the nearest tag is. And the tags can be set to emit an audible signal too, a real shriek that you can hear from a long way off. It sounds a bit like a falcon. And then when I'm safe again I turn that smart phone off. I've only used the trackers about a dozen times – far better than spending days walking around lost and sleeping on the ground.'

'So the GPS on the phone works outside of cell tower cover – I didn't know that. Did you attach those trackers to trees?'

She grinned. 'I just did what Boris said like I nearly always do. He did the research and worked it all out, and then he told me what to do. He says I'm his social welfare project, because he hasn't got any family to worry about. He got some black nylon cord, a whole roll of it – and would you believe it, a pair of folding scissors! Probably so I wouldn't cut my hand again using my knife.' She laughed. 'I tied the tags to trees starting at the mouth of this valley – somehow it's easier to find my way in a relatively straight line going out than it is when I go back in from the road, and I didn't want to have to move them if I went off-course when I put them up. They aren't very evenly spaced, but it works. And the batteries are supposed to work a bit longer than a year. I haven't had to replace them yet, but Boris got me a packet of spares. I'd better do it soon, and now he says he's going to get me one of those emergency beacons, but I don't think I need one.'

And then suddenly she got up. 'I'll just go outside and pee before we go to bed.' She picked up the lantern and left me sitting in the dark, deep in thought about this incredible woman and the isolated, but liveable set-up she had achieved with the help of Boris.

'I'll go too,' I said when she got back. 'It's good that your pee place isn't too far away when you go out in the dark.'

This time she laughed out loud, and I couldn't help smiling. 'I don't normally go outside at night, never actually. I always keep a few empty cans in here in case I need to pee after dark, but I couldn't do that with you here, could I?'

I went outside without the lantern and when I returned she had taken her shoes off. 'I sleep in my clothes,' she said. 'I just take my shoes off, put extra socks on and spread my sleeping bag over me, unless it's really cold, then I get into it. I know I probably smell bad, because I don't change my clothes very often. I have big packs of baby wipes for washing myself, and I wash clothes in the creek, but only when the weather is fine, sunny and a bit windy, so things dry when I lay them out on the rock shelf.'

22

I woke up early the next morning and stayed on my sleeping mat while Sam quietly put her shoes on and went outside. I was still processing what she had told me the previous day, but however openly she had discussed her living arrangements and how she got away, she hadn't said anything about why she was here in the first place. Last night I had been reluctant to ask, but thinking back I felt we had achieved a certain level of trust, and maybe I could ask her.

Breakfast was two pieces of crispbread with peanut butter and water to drink. 'Very healthy,' said Sam. 'I don't think I've ever been so fit and trim in my life – all this walking and climbing hills, not to mention carrying my loads of food. My ex-husband was a superb cook, and we ate far too much.' She hesitated. 'After he left me I didn't care what I ate for a while, before I pulled myself together.'

Yesterday she said she was widowed, now she said he left her. Was it a euphemism for dying or did he really leave her for someone else?

'What happened?' I asked, giving her the option to interpret the question whichever way she wanted to.

'Oh, he left me about three years ago for a nineteen-year old fitness instructor with legs to her armpits and a gorgeous rear end, always dressed in Lycra,' said Sam quite calmly. 'A lovely, sweet girl. We stayed very good friends, though – after the first shock. Well, I think we were each other's best friend since we met when I was eighteen, right up until he died. He was killed for the same reason I'm here.'

The way she looked at me told me everything. She was weighing up if it was safe to tell me, or perhaps how much to tell me. I said nothing, just met her gaze and waited. After a long silence she got up. 'Let's go and sit in the sun. It will be high enough in the sky now to just reach this side of the valley. Take your jacket to sit on, there's still dew on the ground.'

Outside the sun had angled just enough around the corner and high enough over the opposite side of the valley to shine on one part of the flat ledge outside. 'I sit outside and read in the mornings even when it's cold, but where I sit changes with the seasons, of course. In the middle of winter I didn't go outside until nearly midday.'

I folded my jacket and sat down. 'Don't you feel lonely here? How do you occupy yourself? Very little to do and nobody to talk to, it must be monotonous.' It was hard to imagine living like she did. No company and her only human contact was occasional meetings with Boris, talking to Vijay when she got her supplies, and nothing else to break the monotony.

I could see that she was considering how to reply, weighing up if she was ready to frank about her innermost feelings. I remembered from my first months with my foster family how I would sometimes stop myself telling them how brutal my life had been, as if talking about it would bring back too much trauma. But then she said on a tone of careful neutrality, 'I am lonely, very lonely. The phone calls I make every couple of weeks are never very long. And though I didn't know exactly where I would end up, or how it would be when I left Auckland, I realised that by necessity I would have to be alone in a different way than I'd ever been before. You know, no real job, no friends, no internet. But living here is much lonelier than what I had imagined I'd be when I thought I'd rent a cottage somewhere remote. This is true isolation.' For a short moment her expression was one of desolation, but before I had time to think of a suitable reply she continued with a show of composure that didn't fool me for a moment.

'I've always had a Kindle, so two days before I left, before I discontinued my broadband subscription, I loaded over a two thousand dollars' worth of books on the Kindle. The perfect use for a bit of my savings, which was my mother's life insurance payout – she would have approved.' A wry smile of self-deprecation. 'This will sound mad, but I live in whatever book I'm reading at the moment, characters in books become my friends - some of them are close friends now. Sometimes I re-read a book a few weeks later because I felt so connected to someone in the story that I miss them, and reading about them is nearly like communicating with them. And on the way here I bought three big puzzle books with dozens of different kinds of crosswords and soduko puzzles, just to have a change now and then, but they're all used up now.'

She turned her face to the sun and closed her eyes which gave me another opportunity to study her in daylight. Brown hair in a ponytail with only the ends still blond, smooth, lightly tanned skin and long eyelashes, darker than her hair. Boris was right, she was probably early or mid-thirties, and despite her unexceptional appearance she was the most impressive woman I had ever met. The determination and the courage, not to mention the mental stamina to live like this, isolated and with only herself to rely on. And then, as if aware of my intense scrutiny, she opened her eyes and said calmly, 'Are you ready for the backstory now? I've decided it's safe to tell you, but on one condition.'

When I didn't answer straight away she sent a questioning look, and I nodded, 'Of course.'

'Before I start you've got to tell me what your surname is and what kind of work you do that makes it possible to work from anywhere. I don't know anything about you as an adult, only what happened when you were a child.'

'OK, my full name is Thomas Chester. I'm thirty-four and I work online as a consultant for big companies and sometimes for government departments, mostly analytical stuff. I live in Wellington, in a house that's two apartments and I'm in the top one overlooking the harbour, which is nice, part of the reason I bought the place. I have a small circle of close friends, most of them old university friends. I'm single and I've never been married.' What else might she want to know? 'Ah yes, I never sit in bars and drink, and I don't go clubbing. I don't gamble and I can't dance, and I earn shocking amounts of money, which since I bought the house keeps accumulating in a savings account because I'm so boring. That's about it.'

This made her laugh. 'Could you explain the link between the savings account and being boring – which obviously isn't true.'

'It's very simple, I have no expensive habits, I'm dirt cheap to run. I rarely travel overseas because my favourite things are surfing and kayaking and walking along the beach, walking anywhere really, but usually on tracks, and I run a lot. The kind of hiking I've done here is new to me, but I've done quite a lot of it since I got here and learnt a bit about how to stay safe in the bush. I don't go on holidays with other people because I'm happier doing things on my own. I work from home, so I have no social connections from work. I spend very little of what I earn, and the rest goes into that savings account, which I call my retirement fund.'

'Just what I thought,' she said surprisingly. 'It sounds like the perfect life to me.'

'Now then, tell me before I expire of curiosity, what was it that made you abandon your whole life and live in a cave?'

'I found something out, something that's very dangerous for certain people in positions of trust, I suppose you could say, people who have ways of doing things most of us can't. What I know and have proof of would see a couple of dozen people charged with criminal offences and face many years in prison - not to mention that their careers would go up in smoke. It involves a lot of money and probably masses of instances of what's called perverting the course of justice. The worst thing is how easy it would be for them to track me via the access they have to various systems, as I said before. They could follow my trail via CCTV cameras and EFTPOS transactions and the like. They've killed two people already because of me, and another guy died too, but that wasn't my fault.'

She closed her eyes for a moment, and I waited without comment until she collected herself and continued. 'They'll kill me if they find me, there's no doubt in my mind. It was only a couple of days after I made a run for it that they worked out how the story links back to me - they know I was the one who started it and they've been asking questions ever since, trying to locate me. So I'm stuck here. There's nothing I can do without risking my life. I can't go to the police, it's not safe, and from here I don't know how to contact some other authority or even which one might be the right one. I left in a panic, fearing for my life after those two were killed, because I knew it was only a question of time before they made the connection between Dave and myself – and what happened in my garage. But from here I can't achieve anything. All I can do is hope they get caught without my input, so I can go back to a real life.'

Listening to this, even if some of it sounded confusing, made me realise that behind the quiet, determined façade was a deeply troubled woman in a very dangerous situation that she didn't know how to get out of. She had done what she felt she had to in order to save her life, and now she was stuck in a no-man's land with no way forward.

'Tell me what it was, please. I might be able to help you.'

She sighed. 'Oh, no, you can't. I don't think anyone can. The moment someone started making enquiries to help me, my life would be in danger, and I can't do it myself from here. And if I said they killed Dave, they'll think I'm just trying to blame my ex-husband's death on someone. Apart from myself and a couple of others everyone thinks it was an accident. But I know they killed him. He told ... his new partner and she told me.'

She saw the look on my face gave me a wry smile. 'No, I'm not crazy. I don't think he communicated from beyond the grave. He called from the car and said an SUV was trying to force him off the road and it was raining, and the road was slippery, and he was driving as fast as he could.'

'What happened?'

'They did it. She heard a crash, and he shouted, "They hit me again ... no!" and then lots of noise, then silence. They rammed him off the road. She alerted the cops, and they found the wreck, someone had already reported it. His car was way down a steep bank full of trees and boulders, totally crushed, and they told her he'd probably been killed right away. I hope he didn't suffer. He was such a good man, one of a kind – my best friend.'

Her hands were clenched on her thighs, and I felt her anguish like a physical sensation. 'It was my fault!' she cried out, near tears.

'I involved him, I asked him for advice about the information I'd found, and he said the whole thing was dynamite, and not to tell anyone else, and he'd find someone to deal with it – someone who could expose it. And he did, he found an investigative journalist who said she'd take it on. I had all the stuff on a hard drive, so I copied most of it on a USB and gave it to him. He was on his way home from her place when he was killed.'

She took a deep breath. 'They had talked on the phone earlier, and he'd gone to give her the copy USB, but I think she must have made some inquiries after their phone conversations. I don't know exactly how much detail he told her, but it must have been enough for her to ask dangerous questions and involve others. She was killed just after Dave's so-called accident, but nobody made the connection. There was no reason to connect the two deaths, but it was clear to me. At first I thought that if they found the USB Dave gave her they might not look any further, but that was silly - I hadn't thought it through. Just *knowing* what's on the USB makes me a target. And as I said, they made the connection between Dave and me very quickly, so I had to leave, and now I have no choice but to stay here.'

Her voice was cracking, she was trying not to cry. Impulsively I reached out and took her hand and held it tight. 'It's not your fault,' I said after a couple of minutes, giving her time to calm down. 'You didn't make them kill people, that was their decision. You didn't know how it would develop, all you did was ask for advice.'

'I know, but I still feel guilty, and I probably always will. I often think I wish I could wind back time and do things differently. Let's have some coffee and I'll tell you the whole thing. You know so much now, I might as well tell you the lot.'

We sat outside, in stronger sunshine now, both leaning against the cliff wall and I felt as if this was the most crucial moment in my life apart from the day my teacher saved me when I was thirteen. I knew without formulating the thought that Sam and I were now inextricably linked, that we would always trust each other. I hadn't felt this level of connection and trust since that night when Tilda held me tight and told me she was leaving.

23

After drinking some coffee in silence as if she was thinking of how tell me, Sam said, 'I could give you my notebook to read, but reading someone else's handwriting might not be your thing, so I'll tell you. I'll try to get it in the right order – it's a long story. If you want all the tiny details you can read my testament later.'

I glanced sideways with raised eyebrows, and she said with attempted casualness. 'I bought two thick school exercise books on the way because I decided to keep a diary – which I do in one of the books, and then I thought it might be a good idea to write it all down in the other book - how it happened. So if something happens to me too, there's an account of the whole thing along with the hard drive. Someone might find them one day and then the world would know what happened.'

I could sense her pain, she was trying to sound as if this wasn't a deeply disturbing thing to say, to voice the idea that she might perish here alone with only a notebook left behind to explain why she died. Once again I reached out and put my hand on hers. After a moment she pulled her hand away and started her story without looking at me, her eyes fixed on the opposite side of the valley.

'This is how it happened. One night an exhausted, panic stricken man came to my house, which is up a long driveway. He said someone was after him, he wasn't dangerous and asked me to hide him. I only talked to him through a window at first, but for some reason I believed him, so I said he could hide in the garage, which is connected to the house. When I got a good look at him in the garage I could see he was close to crumbling, though I didn't know he was injured then, I just thought he was exhausted. So I told him to sit down on the kitchen chair I keep there, and I would call the cops, but he said no cops, he just needed a place to hide for a few hours. He could see I was hesitating about not calling police, so he told me what had happened.'

She thought for a moment, and I waited. 'He had some evidence, he said, about what he called a corruption cabal, and he thought his car was being tracked, so he took a taxi to the meeting place to hand the evidence over to someone. But his phone must have been hacked because they still followed him.'

Another silence, which I didn't dare interrupt with questions. 'They rammed his taxi, and it hit a tree, but there was a party in a house just where they crashed, and a whole lot of people rushed out to help, so the people who rammed the car couldn't stop, and he managed to get away. I left him in the garage and told him to sit in my car and have a rest, maybe sleep. And then I went inside and pushed the bolt across on the inside of the connecting door.' She frowned, then backtracked. 'And I told him that the automatic light from opening the garage door would go off in a few minutes, but he said he didn't want me to turn on the ceiling light, he was going to rest in the car and then leave when he felt better.'

Once again she paused, as if to make sure she got things in the right order, so I would understand every detail. 'I stayed up because I felt unsettled, but I decided he could stay in the garage until the morning, if that's what he needed. Then after a little while I checked and the crack under the connecting door was dark, so I thought he was sitting in my car having a rest. There was water available if he wanted it, and he could get out if he wanted to by just pressing the garage door button on the wall, so I felt everything was OK.'

Another pause, longer this time, and I imagined she was reliving that night in her mind and maybe experiencing some of the conflicting thoughts she had at the time. I stayed silent and waited.

'Anyway, next the doorbell went and there were two men outside, so I talked to them through a window too. They said they were police officers and asked if anyone had been around, if I'd heard anything. They were looking for a guy who'd had a car accident, and he might be injured, so they wanted to find him. But I thought they might be lying, or maybe the man in the garage had lied – there was no way I could tell - so I pretended I was a bit vague and easily scared and said, no, I hadn't heard anything, and I asked if I was in danger, and did they have ID, and what if the guy was in the house already because I'd had a window open. It was part disguise for protection and part to test the waters. They asked if they could search the property and said they were going to all the houses along the road. Oh, and they said they'd seen the garage light on, so they knew someone was awake.'

She turned to look at me and gave me an ironic little smile. 'When they told me the light was on in the garage I thought it must be the little light that comes on when you open the garage door, and that would mean that man had let himself out just before they came because that light stays on for about ten or fifteen minutes. I thought he'd pressed the button a second time to close the door - you have time to get out before the door shuts. I was so relieved! So I let them in, and they said they'd look in all the rooms starting at that end, which is the garage end, but when I opened the connecting door to the garage the big light was on, and he was lying dead on the floor in a pool of blood!'

'Christ! What happened to him?'

'I don't know,' said Sam sadly. 'The blood must have come from the back of his head – he'd fallen backwards on the concrete floor and split his head open, but he might already have been injured from the car crash. Anyway, they both knelt beside him and one of them said very quietly for the other to search his pockets and have a good look around and to search my car. He said, "it must be here somewhere – we know he had it with him". It had to be that evidence the dead guy had told me about. So I felt that proved they were part of the cabal and not to be trusted. And then the taller cop said he would go and talk to me, so I walked very quietly back to the front hall, so they wouldn't know I had overheard that.'

I was just about to comment, when she continued after a brief pause to catch her breath. She was on a roll now and speaking very fast. I could sense how relieved she was to finally get this off her chest, to tell someone else exactly what had happened. My questions could wait.

'And then it got even more weird. Listen to this!' She took another deep breath as if to prepare herself. 'The one who came to talk to me said they were part of a big undercover drug investigation, and I mustn't mention anything about this man to anyone at all. He said any talk might undermine the whole operation, which was nationwide and had been going on for a year.'

She looked across at me to check I was following the story, and I nodded, so she continued. 'And then he went back to the garage, but I was getting more and more suspicious about the whole thing, and I kept thinking about what he'd said about searching the dead guy's pockets and my car and having a good look around, so I went into the bathroom and opened the window a crack without turning the light on. I could see down the length of the house, right past the garage door if I put my cheek against the glass and looked out sideways. There was a dark utility truck parked a little way down the drive, then after quite a while they opened the garage door and one of them came out and moved the truck right up to the garage. They stood in the open door for a couple of minutes talking, which gave me some interesting insights, and then a while later they carried the dead guy out between them wrapped in something like a body bag and put him in the back of the truck.'

I tried to imagine what shortcuts police might take when they were dealing with an undercover situation but bypassing forensics and just taking a body away in a truck seemed very unusual. 'That doesn't sound right. But something specific must have linked you to those other deaths you mentioned earlier. That information you mentioned, the stuff on the USB stick you gave to your ex-husband – where did that come from?'

When she replied she seemed calmer and spoke slower. I knew I was right, this awful story had festered in her mind, and she had worried that nobody would ever know what had happened, because after her ex-husband died she was the only one who knew the full story.

'You're getting ahead of the story!' she said now, as if she was telling me off, and again I smiled at the tone. 'Sit back and listen to what happened next. The washing machine is in the garage, and I found a little plastic box in the tub of laundry powder a couple of days after the man died, and in it was a little external hard drive. And *that's* why I'm living like this. I got Dave, my ex, to look at what was on that hard drive - masses of detail and videos of police officers filmed in secret meetings discussing extorsion and crime on a scale I wouldn't have thought could ever happen in New Zealand. And lists of names, details about who paid money and for what. Masses of damning information about that cabal.'

She shook her head as in disbelief at what she had discovered and thought for a moment before she continued. 'Dave said to tell nobody, and he'd find someone who could make it public in a safe way, find a good investigative journalist. He had the right contacts because he'd worked as a producer in various media for years. But as I said before, I'm sure the only explanation is that the journalist he contacted mentioned what Dave had told her, started asking questions right away, despite him warning her not to. Perhaps she got others to ask around, people with contacts, and it got passed on, I don't know. I've thought about it a lot, and one idea I had was that when those questions led back to her, they watched her house to see who came. Maybe she'd told someone she would be shown the evidence in a couple of days. Or they hacked her phone when she became a person of interest.'

She looked at me as if she was checking if I believed her. 'I know it sounds crazy, like the plot in a film or something, but I think one of the versions I've worked out after the event probably explains how it happened. Think of it like this.'

She counted it off on her fingers. 'First they hear rumours when someone asks questions, then they trace those back to Liz, the journalist, then they hack her phone and check her connections and find Dave's number and maybe text messages. Then they watch her house, wait for Dave to arrive, check his number plate, see he's the one she's been talking to, a new contact.'

She had run out of fingers now. 'So when he comes out from her house they follow him and then when he's out on the open road they ram his car.'

I stared across the valley for several minutes while I organised all these facts and supposition into a logical picture in my mind. 'Perhaps she told someone that Dave was going to give her some concrete evidence – maybe that fact played into it too. In which case they would have been prepared in advance.'

She shook her head. 'I did think that at one stage, but why didn't they just go directly for him if that was the case? Provided they knew which Dave he was, which of course they might not have known. There are lots of details we'll never know, but I think my theory is mostly pretty realistic. But at that stage there was nothing to connect Dave to me, we had different surnames, so the link to me as his ex-wife wasn't obvious. On the surface there was nothing to connect us.'

Once again I bit back a question, as she started talking again nearly without pause. 'But between the night the man died in the garage and when Dave was killed my house was burgled. Or searched, rather, very thoroughly searched. Like everything moved, emptied, drawers turned upside down - incredible. A couple of things were taken to make it look like a burglary, but it was obviously a search.'

We looked at each other and there was no need to discuss it; they were looking for the evidence the dead man had been on the way to pass on to someone else.

'The search happened after I found the hard drive, so even if they had shaken that tub of laundry powder when they searched the place there was nothing hard to bang against the inside like when I found it. The drive was already in the garden shed, inside the catcher on the lawnmower.'

I laughed out loud; I couldn't help myself. The thought of a team of men searching a house that thoroughly, and it would take a team, and failing to find what they were looking for because Sam had hidden it in such a crazy place, was funny. 'Brilliant! How on earth did you think of that?'

'I don't know – it just seemed like the last place they'd look. It's a rusty old mower of my dad's that's been sitting there since I was a child. I even put some dry grass clippings in the catcher, so it looked innocent. It's here now, safe in my cave.'

'Wouldn't they have felt safe if they found that copy USB drive at the journalist's place? Oh no, of course they would want to make sure you didn't have a copy as well.'

She nodded. 'They didn't know if that USB was a copy or not, of course – I could have given him the original. That was a risk they couldn't ignore, so they were making doubly sure there was nothing at my place, that I had passed on all I'd found. They wanted no loose ends. Oh, but listen – if they knew which files that guy had access to and stole, then they'd know that the USB Dave gave to Liz wasn't the original, because I didn't copy the whole lot.'

We both looked across the valley and thought our own thoughts about this incredible story, and neither of us said anything for a few minutes. I had been so immersed in this dramatic drama that snapping out of the feeling of tension would take time, but unexpectedly Sam wasn't finished. 'I'll tell you what's on the hard drive. It's the only way you're going to understand how important it is for the cabal to prevent anyone finding out what's in those files, why they're prepared to kill people to stop it coming out.'

I waited and after studying my face for a moment, she said. 'There are several spreadsheets on the USB, lots of details. Lists of who they've extorted money from in four police regions in the North Island.'

She ignored my gasp of surprise. 'It's not only regular busi-nesses who pay protection money, *and* some wealthy people who want to avoid trouble with the law, but gangs too. They deal with several gangs and huge money changes hands under the table. There's also a list of names of police who are involved in each region, names and phone number, presumably to burner phones. And last of all three videos which someone surreptitiously filmed, probably the guy who died in my garage. I think he was a cop himself and somehow they found out what he was doing.'

'That's one hell of a lot of evidence! Why was he passing it on, do you think and to whom?'

She shook her head. 'I don't know, but it could be like insurance, perhaps. So he could say, if you try to harm me all this will be revealed, I've given the information to a lawyer. Or were they already threatening him for something he'd said or done, and this was his revenge? Was he an informer or undercover, and they had discovered that? We'll never know.'

'Let's talk about what we do now.'

'What we do now?' She was genuinely puzzled. 'I'll read, maybe write in my journal about this visit from you, and tomorrow, I'll go for a walk to my recharging hill again and charge some more batteries while the weather's fine. I sometimes do it here, but it's more effective on that hill where the sun reaches for hours. And you must set out on your trek back before it's too late in the day, it's a long way to the road and dusk comes early.'

'Don't be an idiot! As someone said to me yesterday - such a good phrase. I'm staying here until we have a proper plan. You obviously can't live here for the rest of your life. What if you couldn't walk out or climb that brown hill to make a call for help?'

Two parallel lines appeared between her eyebrows, and she shook her head. 'Oh, no! You're not getting yourself tangled up in this, no way! I can't allow it. I'm staying here and you are leaving.' Her frown deepened. 'This thing is too dangerous, and I refuse to involve anyone else in it. Those guys are a threat to anyone connected to me. They searched for me after I left, asked around and pretended I was needed for some police matter, contacted my sister in Melbourne. They're very dangerous.'

She attempted a little smile. 'It's been wonderful having some company and someone to talk to, but that's where it ends. I've already involved two people, who paid with their lives when I asked for help. So no thanks, I don't want anyone else on my conscience. But I hope you realise how amazing it's been for me to have a visit from someone I can trust. A real sanity check.'

'I'll leave if you don't want me here, but I'm coming back. I'm not letting this go, Sam, it's not good enough! Anything could happen to you, and nobody would know where you are. Your sister would panic if you didn't make that call on a Friday morning – and then what?'

'I've been here for a long time now and nothing worse than that cut on my hand has happened. I'm fine.'

Now that I had deciphered her face I could pick up on the signs of stress or pain, the tiny lines that tightened at the outer corners of her eyes, the way her mouth straightened from its natural curve. This show of confidence was only a front, and I knew the decision I had made in the last couple of hours was right. Somehow I had to resolve this dilemma and get her out of the deadlock situation she was in.

'That's what they all say until the first time something goes seriously wrong. And that's all it takes - one little thing happens and then you're helpless. This isn't negotiable. You told me the story, so I'm involved now, like it or not. And I'm not letting you stay here indefinitely.'

She glared at me, frustrated and angry. 'It's not for you to decide what happens to me and I'm *not* your responsibility. I'm an independent adult, and I made my own decision after considering all the alternatives – and at the time there was no alternative, so I had to do this, live like this. I'm not stupid! And it's not for you to say it's not negotiable, it's got nothing to do with you. So, thank you for coming - and now, would you please leave.'

All I said was, 'OK, I'll just go inside and pack up my things. But I'm coming back.'

On the way down to the valley floor I thought of Sam going back into the cave and finding the things I had left on her bed. Four self-heating army ration packs and half a dozen chocolate and nut bars along with the GPS device which Marcus had assured me was the best thing I could spend money on.

'I've been hiking and hunting in these mountains and other parts of the country for thirty years and believe me, this is your life insurance,' he had said, handing me the device he'd picked up from a shelf behind the counter. 'I wish we'd had it decades ago. This thing is expensive but worth it. It comes with a really good little manual - there's a lot of clever features and the battery life is amazing.'

I only bought it because I thought I might get more seriously lost next time, but now it was a comfort to know Sam could get help if she needed it. I quickly scanned through the index in the little manual, standing there in the gloom of the cave trying to read the tiny writing, found the page headed "Activating emergency help function" and left it open with the device sitting on top.

When I got to the bottom I changed my mind and instead of continuing to the mouth of the valley I crossed the stream and climbed up to the place where I was when I first spotted Sam. Sitting on the ground under a tree where she wouldn't see me if she looked across I got the binoculars out and trained them on where I now knew the cave was. And there she was, sitting on her little inflatable cushion in the sun, this time a little way out from the deep fold in the cliff, very still and staring into empty space. I watched her for only a moment, suddenly embarrassed to have done it at all, packed up the binoculars and returned to the bottom of the valley to start the long walk out.

24

Twenty-four hours later, I drove into the village after spending yet another night in the forest. I had left my departure from the cave a bit late and preferred to sleep outdoors again rather than try to find the road in the approaching dusk.

'The intrepid explorer is back! God, I'm glad to see you,' exclaimed Bess when I entered the café. 'I know your note said you might be gone for ten or twelve days, but I was getting a little anxious, I must admit. And thanks for leaving that note. Boris came in and asked for you – he'd been to your house a couple of times, and he was worried you'd got lost.' She pointed at the blackboard by the door, where my name and the date I had left was written up with "equipped for 10-12 days" beside it.

'I'm quite tired, but I'm fine.' I pointed at the empty scone basket. 'Are you right out of scones? I was hoping to take a couple home.'

'I'll get some from out the back, just hold on.' A minute later she was back with a bag. 'You can have these three for free, I'll be baking tomorrow. I like the stubble – or is it going to be a beard?'

'It's coming off very shortly, it's itchy as hell. I badly need a shower and a change of clothes. But thanks for the scones, and if you see Boris tell him I'll get in touch tomorrow.'

By late afternoon I had showered and shaved and got into clean clothes, and it felt as if my energy levels had been magically restored. With the ancient washing machine whirring noisily in the bathroom I sat down with my laptop and sent an email to my family to say I had found the mystery woman, and that she was not Matilda, but I would stay in the South Island for another couple of weeks seeing I was there anyway. I copied it to Carter and then my phone buzzed with a message. "I hear you're back. Can I visit? Boris" and I replied, "Any time."

Half an hour later Boris knocked on the door. 'Any luck? Bess said she didn't dare ask you, but she didn't think you'd found your sister, she said you looked too tired, not happy enough.'

'Beer, wine or coffee?' I asked instead of replying. Maybe a few questions of my own would give me enough time to think of how to respond. 'Have you got a partner?'

Boris looked confused. 'What's that got to do with anything?'

'I thought if nobody's waiting for you at home you might like to stay and have dinner with me. The little freezer compartment in the fridge is full of ready-made meals I bought in Greymouth for a quick feed when I've been out all day. And I've got some great wine we could have with dinner – if you drink wine.'

'Thanks, that sounds nice. And I'm not married. I live alone in my great-grandmother's house up the road around the corner from the store. But I'd love a coffee right now. I haven't had time to have one since this morning, it's been a full-on day.'

'What is it you do? You seem to go up and down that road regularly.'

'I've got a part time job as a forklift driver at the mill, and I'm contracted to pick up and deliver mail and parcels from the Greymouth post office and the couriers twice a week – all the way up this road to all the scattered houses. I'm the rural delivery man.' He looked hard at me. 'Now – did you find her?'

'I did. And she's not my sister.'

'I'm sorry to hear that! I was hoping she was, and then you could help her. I worry about her alone up there in the hills. Anything could happen to her, and she'd be helpless.'

I smiled at the disappointed look. 'Oh, I'm definitely going to help her. I'm going to get her out of those hills and make sure she's safe. She doesn't know it yet, and we're probably going to have a major fight about it. She as stubborn as hell, but I'm going to do it. We spent twenty-four hours together and then she sent me on my way and said she didn't want my help, told me to go away and leave her alone. But she's stuck out there in the wild. There's very little chance of the problem resolving itself if nobody uses the material she has and reveals what's going on. The information she has is dynamite, to quote her ex-husband. Two people have been killed because of it, possibly three – one of them her ex. Which means there's no chance of her being able to leave without risking her life, not unless someone takes her to a safe place, and she can't organise it herself from where she is now.'

Boris frowned and stared into his coffee mug for a long time. 'I don't know what's behind it,' he said finally. 'But I knew from the start that she's terrified of those people catching up with her, whoever they are. She said they have what she called tentacles everywhere. Not that I know what she meant by that. Can I help?'

'She knows I've talked to you, and that you're the person who pointed me in the right direction. Would you like to come with me when I go in again? I'm off to Greymouth tomorrow for the third time to get another GPS emergency gizmo and some other stuff.' I got wine and glasses out and continued talking as I moved back and forth. 'And then I'll trek in the next day and convince her. I left a GPS device with her, though she wouldn't have known that until I'd left. If she had, she would have thrown it at me, she was so mad with me for saying it wasn't negotiable, that she had to come out.' I shook my head at the memory of our last conversation. 'Talk about determined! And if you think it's too early for wine, you can just leave your glass until you think it's the right time.'

'Yeah, right! I'll have it now, thanks.'

I fetched the topographical map from the kitchen bench where I'd left it, after marking some key points. 'I'll show you exactly where she is and tell you how she lives.'

Pushing our coffee mugs and glasses to one side I put the map on the table. 'So this is roughly the way in.' I pointed with the pen. 'You follow this slightly lower ground between those hills there, then you climb this very steep east-facing ridge and then the next even higher one, and then you go slightly down to about here on the north-west side.'

Boris followed the path of the pen as I moved it over the map making a line. 'I took note of some of these points as I made my way back out, but I didn't have a pen handy, it was in the bottom of my pack. It's a hard walk, takes hours even when you know the most direct route. When she comes in to get supplies at this time of the year when the days are short, she sets out in near darkness, so she arrives in the village late morning, and sometimes she doesn't make it back before dark and spends a night in the bush.'

'No! I never realised it takes that long. So she sleeps in the bush, eh? My God, that girl, she's something else, isn't she? And where has she set up her tent?'

'It's an unbelievable achievement - I've never met anyone like her. Definitely the bravest librarian in the world. And there is no tent apart from a tiny tunnel tent she used while she searched for the place where she lives now, which is a cave.' I took a sip of wine and continued. 'Anyway, this is her valley, see these very close contour lines, layer upon layer forming a narrow V? That's the steep-sided little valley where she lives. The side the cave is on is a lot higher than the other side.'

I moved the pen and made a tiny cross on one of the contour lines on one side. 'And this is the cave, right here. Way up on the taller, steeper side. I spotted her from the opposite side. It was pure luck - I was resting on the slope and having a drink of water, quite a bit lower than her cave but nearly opposite when I saw her.'

I turned the map over and started a rough drawing on the back. 'From that side it looks like this – a high wall of exposed rock high up on the steeper side with a little shelf in front of it and what looks likes two deep vertical folds in the rock – here and here. It's very striking and once you've seen it you can't mistake it. But one of those folds is a crack, very hard to spot, because it looks like a shadow. It's a narrow passage, just wide enough for a person to walk through, and the cave is about five metres in.'

Next I drew a profile of the cave beside the sketch of the folds in the rock wall. 'The cave is two or three times the size of this room and the roof slopes quite steeply to one side, like this. But I only found it because she disappeared not long after I saw her with the binoculars, and I couldn't understand how she vanished so fast. I climbed down my side, crossed the stream and climbed until I was more or less directly across from where I'd been sitting when I first caught sight of her, and then higher and a bit further on. I found the shelf and there she was, sitting reading in the sun. Do you want to come with me when I go back? Add your voice of reason to mine?'

'I couldn't do it, mate. God knows I wish I could, but I'm slow and if my wonky knee dislocates again, I'll be a liability. I had to be airlifted out last time, major drama. Haven't been in the hills since.'

'I'll tell you the rest, how she found that cave and how she's got it set up. The whole thing's amazing. I'm going to take a photo of this map, just the relevant part and email it to you, so one other person knows how to find her. And I'll write the description of what that rock wall looks like too. I don't know why I didn't think of taking a photo from where I was when I first saw her across the valley. I was probably so excited I didn't think straight.'

Darkness set in while I told Boris everything about how Sam had left her home, found the cave and how she had set up her life there, but I didn't tell him the details about the dangerous knowledge that locked her in place up there; for the moment it wasn't important.

'So there you have it,' I said finally. 'And thank God you've been on hand to help her get the things she needs, like the tracker tags she's tied to the trees and lots of other things – and the phone. I'll just pop a couple of those frozen dinners in the microwave oven now, but one last thing before I do that.'

I looked straight into his eyes, making sure he realised I was serious. 'If everything turns to custard and I don't come back, then you've got to send someone in to talk to her. The key to why she fled, and who's after her, the whole story of what's behind it, is among her things in the cave, and her situation simply can't be left unresolved. The evidence she's got is on a little external hard drive, probably in the little box it was in when she found it. She's also written a detailed account in an exercise book to explain her story - she calls it her testament.'

Boris looked back, equally serious. 'You've got my word. I won't let you down. But tell me what you have in mind, I mean how you would keep her safe.' As I turned the oven on and got plates out, he said behind me. 'And you won't need to email me any photos. I just took some of both the map and your drawings.'

When Boris left late that evening he stopped with his hand on the door. 'I'll write a letter for you to take to her. I'll say you've told me a bit more, just a bit – no need to alarm her, and that I want her to go with you because you'll know how to keep her safe. I'll come over with it tomorrow when you're back from Greymouth.'

25

Driving down the now familiar road to the coast I carried out an internal debate and tried to decide how much more to tell Boris. After he left the previous night I thought of the fact that with Sam's ex-husband and the journalist dead, she and I were now the only people who knew what was on the hard drive. If something bad happened the story might be lost forever, despite the fact that Boris knew about the testament in the exercise book. I had said "if I don't come back" and I hoped he understood that not only must he see to it that Sam was rescued, but also implying without words that he must make sure the evidence from the cave was passed on. In that terrain even a bad fall was more than possible and my trip to Greymouth was vital.

I couldn't risk that the background narrative that explained how Sam's plight had come about would disappear. Her entire story might vanish as if it had never existed. All the decision making and planning she had done, the courage and determination, and the excruciatingly lonely, monotonous life she led in the cave would vanish as if it had never happened. I simply couldn't allow it to be lost, because she deserved to leave a footprint in history. By the time I parked outside the sports shop I had decided to dishonour the promise I had made Sam and tell Boris everything I knew. It was the "needs, must" principle I told myself as I sat in the car and texted Boris. "Please come for dinner again, we need time to talk some more."

Boris replied nearly instantly, "Come to my place, we'll have venison roast."

'What did you get from Greymouth?' asked Boris when I turned up on his doorstep that evening. He glanced at the four bottles in the carrier bag I handed him. 'Did you go all that way for more wine?'

No, I went to get another GPS device and some more army ration packs. They're the most useful thing ever to take. They even heat themselves, so you can have a hot meal sitting under a nylon fly in the middle of the bush on a cold, rainy night like I did more than once. So I got another twelve – you never know, as the guy in the sports shop said to me.'

'Well, thanks for the wine! I've got a nice piece of deer haunch roasting, well hung meat too, so it will be tender. But it's too early to eat it, so let's sit down with a glass of wine and you can tell me whatever it is you think I need to know.'

It didn't take long to tell Boris what was on the hard drive the dead man had left in Sam's tub of laundry powder. When I finished talking and answering questions there was silence for a long while. Boris sat abstracted looking down at the glass in front of him that was still nearly untouched, going over it all in his mind. I watched him and waited until he finally looked up.

'I never in my life thought anything like this could happen here. It's like a film or something. I understand now why she took such precautions, obviously very dangerous knowledge. And how she coped with all the planning while she feared for her life and then got all the way down here without being caught - incredible!'

'I know - she's a very surprising woman. And it's very interesting,' I said, 'that telling you the whole story chronologically has made me see it differently myself. Like it's become a far crisper thing in my mind, as if I've watched it on TV or something, all the details locked in place. But I still don't know anything but the sketchiest details of what's on that damn hard drive – nothing apart from what it's all about, but not the nitty-gritty stuff that's so dangerous, like the names of cops on that list or the details of who paid for various favours.'

Boris went to check the roast and the wonderful smell that emerged when he opened the oven made me sit up straight. 'That smells good! What have you got there?' I got to my feet to have a look. 'Meat, roasted potatoes – and what are those things?' I pointed at the oven tray Boris had lifted out.

'Roasted parsnips, mate.' He laughed. 'A special little treat from the root vegetable section. They might be new to you - you're not a cook, are you?'

'Nope, I only make very simple things like pasta with bits of this and that. And I buy things like smoked salmon and little single serve meals, convenient stuff. I make great pancakes, though, top class, and pikelets. What's in the saucepan?'

'Sauce, creamy mushroom sauce. It's great with roasted venison. I use those large brown mushrooms, the flat ones, and chop them into tiny bits and cook them very slowly in cream.'

'I'm coming for cooking classes when this is over. I'd never have picked you as a guy who likes cooking – no offence intended, but you look like an outdoors, heavy lifting kind of guy.'

Boris raised an eyebrow. 'And I can't be both? You townies have no bloody idea about real life, do you? Offence intended.' I laughed.

'But listen,' I said when we sat down to eat. 'I can get her back to Wellington no trouble, there's no need to worry about that part of it, it's very simple. I'll just buy ferry tickets for me and her and the car. If I have to supply a name for the passenger I'll say she's Matilda Chester, same name as my sister, and they'll just assume she's my wife – or I might call her Tilda. And once we're in my house she's safe for ever.'

'You've got the space, I mean a guest room and all that?'

I reached for my phone. 'I'll show you a photo. It's such a whacky house and I hardly ever have anyone to show it off to. I took a whole raft of photos to show my family when I moved in.'

I handed him the phone. 'This is the view from my balcony, part of the reason I bought the place. And the next one is taken from the steep slope below the house. That bottom part I rent to a middle-aged couple, who seem to be away travelling more often than they're at home. Theirs is a much smaller, two-bedroomed flat.'

'Christ!' said Boris after going back and forth in the photos for a few minutes. 'I've never seen a house like it. This photo from below is amazing. So your flat, as you call it, is the very long part that looks like a bridge when you see it from down below.'

I leaned over to see which photo he was looking at. 'Yeah, that's right. The lower bit over to the right is the flat that couple rent, and it supports about a quarter of the top part – the other end sits on that shelf dug into the hillside. The in-between bit is supported by long I-beams of high grade steel that run across the gap. It was built by an interesting American guy who wanted everything super safe, way above the building specifications. And then he went back to the US for some reason, and I bought it.'

A couple of hours later I looked at my watch. 'Thanks for that fabulous dinner! I must go home and get some sleep. I'm starting out at dawn tomorrow, but my stuff is packed, so I can go straight to bed. I hope to return the day after tomorrow or maybe after another day or two. Depends on how hard the fight's going to be. She's very stubborn, so it might turn into a long battle. Could you write it up on the blackboard in the café, please? I forgot to do it before Bess closed.'

'I will. And maybe you should bring her here,' said Boris after considering the options for a minute. 'You're right – if you're having to do some hard talking and argue, she might be more comfortable with me. She's known me longer, and I've got two spare bedrooms that hardly ever get used and a new bathroom I put in a couple of years ago. We want her to be comfortable and kind of have her own space. That bunk room of yours isn't any good, she'd have no privacy. I'll just give you the letter I wrote earlier and a little thing I got for her from Bess today.'

26

Moving through the bush with the assistance of the GPS device and the map turned the trek into a pleasure rather than an exercise in patience, doubt and hard work, which had been the main components of my previous attempts. That I didn't use the GPS device last time I set out seemed ridiculous now, but at the time I'd thought of it mainly as an emergency beacon. This time the hours I spent in the forest, surrounded by the earthy smell of decaying vegetation and bird song made me feel happy in a way I'd never experienced when I did the Great Walks. It had been cloudy earlier in the morning, but now occasional shafts of sunlight came through the canopy of taller trees and lit the dense undergrowth, as I made my way over and around the obstacles of fallen trees and tight clusters of manuka trees. Not long before I got to the valley a falcon I couldn't see gave out a raucous shriek from high above me and made me smile. It was great to feel competent and independent way out here on my own with no tracks to guide me, to know I could rely on my new knowledge and skills to survive even in a dangerous environment. Different from just being physically strong and knowing how to fight, which is useful, of course, but this was far more satisfying.

Before I started the climb to the cave I put my pack on the ground and walked quite a distance along the stream until I could see the rock wall high above me. I took three photos and returned to the mouth of the valley, satisfied that I had something to show Boris. I got out the letter and the little paper bag I'd put in a side pocket on the backpack, put the pack back on and started up the steep side, this time using the narrow track Sam had made. She had heard me approaching and was standing on the cliff ledge, behind the big fold where the cave entrance was, where she could see who was coming before they saw her, making sure she could vanish if she had to. When she saw me she stepped out onto the larger flat area, stood quite still and simply watched me without saying anything.

'Mail for you,' I said casually and handed her the letter from Boris and the little bag with what he said she'd told him was her favourite treat. 'And a little present from Boris.'

'Thank you.' She sounded subdued, very unlike herself and she looked exhausted.

'You look tired. What have you been doing?'

'Nothing much,' she said evasively. 'Sometimes I don't sleep well,' Her voice was flat, and she didn't smile.

'Let's sit down.' I unclipped the waist strap of the backpack and slid it off my shoulders. 'I brought a thermos full of hot coffee to have with that treat from Boris.'

We sat leaning against the rock wall and drank hot coffee. Neither of us spoke and I kept my eyes on the view across the valley. Sam held the almond pastry in her hand without tasting it for a few minutes before she took a bite and I said casually, 'Wipe your fingers when you've finished that and open the envelope. I have no idea what's in it, but he said it's important that you read it right away.'

She turned her head at that and looked at me properly for the first time and sounded nearly like her normal self when she said, 'Of course I'll wipe my fingers. My mum told me to always wipe my sticky fingers on my trouser leg.'

It made me laugh with relief. 'Thank God! I thought I'd get the cold, silent treatment this entire visit.'

'Thank you for thinking of the thermos! That's the first hot coffee I've had for a year.'

All I said was, 'Good!' I might never tell her that the decision to make a big thermos full of hot coffee was not merely to give her a treat, it was part of my softening up campaign, making her appreciate what she had deprived herself of for so long in a real way instead of just talking about it. That and the letter might do the trick. Not that I knew what Boris had written, but I was pretty sure that, as well as a plea for her to listen to me and come back with me, it would have his assurance that I could be trusted to keep her safe.

When she picked up the envelope and pulled it open I got up and walked a few steps along the rock shelf to give her privacy to read it and time to digest the contents. Standing with my back to her I looked abstractedly down towards the mouth of the valley and didn't hear her coming up right behind me until she spoke.

'I will come with you,' she said quietly. 'I do trust you.' I swung around and gripped her shoulders hard and pulled her against me. An unplanned move, an impulse born by intense relief, and to my surprise she leaned in and said with her voice muffled against my shoulder, 'Bet you thought I'd fight you for several days!'

'I did - I thought we'd have a week-long battle at least. But I brought lots of army ration packs, so we'd have enough to eat while we fought it out.' For a moment I leaned my cheek against the top of her head before I released her, and she stepped back.

'We'll walk out tomorrow or whenever you're ready, there's no rush,' I said when we were eating lunch. Not much discussion had taken place, just occasional comments on Boris's letter and his suggestion that she should stay at his house. I looked up from peering into my ration pack, now nearly empty of spicy chicken with rice. 'We need to talk a bit about what I've thought of as a safe way for me to extricate you from this. Did Boris mention it in that letter?'

'No, he just said it was time to end this and to trust you and listen to your plan, but he didn't go into details.' She reached for my empty food pouch and got to her feet. 'So, please tell me what your plan is. I might want to change the details, but I won't fight you – or not very much.'

The smile she flashed at me made me smile too. 'You'd better not fight me about too many details. I'm as stubborn as you are. I only left when you ordered me to go last time because I knew I was going to come back better prepared.'

'I know - equipped with a thermos full of hot coffee and an almond pastry to soften me up. Ha! Do you think I didn't realise what you were up to?' She laughed. 'You might as well have written it on your forehead with black marker pen.'

'Come and sit down again and I'll tell you what I think we should do. It's a very simple plan. We drive to Picton whenever you've had time to rest up at Boris's house and have long, hot showers and anything else you want. I'll buy tickets for the car and us and say my passenger's name is Matilda Chester – my sister's name. Not that there's any reason why someone would check the passenger manifest, but if they do they'll just think we're a married couple. We drive off the ferry in Wellinton and straight to my place, maybe go to the supermarket on the way, and once we're there you're safe for as long as necessary.'

'Have you got room for me? Without ruining your own routine?'

'Lots of room, far too much for one. You'll have the big guest room which is like a sitting room with a bed for when my foster parents come to stay, which isn't very often. One of their sons lives in Wellington now, so these days they usually stay with him and his wife. That room has an en-suite bathroom and a door to the long balcony, so if you want to regard it as a separate dwelling, that's fine. You'll have to share the kitchen with me, but that's all.'

She was silent for a few minutes, thinking through this simple plan before she asked one single thing instead of the raft of questions I had expected. 'You told me last time that you work from home. Would it disturb you if I kind of moved around in the house during the day instead of staying in the bedroom?'

'Christ, no! Of course I don't want you to stay in the bedroom, I just wanted to make it clear that I don't expect you to keep me company or do things for me. I work in bits and pieces anyway, sometimes I work eight or ten hours in a day and sometimes I do nothing for several days. Very much depending on what I've got to deadlines for, or if I'm waiting for more information.'

'And then? Have you any suggestions for the next step. I can't hide out in your house forever.'

'Oh, you're welcome, I wouldn't mind,' I said casually as if it was a joke. 'But I have a couple of useful friends who might be of help.' I saw her look and added quickly, 'Not with publishing the story, more like finding out background stuff, maybe something that would help us decide how to handle things.'

She was silent for a long time, then she got up and went into the cave, saying over her shoulder. 'We can go tomorrow morning, but I'll have to decide what to leave here and what to take.'

I followed and said after a slight hesitation, 'Can I make a suggestion? Leave everything you don't want to keep, the things that have been really useful.'

'Are you thinking of those guys a hundred years ago, too? Just what I was thinking - that I should leave what might save someone else. The solar panels, the rechargeable batteries and the water filter – oh, and the inflatable mattress and the sleeping bag, of course.' She looked around. 'And all that stuff in the zip-lock bags too.'

'We'll leave the ration packs that are left when we go, they probably last forever. And the GPS device and the manual, so if someone's lost they could call for help.'

'Do you mean that? It's an expensive thing, isn't it?'

'Reasonably expensive, but it's such a great thing to have if you need help, and anyway, I bought another one yesterday in case I got lost again.'

She smiled. 'Very extravagant, but in a good cause. Thank you! I'll sort things out now and see what else I can usefully leave.'

The next morning the pile of belongings Sam was taking amounted to very little. Her clothes, most of which she said she would throw away, her notebooks and the three books about surviving in the bush. And the hard drive. While she assembled what she was leaving behind into a tidy pile, she said, 'No rain comes into the cave itself even in a storm, or at least it hasn't while I've been here, because of the way the ground in the passage slopes a bit, so it's very weatherproof. And did you notice that it stays very much the same temperature in here even at night? Not so much in the winter, but much warmer than outside.'

'It's a perfect cave, couldn't be better.' I took a last look around, pleased I had taken some photos this morning when Sam was outside, before she started dismantling her living arrangements. 'And now it's an emergency shelter, thanks to you.' She didn't reply, just hefted her backpack and walked ahead of me out through the cleft in the rock.

27

We got back to the village early in the afternoon and went straight to Boris's house. I found the key on the hook he had shown me under the edge of the wooden porch floor and unlocked the door. There was a note on the table folded in half with Anne written on it, and I watched Sam read it before she folded it again and put it down.

'He says he'll be home about five and to use the bedroom at the end of the passage – and to have a hot shower and find something to eat.'

'Do you want me to stay here until he gets home?'

'Thank you, but no – I'll be fine. I'll have a shower and wash my hair, the first hot water for a year, wonderful! And thank you for all you've done for me.'

Her voice held a note of finality, she didn't need me just then, so I left with a brief goodbye. As I drove up to my cottage it started to rain and I felt unsettled, as if I no longer knew what my relationship with Sam was in this different environment.

. . .

It was early evening, already dark and the rain had intensified. Everything had been unpacked and sorted, and the washing was on the little rack in front of the fireplace, and I was thinking of what to have for dinner when my phone beeped with a message from Boris. "Come over pls. Need help."

'Coming now', I replied while worried thoughts revolved in my head. I moved the clothes rack further from the fireplace and picked my phone up, put my jacket and boots on and left. I had no idea what this curt message meant, but whatever it was it must have something to do with Sam. Boris was standing on the porch like a watchful sentinel with the light from the front door behind him. He held a finger to his lips as soon as he saw me.

'I don't know what to do,' he said quietly. 'I think she's having some kind of breakdown.'

I kicked my boots off, hung my jacket on the hook beside the door and followed him into the warm kitchen. 'What happened?'

'She had a shower and washed her hair before I got home, and we had a coffee and a chat, then she went back to the bedroom and said she'd sort out which clothes she was going to wash and what to throw out, and suddenly I heard her crying. So I went and asked what was wrong, and she said, sorry, she needed some space, and she's been in there crying her heart out since. She won't tell me what's wrong, she just says she's sorry and to leave her alone for a while. I'm not sure what to do. Maybe I've been too careful, maybe someone a bit firmer will get it out of her.'

'Show me where she is.'

Boris led the way to the door at the end of the passage and pointed. The door was not quite closed and by standing to one side and looking through the crack I saw Sam sitting on the bed with her knees drawn up to her chest, head tilted forward and her hands covering her face, sobbing.

Without commenting I headed back to the kitchen and Boris followed. 'How long has she been like that?'

'At least half an hour. I thought she'd stop and come out when she'd calmed down a bit, but no, she's really distressed now. Do you think she's having a breakdown?'

I wasn't sure what to do, but into my head came the memory of myself as a small boy, when I sat under the neighbour's big hydrangea bush and cried after a beating, and Tilda would come crawling in after me with a cold, wet facecloth and wipe my swollen face.

'Can you give me a facecloth?' I saw the surprise on Boris's face and said, 'Best comfort ever when you've been crying for a long time. Matilda used to do it for me when I was little, cold water, gentle touch – very comforting.'

'Ah! Of course.'

With the facecloth in my hand I went into Sam's bedroom, pulled the door shut behind me, and after studying her for a moment I realised she hadn't heard me come in. I sat down on the edge of the bed, level with her feet. Her posture stiffened and she shook her head, still with her hands covering her face and tears dripping between her fingers.

'Sam,' I said gently. 'Listen to me. I don't know why you're crying, but Boris is beside himself – he's so worried. Please tell me what's wrong.'

Again she shook her head, and her fingers tightened on her forehead as if to hold on and resist any attempt to pull them away. In my head several options appeared, none of them very constructive, then on an impulse I took hold of one of her bare feet with my free hand. Holding her foot firmly I ran my thumb over the inner side, over and over, very slowly, and said nothing. To my surprise she relaxed after only a couple of minutes, lifted her head and revealed a blotchy, swollen face.

'You poor thing,' I said and heard my voice take on the tone of someone talking to a child. 'Look at your poor face!' Letting go of her foot, I took her shoulders in a firm grip and made her lie down. 'Don't fight me, just stay still.'

'I shouldn't have come,' she said, still sobbing and wiped her face roughly with her hands. 'I have to go back and it's ... it's so hard.'

'Shush, let's take it slowly.' I leaned over and ran the wet cloth over her face, and she closed her eyes and sighed.

'I'm going to sit here for a while. There's no need to talk, just lie still and relax. You'll make yourself sick if you cry like that.' Exactly the words Matilda used to say to me all those years ago.

For a couple of minutes I watched her, then I took hold of her foot again and held it firmly, and like the first time I did it, I could sense how comforting she found it. After a few moments she said, 'I panicked. It's the thought of going back ... to be so alone again. But of course I can do it, I did it before. But I can't go with you. It would just put you in danger too.'

'Come on. Let's go and have a cup of something or maybe a drink in the nice warm kitchen. I'll tell you some details you haven't heard yet.'

Instead of answering she asked a question that took me by surprise. 'Why are you holding my foot?'

'I don't know.' I had to chuckle in the middle of this tear drenched drama, because I really didn't know. 'I just thought it might be comforting.'

'It's lovely. Nobody's ever done that to me before.'

Now I laughed, both with relief at how normal she sounded and at myself for doing such a strange thing. 'I've never done it to anyone before, but I'm glad it worked. So, are we going to go and comfort Boris now? He's been very worried.'

In the kitchen Sam walked straight up to Boris and put her

arms around him and leaned against his chest. 'I'm sorry! I panicked when I thought of going back to the cave and being alone again.'

Over her head Boris quirked an eyebrow at me and mouthed, 'What?!'

I held my hand up and shook my head. 'Let's sit down,' I said and tried to sound as if this was a perfectly normal social situation. 'Do you think you're up to having a glass of wine, Sam? Without falling over? I gave this guy a few bottles of a very good red a couple of days ago – unless he's drunk them already.'

Sam stepped back from Boris, who said pretend indignantly, 'Of course I haven't drunk four bottles on my own. I'm keeping them for a special occasion – like now. I'll get some glasses.'

We sat at the round kitchen table with wine and a couple of cheeses. 'Sorry, no crackers,' said Boris. 'I just eat cheese on its own when I have it with wine.'

I drank some wine and wondered how much detail to include, decided there could be no shortcuts and set out on my convince-the-reluctant speech. 'I know a guy called Jasper - I met him at a wedding a few years ago, and we've become good friends. He's in a weird job for a nearly secret government agency that I don't even know the name of, and he's never told me what he does. My guess is that he's some kind of specialist in communications security, but he's never specific about his job, it's just an idea I've developed over time.'

I picked up a piece of a perfectly ripe Brie-style cheese, licked my fingers and drank some more wine. 'Anyway, because of what I do as a consultant to big industries and sometimes government departments, analytical stuff - analysing data, reporting on mistaken conclusions and that sort of thing, Jasper and I sometimes share insights, so we've talked about work a few times. I'm telling you all this, so you'll understand that I trust him completely, he's like the proverbial oyster - he's used to keeping secrets and being evasive. I had just finished talking to him when I got your text, Boris.'

Two pairs of eyes were fixed on me now, waiting for what would come next. Maybe this would work, after all.

'I thought Jasper might have some clever ideas, and he certainly did. He's the only person I could think of who can be trusted with this problem, so I told him the basics. The plan I put to you in the cave, Sam, is just the physical plan, how to get you back to Wellington and all that, pretty simple. But what I wanted to talk to Jasper about was how to release what you have on that hard drive, how to do it safely, so the source can't be traced. I thought he'd be able to tell me how to do it via the internet, but he came up with a very simple, very clever idea. He suggested going back to old-fashioned basics and I think it's foolproof.'

'I didn't think it could be done, well, I was sure it couldn't.' Sam's voice was rough from so much crying, but to my relief she sounded more like her usual self. 'When I left Auckland I thought about it a lot. I truly couldn't think of any way of doing it without maybe telling the wrong person, or someone tracking which phone or computer it had come from - and risking my life or someone else's. I know it would be too late for them to stop it once it was out in public, but they might want to silence me for ...'

Her voice tapered off and she looked into the middle distance without focus for a moment, as if she was trying to remember what had gone through her head those panicky first few days of her flight. 'I was terrified they'd link me to Dave, despite our different surnames. Because just having seen the stuff on that hard drive is a death sentence. And they did trace it back to me, so I was right to do what I did. After I left Auckland they asked around, tried to find me, and they're still doing it. One of those two friends in Auckland I call once a fortnight told me. And only a couple of months ago someone turned up on my sister's doorstep in Australia and asked her too, but she got rid of them, thank God. So I have to go back to the cave.'

Then she added quickly, 'I forgot what I was going to say earlier - even if it would be too late to stop it, Brown might want to punish me, like revenge for what I had set in motion. He'll be furious about how I tricked him to underestimate me.'

Her face was calm, but her voice betrayed her, she was getting upset just thinking of her life in the cave, the cold and the utter isolation that she thought she must return to in order to be safe. I wished I could take hold of her foot again and calm her down, but common sense intervened, so I continued with my explanation without responding.

'This plan that Jasper and I discussed has two parts. One is how to keep you safe, which we've already talked about. You stay in my flat, out of sight, and nobody has a clue you're there. I already told you how boring I am, not the kind of person people drop in to see on a whim, very few close friends. So that part's perfect in itself.'

'No, I can't do it, I have to go back to the cave! Two people have already been killed because of me. I *can't* let it happen again!' She was deadly serious, only just managing to hold back her desperation at the prospect.

'Why won't it work?' Boris asked, frowning at this sudden change of mood. 'As Thomas just said, it's pretty simple. What could go wrong?'

'Facial recognition! There are cameras everywhere and these guys can access everything. I bet my face is loaded on the surveillance systems at the ferry terminals and on the ferries, everywhere. And then they'd link me to the car, and from there to Thomas. It's too risky, I can't let it happen.'

Boris had stopped frowning. 'Really? Surely they aren't going to keep feeding your face into the systems all over the place after all this time just on the off chance they'd find you!'

She shook her head. 'That's not how it works. They just upload a photo of someone they're trying to locate in the systems everywhere, and then whenever a camera spots that person it triggers an alert even months or years later. I told you, they have the resources, and they can do these things. I can't risk it.'

28

This was a serious set-back knowing how stubborn she was, and I had to get around it somehow. I couldn't drag her back to Wellington against her will, so I needed a new plan, but first things first.

'I hadn't thought of that.' I tried to sound as if it was no major problem. 'We'll redesign that part of the plan. But you're not going back to the cave, no way.'

I just managed to stop myself saying I wouldn't let her go back, which would have led to more problems. 'Let me tell you about Jasper's idea for how to get this information out into the public arena without risking someone tracing it back to us. I think it's very clever.' I turned the plate with cheese and studied what was left.

'And?' said Boris impatiently. 'Would you stop eating bloody cheese and get on with it. Do I have to shake it out of you?'

'Do you think you could?'

He grinned. 'Wouldn't even try, mate. But carry on.'

'Jasper will help with this, because he knows how to do it. First

Sam and I write a script describing how this happened, step by step, nothing left out and we fine tune it until it covers the full story but leaves Sam anonymous, so we don't mention that Dave was her ex or which city this started in. Keep her right out of it.'

'But where would you publish it?' Boris looked doubtful. 'And would anyone believe it? It could be a made up thing, like a scam.'

'No, hang on, there's more. Jasper is going to teach me how to get an artificially generated voice to read the script, like a narrator in a documentary, and the voice-over will play while images of the documents on the hard drive appear on the screen – and the videos of those meetings, too, of course.' I saw doubt on both their faces and drank some wine while I thought about how to explain it.

'Imagine you get a USB in the mail, and you plug it in on your computer. First you see the list of the files that are saved on the hard drive, just like Sam did. The voice is already telling the beginning of the story. And importantly, this script never mentions gender, we just call Sam "they" or "X" or something, we tell it from an observer's point of view. Then the files are opened one by one while the voice continues, maybe reads out the words on the screen aloud. And so it continues, one document after another is opened – and left open for long enough to read – and all the time the voice-over continues.'

I took another sip of wine. 'Let's say that by the time you get to the videos of the meetings the narration has covered how Dave was forced off the road. Then the voice-over stops while the videos play, and last of all, the voice reads out the names and contacts on the final two files while they stay open on the screen. The name list stays open on the screen while the narrator continues the story with details of Dave's link to that journalist and why they were both murdered. And there it ends.' I took another sip of wine. 'We spent over an hour on the phone working on this idea and I think it's good. I had to tell Jasper what it was all about, sorry Sam! But he's used to keeping state secrets to himself, so he's not a risk.'

There was total silence for a long moment. Sam opened her mouth as if to say something, then closed it again and sat back looking thoughtful. Boris sat staring into space, and I looked from one to the other. 'Any thoughts? I was expecting plenty of comments and maybe other ideas, but silence?'

Boris got up and clapped me on the shoulder. 'Lots of questions! I put two frozen pizzas in the oven while you two were in the bedroom, and they smell as if they're ready now. Sorry, girl, you missed out on the roasted venison that Thomas and I had. I ate the leftovers last night. Let's continue this over dinner. I'm hungry.'

With plates of pizza in front of us and our glasses topped up Boris reverted to my idea. 'So, tell me a bit more,' he said, as if it was of no importance and he was just making a passing observation, none of which fooled me. 'This little whatever we should call it – documentary perhaps – will be published, right? And without any risk for Sam, which is what worries me, but how?'

'We copy it on a few USBs, distribute them to the Police Commander and the Minister of Police and a few carefully chosen media. Then we sit back and wait.'

I ate some pizza and waited for Sam to comment, but she said nothing, so I continued. 'Jasper is very intrigued and has offered to help in any way he can. He's a very useful guy. He's got a laptop he's modified, so it's not Wi-Fi capable and it can't be linked to the internet even with a cord, and it's got some very useful software on it, like the AI voice generator app. He said it exists in a vacuum, and don't ask me why he has it, I wouldn't dream of asking. But he's going to lend it to us, so we can create the documentary, as you called it, and copy it to USBs without using a computer that can be traced.'

Frown creases had appeared between Sam's eyebrows while she listened and now she wiped her sticky fingers, picked up her wine glass and said doubtfully, 'So how do we send the documentary out and still stay anonymous? We can't email it as an attachment, and if we use USBs we can't use courier bags because they can be traced, and we can't deliver them ourselves.'

'This is where Jasper's idea of going back to basics comes in. We put them in those padded paper envelopes and mail them – a nice old-fashioned way to do it, envelopes with stamps, just like a couple of decades ago. He'll order the envelopes online for us and then he'll mail them and keep us right out of that loop. If they go into different post boxes, one at a time they're not memorable, not like six or eight identical envelopes going into the same box would be.'

I finished talking, went back to eating pizza and waited for the next comment or question, and after thinking a moment Boris said, 'That's pretty clever, nice and simple. I like it. No way of tracing it to Sam or you, media will write about it, TV will screen it, and all hell will break lose.'

'And what about that Box guy?' Sam asked, and then she said quickly, 'Oh, no! Maybe I didn't mention him when we talked in the cave. Hang on, I'll show you, I'll just get the prints.'

She returned from her bedroom with a plastic zip-lock bag and pulled out a bundle of papers. 'I printed these when I first discovered how important this was. I've kept them in the bottom of my pack under that hard layer you can take out, so if those guys caught up with me I'd hand over the hard drive, and then after they killed me, someone might find the pack and these prints. Like some kind of crazy insurance, making sure the information was still available for someone to act on.'

Boris and I looked at each other in silent disbelief at this calmly voiced disaster plan, then Boris found his voice. 'What did you print?'

'I printed all the spreadsheets and the lists of names and contacts - and a few clips of faces from the meeting videos. See, here in the list of names, in a row that someone had whatever-it's-called, folded in or hidden like you can do in Excel, is one word, Box, and a cell phone number. I'd missed that hidden row, but Dave pointed it out to me, so I got the hard drive out and opened up that row, so I could print that sheet with the Box name showing.'

She pushed one sheet into the middle of the table and pointed. 'See, down here, row seventeen. And I think they've got him online so to speak in those meeting. There's always a phone in the centre of the table when they meet, and sometimes everyone's looking at that phone while someone speaks, so Dave and I reckoned that's how Box takes part, he makes a call to that phone, and they put it on the table in speaker mode. I bet he's the mastermind. Maybe the others don't know who he is. He probably takes a commission, like a percentage of what their racket brings in.'

'Christ, Sam! Getting this Box person identified is vital. If he's the driving force behind all this, we can't have him warned off by articles in the media before we know who he is. We can't release anything until we've figured it out. But how?'

'All their phones will be throw-away phones, won't they? Like in the movies, and you read about it when they report on drug dealers. Do you think we should call that number and see who answers?' Boris looked hopeful, as if hearing the voice might tell us something.

'Shit, no! Leave that kind of stuff to the authorities, but ...' I thought for a moment. 'I'll call Jasper again. There's something I want to ask him.'

'Hi again,' said Jasper a moment later, and I pressed the speaker button so the others could hear. 'You thought of something else?'

'You know how I told you there are videos on the that hard drive and not just images, audio too. There's one person who takes part in meetings via a phone, but he's not named. I think we need that software that identifies the audio pattern of a voice – I've seen it on TV and it creates a graph, like a voice fingerprint. The trouble is that the voice is coming from a phone in speaker mode, which was filmed. Like two degrees of separation. Would it work?'

There was a long silence, then, 'Would you like the full lecture or the short version?'

Boris grinned. 'Short!' and Sam nodded.

'Short version, please,' I said. 'And only use words we'll understand, like normal English words.'

'The science of voice identification is complex, and you need the right software, plus a longish sample from the person you suspect, so you have something to compare it to. Preferably you should have a top quality sample to match your recording to. If you have nothing to compare to you'll still have no ID.'

He waited, but nobody commented. 'Recordings from phones and secondary device are prone to distort and corrupt the original, so what you call two degrees of separation will make it doubtful, I think. The best thing is to have one sample recorded on the analysis software via a good microphone. So your two degrees of separation is probably not worth thinking of.'

He paused for a moment, and we waited, all looking at my phone on the table, just like those guys in the meetings. 'So thinking of the possible distortion and unless you have someone specific to compare the recording to, I don't think that's an option. But what you can get, with the help of a voice biometrics expert, is useful information about the speaker - like where they likely grew up, country of origin, identifying idiosyncratic little habits, slightly odd ways of pronouncing certain word or letters.'

He chuckled. 'Remember John Key, the prime minister? Classic case. He can't say words starting with the letter combination s-t-r and sometimes just s-t without making the s what's called sibilant. He says *strong* as if it's written *shtrong*.'

Total silence followed this flow of detailed information, then I laughed. 'You're a bloody marvel, Jasper, many thanks! You can go back to your crazy IT cave now and continue whatever you were doing. We'll catch up when I'm back.' I ended the call and pushed the phone to one side.

'An IT cave?' Sam raised her eyebrows. 'Is that his study or something?'

'Yeah, his version of paradise. It's chaotic - cables linked to mysterious black boxes, Post-it notes in different colours stuck to the walls, pens and tiny screwdrivers scattered all over, and boxes of miniature tools - and quite a bit of dust. His got this long desk built right along one wall with several screens and he just wheels his chair along to whatever he's working on. He claims he knows exactly where everything is, but I have my doubts. I've never seen anything like it – geek heaven.'

Then my phone beeped. 'Jasper again,' I said, took the call and pressed the speaker button.

'Hey, just a thought about this enterprise of yours , which is getting more intriguing by the minute. I hope I'll get to meet the mystery woman - what a staunch character, eh? Is she built like a warrior and wears a Viking helmet?'

I looked at Boris to avoid meeting Sam's eyes and tried not to laugh. 'She's a big unit, Jasper, she could take anyone on. But seriously, she reaches just up to my shoulder, I guess, and probably weighs no more than 55 kilograms, no, probably less. My phone is on speaker, and she's sitting right beside me laughing. You'll meet her when you're back in town.'

29

I was about to return to my place hoping to avoid any further debate about Sam going back to live in the cave, but when I was putting my boots on she came out on the veranda and just stood there watching me zip up my jacket for the walk home. I could guess what she was thinking.

'I can't let you help me, I just can't' she said again, calm and very serious. 'If I let you become involved you're at risk, and I couldn't live with another life on my conscience, I truly can't. But thank you for putting all those preparations and ideas into place. You're amazing.'

'Come here,' I said instead of replying, pulled her into a hug and said close to her ear, 'Now don't lie in bed and worry, please. We'll sort it out tomorrow. Think of something nice, have another glass of wine and go to sleep, OK?'

With her forehead against my shoulder she said very quietly, 'I'll try.' But I knew she would worry whatever I said, and though I understood what was going on in her mind I didn't know how to fix it. Her feeling of being hunted, of being the prey just one step ahead of danger, was so ingrained in her psyche now that reason couldn't shift it. Maybe it would take a long time for her to get out of that constant state of fear even when this was over, to regain real peace of mind instead of always worrying.

'Think of me holding your foot,' I said and felt ridiculous as soon as the words were out of my mouth, but to my surprise she laughed quietly. 'Perfect – I'll do that.'

I waited until the door had closed behind her before I set out in the rain and tried to focus on a new plan for getting her back to the North Island. One that she would accept as not involving me directly, to remove the obstacle of a potential threat to my safety.

Lying awake in the pitch dark of my bedroom I thought of and discarded various ideas before I finally went to sleep, and then at half past two it came to me. Some sound woke me up and just as I turned over to go back to sleep I had it, the perfect solution. In the morning I got up and started my research before I even turned the coffee on, and after twenty minutes it was sorted. I picked up my laptop, put on jacket and boots and ventured out into a chilly morning to walk to Boris's house once again. Now that I had hit on the perfect answer I couldn't wait to tell Sam. I caught Boris just as he was putting on his boots to leave for the coast, so I gave him a brief outline and he nodded, apparently satisfied.

'This looks OK,' he said, after listening to my explanations and studying the map with lines and arrows on the laptop, which I was holding steady on the veranda rail. 'I'm glad you brought this instead of sending it, I couldn't see all this detail on a phone. This separation between you might do the trick, so long as she feels it's enough. This thing she's battling with in her head, it's like a demon. I got nowhere trying to reason with her after you left last night. I had to stop - it was driving both of us crazy.'

I nodded and thought back to my various speculations in the night, how one thing kept coming up; the way Sam kept saying, "I can't involve anyone else, they've killed two people already because of me." They weren't killed because of her, of course, but it was pointless to say that when she had spent so long infused with perceived guilt without anyone to discuss it with.

'I know. It will be hard for her to move on from feeling guilty, but the main thing is to get her back to my place where I can be around all the time for however long it takes. I'm not about to let anyone get to her – or to me.'

Boris nodded. 'Go in and make yourself a cup of coffee and some toast or whatever you want – there's cereal in the cupboard. Let her sleep. I'll see you tonight.'

I spent an hour reading news online and responding to emails over breakfast and then Sam spoke directly behind me. 'What are you doing here so early?'

'Waiting for you to wake up, so I can show you the perfect plan. I had to bring the laptop to do it, so I've been passing the time having breakfast and catching up on the news.'

Once we were sitting side by side at the table I pulled up the images I had saved and drawn on. One was a map of Wellington with a red line showing the path I thought she should follow, and the other was a screenshot from Google Earth of the same part of the city.

'First up, Boris books you on the ferry as a foot passenger, so it's not my credit card being used,' I said. 'And I book myself and the car on the same sailing. I drop you in some suitable spot in Picton and you walk with your backpack to the ferry terminal and go onboard. I'll sit in the forward cabin on the port side, and you'll keep clear of me.'

'I thought you'd go to the café for a coffee or two.'

'I can get coffee and a sandwich from the café on the way up from the car deck. So, we dock in Wellington, and you get off with the other foot passengers, take the shuttle to the railway station and walk across to MacDonalds. Here, where the X is on the map, right across from the station. You have a coffee or something, then you go to the toilet.'

She laughed. 'When I was little my mum used to say, "have you been to the toilet?" before we left the house, every single time.'

'So, locked in a cubicle you pull out my satchel that you'll have inside the backpack, already with your stuff in it. If I take most of your things in the car you'll have room to fit the jacket you've worn up to this point into the satchel before you exit the toilets. It's just a big rectangular canvas satchel that I carry my laptop and stuff in when I take it to meetings, so you can carry it over your shoulder. You leave MacDonalds looking completely different. Now you have no backpack, and you're not wearing a jacket - you're wearing my black cap and the sweatshirt you've got on now. The empty backpack is left in a corner for the cleaners to find. Don't forget to take out those print-outs, if you put them back there after you showed us last night.'

I waited for questions, but she said nothing, so I continued, feeling slightly more optimistic. 'You follow this red line.' I pointed at the screen.

'The line starts here at McDonald's and continues to the left, then left again into that street, then around another corner where you take the cap off and pull the hood on your sweatshirt up instead. Just chuck the cap in a waste bin somewhere along the way. Then you go around three corners to this point here, where you head straight towards Mt Victoria, where there are meandering paths and tracks and a road or two. Now look at this.'

I pulled up the screenshot from Google Earth. 'This is Mt Victoria from above, and you can see some of the tracks here and there, where they're not obscured by trees. But I know where they are – I run up here a lot. So by following the line on this image you'll end up here, on the far side from where you climbed up Mt Victoria on the city side. Then you go down these steps, turn right and walk along about a hundred metres and there's my place – marked with an x. I'll be there before you, the front door will be unlocked.'

She sat silently looking out the window without focus for so long I thought she was going to refuse, but finally her attention moved to me. 'That would work, I think. There would be nothing to connect me with you or your car, which is the main thing. But you can't send me those images.'

Now why would that matter? The phone was registered to Boris, so sending message attachments shouldn't be a problem, but no way was I going to argue the point. I couldn't to risk upsetting this. If it made her feel safe, then I must find a printer. Her concern was focused on keeping me from getting involved in her drama, but I knew any danger would probably affect her too, so no protests from me.

'Boris has one,' she said after a moment, and I blinked in surprise.

'A printer. It's over there on the little table in the corner.' She smiled. 'I could read your mind, but there's no need to go to Greymouth and being complicated. We'll do it here. I think that thick red line will show up just as well in black.'

After we booked the ferry tickets I realised that leaving the village in a few days would be a real wrench, as I said to Boris when we met outside the store one morning a couple of days later. 'I seem to have grown roots here. I've only been here for a few weeks, and I feel I'm part of the scenery.'

'Just what Bess said yesterday, we'll miss you when you leave.

But you can always come back for a holiday and do some more exploration in the bush now you've got all the right gear. You can stay with me, if you want to. Let's go across to Bess and have a coffee.'

We sat at the table just inside the window where I used to sit filming Vijay's shop when I first arrived. Bess had just opened, and we were her only customers. 'What's she up to?' I asked quietly, reluctant to use Sam's name in the cafe. 'Having long hot showers? I must invite myself around for dinner again. Is there any of that venison left?'

'Come over tonight,' said Boris. 'I got a chunk of venison out of the freezer yesterday morning and I'll pick up some of those flat brown mushrooms when I go down to the coast after we've had our coffee. It's a mail and courier day.' He turned and scanned the café, before he continued. 'Just checking Bess is out the back and there's nobody to hear us. Sam's online on my computer, making notes about clothes she wants to buy. I said she can use my credit card to buy some clothes before you leave, but you'll have to give her your address, so she can have them delivered there.'

'She'll need a lot of new gear, she said she'd throw out most of what she's been wearing the last year after all those rudimentary washes in the creek. Has she got enough for a change or two until we get to my place? I can go to Greymouth and buy some, so long as I know what she wants.'

'No, she's fine for the moment. She's got a pair of jeans she's hardly worn since she first moved into the cave and a couple of tops that are OK – and a jacket of course, the one she wore when you walked out. Everything's been through the wash. Lucky I bought a dryer not long ago. Any news from Jasper?'

'He's found one of those biometrics specialists he talked about, who can decipher people's background from their voices. He said she's been used as an expert witness in a couple of court cases, and she's got a good reputation, so we'll get a sample to her once we're back in Wellington.'

Dinner that night was more relaxed than at any time since Sam had been in Boris's house, and she looked calm and rested.

'God, you're such a great guy to know!' I said when we tidied up after the main course. 'I'm so glad I accosted you outside the café that day when Vijay said to go and talk to you. And you've made dessert, too – I noticed the spoons.'

'Nope, I never make dessert. But Sam's been eating ice cream every day since she got here, so we're having ice cream. We've got three flavours in the freezer now.' He laughed. 'We ran out yesterday, and I had to nearly hold her down to stop her running off to Vijay's to buy more. She was so desperate she nearly forgot she can't go out.'

'Not true! But you don't know what you're missing until you can't have it.' Sam was already putting the three ice cream boxes on the bench. 'Like ice cream, and pastries and scones. Well, I could have, of course, but I decided when I first had a look at the village that I'd only ever go into the one place and get the necessary things and just forget about the luxuries. The fewer people who talked about me the better.'

'Probably very wise and Vijay proved to be a good ally. He wouldn't tell me a thing to start with. ' I grinned at the memory. 'I had to wear him down by talking to him, no, correction – talking at him - for half an hour every morning until he gave up and told me your name was Anne, and a couple of days later he said to go across the road and talk to Boris. And he was just as hard to crack. Hardly said more than one word at a time for the first half hour. Like talking to a lump of granite.' I felt absurdly pleased when Sam giggled, the first time I'd heard her do that. One of those little things that signal a degree of normality.

'I had to get a grip on what kind of person you were first,' said

Boris, unperturbed by being likened to a lump of granite. 'But I'm very sorry you're no closer to finding Matilda. It's what you came for, after all.'

'I know. But look at what we achieved together instead, a different woman, yes – but she needed rescuing too.' We both turned to look at Sam, who was already sitting at the table eating ice cream, pretending she was not listening.

The day we crossed Cook Straight was breezy, but the sea wasn't too rough. I found it hard to sit still and read instead of going out on deck, but I had to stay in one place and maintain the constant physical separation between us that I had promised Sam.

Back to the house after stopping at the supermarket, I was putting things away while I tried to create a mental timeline of where Sam was. I calculated how long it would take her to walk across town, and how long I had spent in the supermarket, but before I had worked it out I heard the front door open and headed for the front hall.

'What a long house!' Sam dropped the satchel on the floor. 'Can I have a glass of water, please?'

'Come over and see the reason I bought this house.' I poured her a glass of water and led the way to the glass wall and smiled when she exclaimed, 'Oh, wow - what a great view! Boris said the house is like a bridge and that you'd show me when I got here.'

'You can see how it's built from down below, or on Google Earth. That path around the far corner leads to the tenants' flat down below, but they're away for another few weeks, so there's nobody to see you if you want to go down there. I've got some photos I took for the insurance company and to show my adopted family. They were very interested when I said I was thinking of buying a house.'

I handed her my phone with the photo folder open and watched her study the photos with an intent look on her face. 'Good lord, Boris said it was amazing. So right now we are really standing on a bridge - a long part that spans that gap, way more than half the house. Does it vibrate in a wind? Was it super expensive?'

'Medium super expensive, I suppose. When I heard the American was going back to the US in a hurry I offered him instant payment if he cancelled the auction, so I got it for a bit less than it's probably worth.'

She turned back to study the long room. 'It's lovely and I'm not surprised you bought it, view or no view. And no wonder your armchair faces this way. That one's yours, isn't it?

'We'll put another one over here too. There's no reason why you shouldn't enjoy the view as well. Now, let me show you the room you can have.' I led the way to the far side of the living area. 'I haven't had time to make the bed, but there are sheets on the top shelf in the wardrobe, so make yourself at home while I finish unloading the car, and then we'll have a cup of coffee.'

That evening Sam called Boris to tell him everything had gone to plan. While I chopped bacon into pieces and grated parmesan for our pasta dinner I listened to Sam's side of the conversation and thought, not for the first time, that their relationship was a bit like a father and daughter bond. When we first talked in the cave she had said that she was Boris's welfare project, but I had watched them together and formed my own opinion. From his side it wasn't just concern about her safety, it was deep affection, and from hers something similar. The way she had hugged him after her crying bout, when she realised how worried he was, and her tone now, showed how close they had become.

She finished the call and came to see what I was doing. 'He said to say hi to you, and to check if you have a freezer full of frozen dinners – do you?'

I took three steps to the left and pulled the freezer door open, and she laughed. 'And is it true you make great pancakes? I love pancakes, those thin ones, not the American ones that look like large pikelets, the crepe kind.'

'I make great pikelets of regular size and very thin pancakes too. And there's raspberry jam in the cupboard, which is my favourite thing to have with them. Would you like pancakes for dessert?'

We ate pasta followed by pancakes and I promised to put cream on the shopping list, so we could have them with jam and whipped cream next time.

30

The next morning, before I even had a shower, I sent messages to my family and said I was back home with a visitor who was staying for two or three weeks to be looked after while she recovered from a serious bout of the flu. The odds were that everyone would get so excited about any visitor staying with me, let alone a woman, that if I hadn't lied about her health they'd invite themselves to meet her, particularly my adopted mother. I knew Linley would call within a couple of hours to try to find out more, but she called nearly instantly, 'So we'll have time to talk before I have to leave for work,' as she said, but I managed to hold her at bay, and she laughed at my various attempts to stall her. 'Don't panic! I'm not coming down to inspect her - but good luck!' Whatever that meant.

When Sam came appeared I was standing by the window looking out at the dismal view. 'It's going to rain, bound to. And probably for two or three days. When the wind is in that quarter it always rains for a couple of days. I like that colour on you, it's nice to see you out of camouflage colours for a change. Were most of the clothes OK?'

She looked down at the light blue sweatshirt that had arrived in a large courier bag the previous afternoon. 'I'm such a standard size ten that shopping online is easy. And it's lovely to have new underwear too. You don't realise how good clean clothes feel until you can't change every day. There's another big bag on the way, and I want to buy even more things. It's weird to think that lots of my clothes are in a storage unit, and I can't get to them.' She glanced sideways at me, hesitated. 'Can I please use your credit card to shop online? I've still got loads of cash, so I can repay you. I used Boris's card before, but I can't do that now.'

'Of course. But listen, when you left Auckland you obviously made dozens of minor decisions – and in a hurry, so I'm curious. Why did you have so few clothes in the cave? You said you left your place with a suitcase, and then you got the big backpack and got rid of the suitcase and bought all the bush gear. What happened to the clothes you started out with?'

She made a face. 'It was one of those needs/must situations. Once I read that old book on one of my first bus rides and leant about the cave, I knew it would be the perfect place, untraceable and much safer than renting a granny flat or something. So I discarded clothes in various towns, left stuff on park benches and in backpacker lodges, because I knew I'd need things that were suitable for a very different life. I had no choice - I couldn't lug all of that stuff around in the forest. But some of the things I got rid of were favourites.'

She shrugged. 'You saw me – dark grey and brown, camouflage colours, practical things. And weatherproof clothes, warm base layers, all that stuff. I got rid of the last non-essential clothes and things in Greymouth, and suddenly the pack was half empty, and I only had the things I'd picked up here and there on the way, my bush clothes, lots of them from second-hand shops. Then I bought some gear in a big sports shop there – rechargeable batteries, a lantern and a foldout solar panel, the sleeping mat and a sleeping bag. I thought I'd got all I would need.'

She shook her head at her own ignorance. 'But I didn't have a clue at that stage, of course. Camping was never my scene. I didn't even know there was such a thing as a tunnel tent until I saw it in The Warehouse in Westport where I went to avoid attracting attention in Greymouth by buying everything in one place. But the little tent I got was perfect and it had those wands that just pop it up in the right shape when you unpack it. Easy to carry and very easy to put up each night all that time I searched for the valley.'

'And then Boris got a lot of things when you discovered what you really needed?'

'He saved me, he really did. I wouldn't have survived for long without his help. My dad died of cancer when he was only fifty-six, and sometimes I'd sit in the cave after picking up something Boris got for me and think how he would have enjoyed knowing how much I've learnt. And he would have liked meeting Boris too, just the kind of man he admired.'

'And you mother's dead too, so both your parents died too early. What happened?'

'A stupid accident, totally unnecessary. She broke her neck when she was helping a friend put up a new light fitting over a circular staircase - the light hung over the centre of the spiral. God knows why they thought they could do it themselves instead of getting a tradesman to do it, totally mad. But they rigged up a couple of planks across the top for my mum to stand on, because she was the one who didn't mind heights, and one plank slid off the railings it rested on and tipped her down the stairs. She broke her neck and died instantly. It's put me off ever doing anything dangerous.'

'Really?' I had to laugh at this piece of nonsense. 'Sorry, I'm not laughing at how your mother died, I'm laughing at you and how you underestimate yourself. You have done more dangerous things in the last year than most people do in a lifetime.'

I counted on my fingers the way Sam did sometimes. 'Living in the bush for weeks while you searched for the cave, on your own and with no knowledge of bush craft. Not dangerous? And making a rapid escape from killers without being tracked? And surviving in that cave for a year, not to mention hiking for hours to and from the road, crossing streams and God knows what? As Boris said, you're one of a kind. You've done some extremely dangerous things in the last year.'

She changed the subject, her usual reaction to praise. 'I'll call Emily today and my friend Jill, and maybe the other one I've kept in touch with this last year. Can I use your phone, please? I left the phone Boris got for me, so I used the burner phone when I called him, but I shouldn't use it to call them from here.'

Now I understood why she'd said I couldn't send the Wellington map to her phone; she had left the smart phone behind. 'Why did you do that?'

She shrugged. 'It's an expensive phone, much better than his own. I think he should use the one he got for me and sell his old one, and the contract is in his name already.'

'Didn't he say you paid him cash for everything he got for you?'

'Of course I did, but I want him to have a nice phone.'

I passed her my phone and watched as she looked up the first number she wanted on her burner phone and walked away towards her bedroom. She didn't return until half an hour later, when I was still standing there looking out over the harbour I could hardly see though the rain, immersed in thought about a statistical analysis I must sort out before Monday.

'Here's your phone, thanks! Emily knows now, or at least the basic facts. You and Boris are the only people who know nearly the whole thing, but she understands why I can't fly over to stay with them like she wants me to. She kept saying it nearly every time I called her from the brown hill. And I kept saying I couldn't, it was dangerous in case they turned up to ask her about me – having me in the house was a risk. Never mind, now she knows I'm safe here and there's a plan in place.'

'And?' She was holding something back. 'What else?'

'She's had a few calls again from people wanting to know how to contact me, which is bit weird because it had nearly stopped, but now it's ramped up again. People pretending it's something urgent about the house or that's it my boss at the library, and recently a guy, who said his name was Johnson, called and pretended my friend Jill had given him Emily's number, which I know isn't true. He had some story about a court case in Auckland where I was a witness, he said he represented the prosecution, and they needed to talk to me urgently. I know who this is, but Emily just said what she always says, that she has no idea where I am.'

I turned and looked closely at her. 'Does it exhaust you to talk about it again? You sound as if you need another cup of coffee.'

'It does get tiring, yes. I'll make coffee, I know where every-thing is.' She walked to the kitchen end of the living area and said with her back turned, 'Every time I have to discuss it again it's like something catches me and pulls me in, makes the threat feel real. And of course, the fact they that guy who called himself Johnson talked to Emily – that's very scary, he's the one I have nightmares about sometimes. I can't figure out why they've started asking about me again after all this time, it seems weird."

I decided to say what I had been convinced of since she first told me the whole story when we sat outside the cave that day. 'I think you're probably suffering from PTSD, you're in a state of shock still. Think about it - from the time that guy died in your garage, right through to getting away safely without anyone to help you, the whole thing was endless stress and fear. And then you cut off contact with nearly everyone and lived in isolation for a year with nobody to talk to, leaving the whole series of traumatic events festering in your mind.'

She made no comment, as I had known she wouldn't. 'I'm going to call Sasha, too. But before I do, I think I need to tell you the part you haven't heard yet. The very last bit of this endless drama.'

I took the mug she handed me and sat down. 'I don't think I've heard you mention her before, just one friend called Jill. Is this last bit to do with what you said before, when you said Boris and I are the only ones who know *nearly* all of it?' At the time I had wondered if it was something personal, something she felt embarrassed about.

Her face betrayed her conflict; I saw it as soon as those questions were out of my mouth. She was trying to decide if she should tell me after all, or maybe how much to say.

'Never mind,' I said quickly. 'It's not my business. There's no need for you to tell me anything personal.'

'Don't be an idiot!' She sat down in the chair beside mine. 'You know so much about me, personal or not personal, that some more doesn't even count. Of course, I'll tell you - but it was so strange.' For a long moment she said nothing, just looked out at the harbour hardly visible in light rain and low cloud. 'This is something nobody apart from Sasha and I know about. You might be shocked by what I did. That call Dave made from his car moments before he was killed was to me, not to Sasha, his new partner.'

She had me now, no way was I going to pretend I didn't want to hear this. 'OK, please tell me why you said he called her.'

'When they were trying to force Dave off the road and he called me, he didn't just say someone was ramming his car over and over, he mentioned what type of vehicle it was, he said my name, he knew he was talking to me. And when the call ended with that dreadful scream, I didn't call the emergency services. I called Sasha, his new partner, who some months earlier had screamed at me that she hated me and accused me of trying to get Dave back. Partly because I thought she might know which road he was on.'

A long pause I didn't dare interrupt. 'But when I was talking to Sasha I had an idea – which had probably been in the back of my mind when I called her to be honest. And I persuaded her to say that he'd called her, not me. I said that letting anyone know he had called me, which I said was obviously because our names both start with S-a, and he got it wrong while he was driving, that would be awful for her. People would gossip, and I said that was the last thing she needed if he was injured.'

She made a face and shook her head. 'I was trying to make sure that nobody would find out that it was me he'd called because it would link him to me. Even in the turmoil of not knowing if he was dead or how badly injured, or even where it had happened, I knew I couldn't call the police, they mustn't connect Dave and me. It sounds hard-hearted now, but I was kind of functioning on two levels, one traumatised and one rational. I've thought a lot about it since, how strange it was that my brain kept working in that agonising situation. I didn't know he'd been killed when I talked to her, or course, but I knew it must be very serious. With different surnames, the connection between Dave and me wasn't obvious.'

'I remember – that day we sat outside the cave you told me an outline of how it all linked up. Of course you didn't want the cops to know he called you. And did Sasha do it?'

'Oh, yes, she was so grateful I'd suggested it, so before anyone had found the wreck of his car, she called III and pretended *she* had received that call, and nobody ever questioned it. Well there was no reason why they would, I suppose. But she was grateful I'd spared her gossip, and she kind of appointed me her mentor and kept calling me asking for advice, sometimes twice a day. About what to put in the notice in the paper, what music to have at the funeral, flowers or a wreath - every single decision. It nearly broke me. I became her go-to support person.'

'That must have been hard.'

'It was.' She gave me a forced little smile. 'But when I first talked to her after Dave called me - she was so trusting and sweet, and we talked through what she would say when she called III, and then she asked if she could call me again after she talked to the police, which she did, and I tried to comfort her. And then she called back a second time to tell me that they had found the wreck, and that Dave was dead – and that was awful. She was crying, devastated, and right after she'd told me he had died, she apologised for screaming at me that time and said she didn't really hate me, she was just jealous of my friendship with him. Such a kind thing to do in a situation like that, when her life had just been shattered. So I understand why Dave fell for her, she's a lovely, sweet girl. She's got a rare quality, and I don't know what to call it - a kind of naturalness and honesty, no pretences, just head-on kindness.'

She stopped and closed her eyes for a moment. 'At the funeral she asked me to sit at the front with the families, she insisted, sent her mum to drag me up to the front. And afterwards she hugged me in front of everyone outside the church and thanked me for being kind to her and helping her.' Another long pause. 'But this might surprise you. After the first couple of times I spoke to her after the accident – which wasn't an accident - I realised I was truly concerned about people gossiping about Dave's friendship with me, and how hurt she would be by unkind rumours. I *was* trying to protect her, that was the weird part. I did it initially, so the cops wouldn't know about Dave's connection to me, and then I was genuinely glad I'd been able to save her extra pain.'

I nodded. 'I'm not surprised. You're a very kind person – once again, don't undervalue yourself.'

'When I could get to the brown hill I called both her and Jill every second Friday morning after I'd talked to Emily, just so they knew I was safe. I didn't really tell them anything more than what I'd said before left town, just that I was in the South Island living in a good place where nobody would find me, and I was fine. There was nothing more I could say really. They all kept asking questions, but I never gave them a clue about where I was or how I was living.' She gave me an ironic smile. 'I told them I was living in a nice little place on a hill with lovely views.'

That evening we had a half hour discussion in a phone call with Jasper about the scrip we were going to write, and how the narration would work with the images from the hard drive, both of us making notes as we talked. Sam proved equal to dealing with Jasper when he got dogmatic as he did a couple of times. No arguing, she just quietly dug her heels in and repeated what she had already said until he listened; another discovery about her, but not one that surprised me.

31

The next day we started working on the script and it turned into a marathon of debates and discussions. By late afternoon we had spent practically the whole day side by side at the dining table with my laptop. I was doing the typing, while Sam checked the notes from our discussion with Jasper. What had seemed simple to start with proved to be riddled with problems, most of them relating to Sam's safety, and to my surprise I was sometimes the one who was most concerned about the risks.

'No, we can't, it's too dangerous,' I said for the second time, when we went back to the very start of the script where Sam wanted more detail about the man who knocked on her door. 'Even if we say *someone* or *a woman* let someone into a garage, we've straight away alerted these guys to the fact that you're involved in compiling this. You're the only person, apart from those two cops, who knows about the man in the garage. We have to leave it right out of the script. Let's face it, you might not be safe until all those guys on the list are caught, because we can't ID Brown. So the man in the garage, and whatever you overheard one cop say to the other about searching the place, can't be included.'

'OK, you're right, of course we can't include any of that. I think my mind is misfiring today, I didn't sleep very much last night. And I didn't think of the angle that there might be some new ones who aren't on the list. We'll have to tell it like someone's fed all the information to a third party, who's now providing the voice-over text. And no mention of the garage.'

Half an hour later Sam interrupted herself in the middle of constructing a paragraph about the burglary that was really a search. 'No, we can't include this either! It's the same as with the beginning, they'd know I was involved in outing them.'

'I need to think,' I said and got up. Standing in front of the window with my back to the room I tried to reason it out and after a while I thought I had it. I went back to the table where Sam was quietly waiting and sat down again.

'I think we could introduce a little fib here, a hint of something that isn't true. If we can manage to get the wording right we could imply that this narration was put together by someone within the police. Someone who had found out about the search, maybe heard it discussed, but without any mention of whose house it was.'

But Sam vetoed it. 'No, let's just leave it. You were right to start any mention of the garage or the search would link this video to me. It's great evidence, but it's much safer to not mention it at all.'

We had got to the point of Dave's phone call and Sam said suddenly, 'No, no, we can't include this either! We'd have to say he called his partner, and those people might think Sasha knows what's on the hard drive, which puts her in danger. We'll have to leave that phone call right out of it. His death will just be an accident on a wet and slippery road.'

'It's a pity, though. It would be good to have it known. I wonder

... no, we can't include it, because how would our fictional narrator know about it? We'll just say he was killed in a tragic accident after visiting an investigating journalist and giving her the evidence. Followed straight after with how the journalist was stabbed to death. I think people will draw the right conclusions even if we can't say it outright. Do you mind?'

In the back of my mind was the thought that she would resent not having it known that Dave was murdered, that she would feel he deserved that it was made public, feel hurt on his behalf.

But to my surprise she made no objection, just said calmly, 'Some things just can't be done, however much we want to, so let's just describe it. And as you said, the implication that he was murdered is very clear. Is there a bottle of wine somewhere or have we run out? This day's been such a marathon of talking, I need a drink.' She got up and stretched and I tried to look as if I hadn't noticed her top riding up showing a firm midriff.

I pointed. 'Open the door in the corner beside the hall and have a look. There should be at least a couple of bottles left.' I sat back and watched her open the door.

'Oh, my God! Thomas, this is insane - there are hundreds. And there's a fridge in here, also full of bottles.'

She turned around laughing and I couldn't help laughing too. 'You're mad, do you know that? You live here on your own, you told me you hardly ever entertain at home, just visits from your adopted family and the odd friend. And you have hundreds of bottles of wine!'

'I like buying good wines, it's my only extravagance and it's nothing compared to what others spend on overseas travel. And now you're here, and I'm sure Jasper will come and go more often, he's fascinated by you. And maybe Boris will come for a visit. It's like I've got a home-based social life all of a sudden, so isn't it great we won't run out of wine? Grab one and we'll have a glass with those cheeses I got on the way home from the ferry.'

'I'll print what we've written so far and read it aloud, so we can hear how it sounds,' said Sam after a dinner of lasagna from the deli department in the supermarket, one of many ready-made meals in the freezer. 'I think it's important we don't just look at it as texts on a page, it's got to sound convincing.'

I leaned my head back against the back of my chair and listened with my eyes closed as Sam read their script aloud. 'You've got a nice reading-aloud voice,' I said when she reached the end. 'Very nice. But it seems too short. Do you think it's long enough to cover those places where we want the image of each open document to stay on the screen for a while?'

We looked at each other and shook our heads at the same time. 'Ha! Synchronicity,' Sam said. 'Such a great word. Perhaps if each open document is only on the screen a few seconds – then people can go back to them, pause them and study them properly if they want to.'

'Or we can read out the cabal names, when that file is open as we said before – that would be effective. And maybe read out the names of those who paid protection money, too. That will let people both hear and read all the names – maximises the impact.'

I held my glass up in a toast. 'Here's to the night when those guys hear their names read out on the TV news or wherever, posted on media websites and YouTube. Imagine the shock and upheaval. Poor parents and families, though. There will be a lot of devastation.'

'I think of that often now that we're working on this. The worst thing is thinking of those kids who grew up saying proudly, "my dad's a policeman". But we can't stop for their sake, this is far too important. When's Jasper coming?'

'Tomorrow morning.'

At one in the morning I woke up and tried to identify what had woken me, got out of bed and went into the dimly lit living room. Sam lay curled into the bend of the curved sofa, and she was having a nightmare, making little moaning noises and twitching slightly in the grip of whatever terror the dream inflicted on her. Should I wake her, or would that startle her and make her even more scared? After a few moments it came to me, and I sat down, took one of her feet in a steady grip, just as I had once before, and ran my thumb slowly over her foot. The twitching stopped and her leg relaxed, then she said, 'Why are you holding my foot?' in the same surprised tone of voice as the first time.

And once again I replied, 'I don't know.'

'I was having a nightmare.'

'I know.'

She made no move to pull her foot away and I continued to sit there. After a few minutes she spoke again, sounding more awake now. 'Until you came to the cave the second time, nobody had touched me since Boris fixed my cut hand nearly a year before. Until you touched me that day I hadn't realised how it made me feel – that nobody ever touched me, I mean. Like I wasn't part of life, less than human. It's the ultimate definition of isolation.'

'You're here with me now, you're not alone. Just say if you need a hug now and again.'

Why the hell did I say that? Talk about opening Pandora's box, she was vulnerable, she didn't even know how much herself. She thought she was reasonably OK, but it was quite clear she wasn't.

But all she said was, 'OK, thanks.'

I let go of her foot and got up. 'Are you more comfortable on the sofa than on the bed? Is the bed too hard, too soft?'

A slightly disconcerting silence, I could sense her hesitation. 'No, the bed is fine, don't worry – I was just being silly.'

Something was wrong, but after a few moments I thought I knew what it was. It was the proximity to another human being that had drawn her from her bedroom on the far side of the long living room to the sofa. Probably in part because of how I never close my bedroom door completely. From the sofa she would feel she was nearly in the same space as someone else.

I sat down again, took hold of her shoulders and half lifted her, and slid myself down behind her. 'Come on, lie down.' I gave her a little tug. 'Let's get you to sleep again.' I put my arm across her body and pulled her back against my chest and after a few moments of tension her beathing changed and she slipped into sleep surprisingly quickly. As I lay there wide awake I wished I could tell Tilda how useful these comfort fixes of hers were all these years later. This was how she used to hold me when she came into my bed at night when I had nightmares.

It was hard to imagine how Sam had managed to be so composed when she told me most of her story at the cave. She was obviously still affected by unresolved trauma. Apart from the death of Dave and the agony associated with his funeral, the things she had related with obvious fear were her interactions with the man who called himself Brown. His behaviour had affected her deeply; the pretend concern and the underlying hint of threat, and the way he had touched her, had turned him a monster who haunted her dreams. And on top of all that, her flight. I pictured her hitching a lift from the coast to the village, buying food from Vijay and setting out to find the valley. Day after day in the hills, alone and struggling to learn the ins and outs of the contour map and the compass, sleeping in her cold little tent, having to return to the road to re-orientate herself and try a different tack to find the cave mentioned in that old book.

Exhausting and, I imagined, with the thought always in the back of her mind that she might get irretrievably lost and die there. Cold and miserable, nothing warm to eat or drink, dirty and probably in damp clothes from dew and rain. And then living in the cave, cold and alone with nobody to talk to, truly isolated from the rest of humanity apart from on her brief visits to the village and her meetings with Boris. I knew I was right; she was badly damaged and needed time and probably help to get back to normal.

In the morning I woke alone on the sofa and heard the coffee machine whirring into life behind me at the kitchen end. I stayed where I was for a moment, sorting out what had happened in the night and decided to leave the things to Sam. If she preferred to treat the incident as if it never happened I would go along with that and never refer to it. I sat up just as she came around the end of the sofa with a mug in each hand, put them on the coffee table and sat down beside me.

'Thank you!' She reached over and curled her fingers around mine. 'I haven't slept so well for a long time.'

32

It wasn't until I opened the door for Jasper that I realised I might have a problem. He was very interested in how Sam had lived after I described how I spotted her from across the valley, and I had told him I had some photos of the cave, but I hadn't told Sam for some reason.

But while I was making coffee for Sam and myself, and industrial strength tea for Jasper, the situation resolved itself.

'I can't believe you lived like what Thomas described to me over the phone,' I heard Jasper say behind me. 'Now I've met you it seems incredible you carted supplies and stuff in through the bush and up the steep side of that valley. I wish he'd taken some photos.'

I turned to look at them standing by the glass wall looking out over the harbour. The difference in height and breadth was comical. Jasper is built like a tank and Sam is quite small, a very disproportionate pair. As I turned back to the coffee machine I heard Sam say, 'He did take some photos, but I haven't seen them yet – let's have a look.'

'Come over here and get your cups, guys. I left two teabags in your mug, Jasper. I don't know quite how black it's supposed to be.' As I handed Sam her mug I said, 'Sorry, I didn't tell you about the photos, I should have shown you before now.'

'I'm not worried. Let's have a look.'

'Christ, that valley side is steep!' Jasper was holding his mug in one hand and my phone in the other for him and Sam to look at together. I knew the photo they were looking at, a shot from the mouth of the valley slightly angled to the cave side.

'See those big creases in the exposed rock face way up there?' Sam leaned over Jasper's arm and pointed. 'One of those folds, the one furthest to the right, is actually a cleft you can walk into, but the opening looks like a shadow from where Thomas took the picture. It's a narrow passage just wide enough for one person, only a few meters long and the cave is in there.'

They continued to discuss the photos I took inside on my visits, when Sam went outside and before we left that last morning, then the view from the rock platform outside the cave and then the last one straight up the valley before we crossed the creek.

Jasper put the phone down and turned to me. 'Don't get rid of these. One day when this is over you or Sam might want to write a book about it and those pictures would make great public relations material.' Then he laughed. 'I spend a lot of my working life making sure nothing gets out into the public arena, so it's not as if I'm an expert.'

What is it you do?' Sam sat sideways on the sofa so she could look at him. 'Thomas says he doesn't know.'

'I can't tell you, it's classified. Let's say there are some places where this country has personnel in other parts of the world, some moving around, which can make things tricky, and all communications between them and people back here have to be kept secure. Which is what the outfit I work for does, or part of what we do. We do a lot of stuff most people have never heard of.'

'On the move - like ships and planes and units of army guys? Or maybe diplomats moving around to attend meetings, maybe secret meetings nobody knows about?'

'Stop!' Jasper held up his hand, palm out. 'No more questions. You're too smart for your own good.' He grinned. 'Or too smart for my good. Looking innocent is such a great cover for being clever, I was nearly tempted to reply then.'

We spent a couple of hours discussing how to set up the project we now referred to as 'the documentary' and then we stopped for lunch. 'You know I don't cook,' I said to Jasper, who had brought pizza the last two or three times he came for a meal at my place instead of picking a frozen meal. 'Pick out what you want.' I pulled out the freezer drawer with single-serve frozen meals and pointed. 'I'm going to have salmon pasta bake and there are multiples of all my favourite food. Sam wants cottage pie. And then we can have ice cream – I went to the supermarket on the way home from the ferry to get some supplies and bought four different ice cream flavours. Good thing I've got this giant freezer.'

Over lunch Jasper asked questions about how Sam had arranged her life in the cave, and she mentioned the phone calls she made from the brown hill every couple of weeks. While she was telling him how her three confidants had all been approached by men trying to find out where she was and how to contact her, Jasper's habitual frown became more pronounced.

'That's not good! We need to be really careful both with the voice-over script and what you say to your friends, maybe a long time into the future.' He looked at me. 'I hope you're going to keep her here - don't let her take any risks. A lot of people will panic when this docu gets out, cops who aren't on that old list and maybe others, who knew and turned a blind eye. Very dangerous.'

That night I woke again not long after midnight when little moaning noises told me that Sam was back on the sofa; it seemed to be turning into a midnight routine. I sat down by her feet, took hold of one with a firm grip and waited for the question, which came out in the same tone of surprise as the previous two times. 'Why are you holding my foot?'

'Come on, this is ridiculous. These nightmares aren't good for you and you're not getting enough proper sleep.'

'I know, I'm sorry.' She hesitated for a moment. 'It's like I never feel quite safe now. Not like before I fled from Auckland, but different from when I was living in the cave. The threat seems closer somehow, like someone could be outside right now.'

'And that's why you're on the sofa. I know that, and I do understand. But as far as sleep goes you're no better off here, are you? Unless I join you, which is bloody uncomfortable. So would you get up, please, and come with me.'

We got into my bed and within minutes her breathing changed, and she was asleep. I lay there for a while listening to her nearly inaudible breaths and tried to imagine what would happen in the morning. Unless I put a pillow between us anything could develop, and no way was I going to take advantage of her sleeping in my bed. I knew the attraction was mutual, but a relationship was probably the last thing she needed. In the morning I woke up and found Sam right beside me, sound asleep with one leg hooked over mine, but before I could think of exactly how to extricate myself she woke up. She said nothing, just moved closer.

'It's not that I don't want to,' I said and moved her arm off my chest. 'There's nothing I want more, but it's not what you need until you've settled down, I don't think.'

She giggled. 'You're so sensible, Thomas! Sometimes you

sound like an old grandfather. Let me tell you what I think. I think we should take the risk and just go for it. I think a healthy dose of sex might fix my nightmares. I dreamed about it just before I woke up.' Then she giggled again. 'And here you are like a tempting ice cream dessert right beside me. How could I not crawl all over you and seduce you?'

We didn't talk much after that.

33

We had finished an early dinner and were sitting at the table talking, in no hurry to get up, when a text message arrived from Jasper. 'Coming over right now, Stella called.'

I read it out to Sam, who said exactly what I was thinking. 'Stella? Isn't that the biometrics woman he sent the recordings to?'

We had only just got the table cleared when the doorbell went; Jasper had arrived in less time than seemed possible.

'Did you fly?' asked Sam. 'Or were you going to just turn up, and then you decided to stop and send a text when you were nearly here?'

'As I've said before,' said Jasper, put his satchel down and gave her a hug. 'You're too smart for your own good. I was going to just turn up, and then I thought I might catch you two at some kind of awkward moment, so I stopped and texted just to warn you'

He saw the glance Sam slanted in my direction. 'No, he hasn't told me anything, but I've got eyes in my head and I'm not stupid.' He opened his bag. 'But I had to come over right away, she's calling at half past seven and I want to take her call on a secure computer, so I've brought my own laptop. I must have a look at yours some time – bet it's not what I would call secure. Where shall we sit?'

'Dining table,' I said, 'so we can sit on either side of you. Do you know what's she found out?'

'Not a clue, but she sounds excited, so it must be something special. I've never met her, but the first couple of times I talked to her she didn't seem like someone who'd get over-excited very easily.'

He had no sooner got himself organised than his laptop buzzed loudly. On the screen appeared a middle-aged woman with curly grey hair and a big smile. 'Hi Jasper,' she said quickly. 'Sorry I have to make this call at such short notice, but I'm due at choir practice in the cathedral in an hour and you said you were busy tomorrow night, so here I am.'

'I'm at Thomas's place – can you see us all?'

'Yes, fine. Those voice samples you sent are very distinctive. He's a Southlander, raised there and probably only lived elsewhere for relatively short periods, perhaps in his early twenties, definitely after he left school. There's very little trace of cross influences or overlays. Probably raised not far from of Invercargill, I would guess.'

'How do you know he's a Southlander?' said Jasper in a tone of mild disbelief. 'Not that I doubt your word, but this is interesting.'

'He has the Southland R-sound, very pronounced rhoticity, which is common down there, nearly universal, but not anywhere else in the country. I'll play you a couple of sample words from your recording. Listen for the way you can hear the R in words where most people kind of skate over the R after a vowel. He says "of couRse" instead of "of cause" which is how most of us say it. And check out how he says the word "hard".'

"Of couRse," said Box's voice, and then "it's haRd to decide". Both times I heard what she meant, though I'd never thought of it before, and Sam laughed. 'Of couRse, just like that sports reporter on TV, the skinny, dark haired one - he does that R-sound very strongly.'

'Exactly! He's from down south too. But here's the best bit – I know who he is.'

To say we were stunned is no exaggeration. Stella watched our faces and grinned. 'It's not only the Southland "sounded R" it's also some phrases he used in a few places. I've cut a few bits from your recordings, and I'll play them now, immediately followed by this man using the same phrases in video clips from press conferences and the like. You'll be able to find those news clips online if you want to use them.'

The recordings had the same voice, with the same phrases said exactly the same way. And not common phrases either. The first one was "let's agree to agree" which was an unusual thing to say, followed by "it's too late, the clock has struck" with two instances of a man's voice using exactly those words in other contexts.

'Definitely the same guy,' said Jasper. 'How did you work it out?'

'Oh, it was easy. As soon as I heard him say "let's agree to agree" on one of your recordings, I thought of Mark Carton. I tend to remember the unusual things people say, and this time it was extra easy. I'd heard him just a couple of weeks ago when he made that public appearance to announce he's standing for parliament in the next election, it was on the TV news. He's very popular at the moment. I think his views resonate with a lot of people. He used that "let's agree" phrase in the video clip, he's always saying it. Like a signature thing.'

I laughed; this was so silly, like some kid's joke. 'He calls himself Box because his name is Carton – what a weird surname. Maybe he was called Box at school.'

'It's originally French,' said Stella. 'Could be some ancestral connection from when the French had Akaroa perhaps. I looked it up because I'd never come across it before.'

'What's his job? Is he in the police?' Sam was on the edge of her seat, getting more and more excited.

'Yep, pretty near the top for the region, and he's been very vocal about the need to invest more in pursuing those bikie gangs that import drugs. I think he's got a good chance to get in. So, now I have some questions. Is this likely to end up in court? And if it is, are you counting on me to play a part?'

There was silence for a moment and then Sam took the lead. 'I hope it will lead to a court case about police corruption. And when that happens we'll have to involve you as a prosecution witness. Does that mean we can't quote you now?'

Stella frowned. 'Don't quote me by name. I don't think it's against the rules, but it might be prejudicial. I've never come up against this before, I'm usually just called in as an expert witness. This is the first time I'm involved in the initial stages, I mean before there's even a case waiting to be heard.'

'OK, I get it.' Sam thought for only a second. 'So how about this – when we put our evidence together, could we use those comparative recordings you just played and pretend we worked it out ourselves? Not that we're going to tell the world who we are until these guys are out of circulation, of course. And then when you're a witness in the court case you can comment on them from your scientific point of view? Would that be OK?'

Jasper and I looked at each other, impressed by this instant plan and Jasper shook his head in disbelief. I knew he was think-ing, 'She's done it again.'

'Yes, fine with me.' Stella smiled. 'It's a very good idea, because it gives you a chance to reveal who he is yourselves, but I have a suggestion to make. Don't say his name, just use the recordings. I'll send Jasper the video clip where he says, "let's agree to agree". It will be somewhere on the TV news page on the internet. If you use that clip people will draw their own conclusions.'

I realised I had no idea how much Jasper had told her. 'Did Jasper tell you we're going to release some very damaging stuff without revealing who we are?'

'Yes, he said it must stay confidential. I don't have the details, but as I said, I think you should let people draw their own conclusions, so don't mention his name.'

'And you'll let us have those recordings so we can include them? You don't mind us kind of taking advantage?'

'Oh no, not at all. The moment Jasper warned me about how sensitive this is and mentioned the word corruption, I said I'd do whatever I can to help you. Sorry, I have to run or I'll be late. Bye!'

And there we were, slightly overwhelmed, then Jasper chuckled. 'Well, isn't that amazing! Let's have a look at this guy.'

'God, how disappointing!' said Sam a few minutes later as she studied Carton's face. 'What a bland looking villain. I was hoping for someone who at least looked a bit shifty, preferably dark with a moustache. Bald and ordinary looking just doesn't do it. I bet he's got a regional cabal or two going down there, too.'

34

For the next few days Jasper came over straight from work and we worked together on how to get the so called documentary to work for best effect. The discussion about Box and how much to reveal or not reveal became intense when we discovered we had very different opinions about how to deal with it, particularly Jasper and Sam.

'We create a copy of the spreadsheet with all the names apart from Box and with no hidden row, just leave him out of it until later,' said Sam stubbornly, an opinion she had repeated more than once since we found out who he was. 'We must get the others out of circulation first to stay safe, and at the same time we can make Carton think he's safe and think nobody knows about him. I bet he doesn't know this list exists. I think Brown is the top guy for Auckland, maybe for the whole of the North Island, which explains the several regions on the hard drive - and he made the list for his own convenience.'

'I still think we should show his real name and the phone number and include the stuff Stella gave us in the documentary.

Let's get rid of the whole lot in one go.' Jasper was in repeat mode too. Those two were equally stubborn, but so far I had stayed out of it. 'Maybe it was just the guys, who organised the recruits for each region, who knew who all the people involved were – or who Box was. They wouldn't want everyone to know everything.'

'Oh, for heaven's sake!' Sam was getting irritated. 'It doesn't matter, does it? They sat in the same room talking in those videos, so at least each regional group knew each other and presumably each other's phone numbers. They must have coordinated what they did, it can't have been done ad hoc by individuals. Each extorsion or whatever we'll call it would have needed co-operation. We should definitely leave Box to later.'

After a few minutes of this debate being repeated once again I intervened. 'Let me suggest something. I presume that when Box has something to tell a group of them he orders the guy in charge of a region to call a meeting, then he calls that top guy, who puts his phone in the middle of the table in speaker mode. Agreed?'

They both looked at me without comment, probably thought I was a bit slow on the uptake. 'I also suppose that each regional leader informs Box about new recruits somehow, and their phone numbers as well, in case he should ever want to contact an individual himself. Or maybe there are introduced live for Box to record and make a note of. I bet they don't email lists and stuff, Box wouldn't want to expose himself by giving out even a secondary email address - he wouldn't risk anyone figuring out who he is, that's why he has an alias. I agree with Sam that Box has never seen the list from the hard drive, and he has no idea he's on it.'

'Right, but the man who died in my garage got hold of this list somehow, and he's the one who sneakily filmed the meetings,' said Sam slowly. 'Early on Dave and I discussed how he got to be at all the different regional meetings, and I remember saying maybe he had been Brown's trusted lieutenant, the guy Brown takes with him to all the North Island meetings. And that would also explain how he got hold of the list, he was close to Brown or kept records for him. And then he turned on Brown, decided to become a whistle blower, perhaps, or he was undercover the whole time.'

She thought for a moment and shook her head, as in disbelief. 'For God's sake! I can't believe I didn't think of this before, why is Brown not in any of those meetings? If he's the boss he would have been there with his second in command, wouldn't he?'

I hadn't thought of this either. 'We know the meetings were sneakily filmed. As you pointed out early on, you can see the knee of the guy sitting there holding the phone in two of the recordings. Let's presume he is the man who died, he was Brown's lieutenant and those two travelled to regional meetings.'

'And,' said Sam, 'if those two worked together maybe they sat beside each other, so that explains why Brown's never visible in the videos!'

'Very clever! So the man who died made his sneaky videos and had access to those spreadsheets. And once he had copied those on his hard drive and added the videos he had a perfect record of the whole set-up – apart from the identity of Box.'

'And here's another idea about the videos. How about this? Let's assume Sam is right and Brown is the head honcho for the North Island. Perhaps he sent the dead guy to meetings to record them for him, perhaps he was never present himself? Perhaps Brown got the dead guy to film the meetings in that sneaky way, so he could watch them later. Or maybe he just didn't want those at the meetings to know they were being filmed.'

There was a silence. Sam stared vacantly at the fridge and Jasper drank some beer and looked as if he was still computing facts and assumptions in his head, possibly about to come up with yet another theory.

Finally he said reluctantly, 'OK, I think one of these various theories is bound to be right. They all sound reasonable, and I agree now that Sam is right about leaving Box for later. So, we include that name list in the docu with no mention of Box, no hidden line – we just take him out and put him on the back burner until the main firestorm is over, and then we expose him. Meanwhile he'll sit down there in Southland, sounding his R's and pontificating about drug deals and gangs, and how he's standing for parliament, and he'll have no idea he's identity is known.'

Sam laughed, relieved and cheerful. 'And he'll chuck his burner phone away and pretend he's shocked and appalled at what corrupt police get up to. I wonder how they managed the money, sharing it out and paying Box his dividend. Bitcoin?'

'God knows, and I don't care.' I was deeply relieved that this repetitive debate had finally been put to bed. 'There are so many crypto currencies and sneaky ways of hiding money. Let's get this thing finished, and then we sit down separately tomorrow and go through it as if we've never seen it before, like we just got a USB in the mail and plugged it in. Then we do the final tweaks, get the AI voice to read that perfect script and send the USBs out.'

By half past ten we had finished and played it once right through, sitting side by side at the dining table watching it on Jasper's laptop, the safe one he was leaving at my place until this was done.

'Bloody fantastic,' said Jasper when it ended. 'But we still need to decide exactly how and when we're going to expose Box.'

We were standing in the hall talking to Jasper, who was ready to leave, when my phone buzzed with a call from Boris. 'Sorry, guys, I think I'd better take this.' I took the call, a bit worried about this late call.

'Thomas!' he said urgently, and I turned speaker mode on. This sounded like something we should all hear. 'I've just had a long talk with Bess - she called as soon as I was back from doing an evening shift at the mill. Someone's been around asking questions about you and Sam. Well, Bess knows nothing about Sam, of course, but she knew you were searching for Matilda.'

'Shit! What did they ask?'

'I think between us, Bess and I have more or less figured it out. Is Sam up still?'

'Yep, she's right here and so is Jasper.'

'Could you turn your phone to speaker so you can all hear this?'

'It's on speaker already.'

Sam and Jasper shared a worried glance, and I felt urgency mounting.

'So this is what happened. I got home from an evening shift at the mill half an hour ago, and I had an urgent message from Bess to call her whatever time I got in, first time that's ever happened, so I did. A guy's been asking questions about you and probably about Sam. He turned up at the backpacker lodge two days ago, and he seems to have talked to quite a few people. He claimed to have heard that an old mate of his had stayed in the village, a guy he'd lost touch with, and he had this little story he trotted out wherever he went, a way of leading on to asking what you might have been doing here and if you had your wife with you, all kinds of things.'

'What did he look like?' asked Sam. 'Middle-aged, tall and skinny?'

'Bess has a photo of him on her phone, she's going to send it to you, I gave her your number. She snapped him through the window when he was standing outside the café talking to someone. She's worried about the way he's asking things that seem to be about you, Thomas. Said he seems more like a cop asking questions than someone trying to find an old mate, so that made her suspicious. And as she said, if he really was a cop he would have said so. She fond of you, and she can't believe you've done anything wrong, so she wanted to check in with me.'

Jasper broke in. 'Hi, Boris, it's Jasper. Did anyone find out how this guy knew Thomas had been there?'

'Bess and I think we've tracked backwards through all she's picked up in the café and we have a theory. You know how everyone talks to her when they come in for coffee, that café is gossip central – well, now she's kind of sorted out in her mind who's been telling her things second or third hand, and who's told her what this guy has said directly to them, so she's pretty sure she's got it right. As I said, she really worried about why he wants to find you.'

I glanced at Sam, who looked calm, but that meant nothing. 'Let's all sit down,' she said, 'and you can tell us what Bess thinks.'

'I'll tell you first up why she even called me. She has no idea of that Sam was living in the cave or why, but she's heard people comment on her before, wondering where she could possibly be living and why. And then when you spent over a week in the hills, Thomas, she brought it up when I called in for a coffee. She said, she hoped that woman would turn out to be your sister, and she mentioned how strange it was she only comes into the village now and then and buys stuff from Vijay's, and then walks away, because nobody can figure out where she's living. Some people had discussed it in the café, speculated on why, and how she obviously didn't want to be found, so it's out there, and more so than ever after you turned up.'

'Christ! I only told three or four people I was looking for my sister before I talked to you.'

'Anyway,' continued Boris, 'after you came back and said it wasn't your sister, Bess commented when I called in for a coffee, said she had hoped it would turn out to be Matilda. So now, when this chap came in behaving so strangely - and she said he was very focused and probing, she got worried. And others told her he'd talked to them too. And he knew you had taken Marina's house for a couple of months.'

A horrible string of possible connections was developing in my mind, various ways this man could have found out more. 'I must check with Marina, see if he contacted her and what she might have told him.'

'I already did,' said Boris. 'I've known her since we were teenagers, that cottage was her granddad's, her family lived in Reefton, but she was often here in the holidays. I just called her, and she said he called her yesterday, got her number from the Book-a-batch website and spun her a story about a long lost friend, and could she confirm if you were called such-and-such, and had you possibly come from Christchurch, used some made up name. And she said, no, it can't be the same one, this guy's called Thomas and he lives in Wellington. She didn't mention your surname, though, she's quite sure about that.'

'Is he still there?'

'He left today, just after lunch.'

'Oh, no!' exclaimed Sam. 'I bet people told him that Thomas left suddenly and didn't stay the two months he'd paid for. He'll have found out what kind of car Thomas drives, so now it's easy for him to find us. He'd be able to check the vehicle register for that model car owned by someone called Thomas, who lives in Wellington.'

'But why did he go there at all? It seems crazy,' said Jasper. 'It can't have been random, so what led him to the village in the first place?'

We looked at each other, baffled and Boris said, 'It doesn't matter what led him to come here, something did, and now you must take precautions – immediately.'

Again I glanced at Sam, who was staring vacantly at the phone in my hand, seemingly lost in thought, and wondered what was going on in her head. Suddenly she looked up.

'The Friday phone calls! Of course, that's what it is. They must have monitored the calls on Jill and Sasha's phones and seen that every second Friday the same number called first one and then the other. They probably have software that can scan for that sort of thing, find patterns?' Her gaze was on Jasper, and he nodded, yes. 'So they'd be able to find out which cell tower those calls came from, always the same one and that's why he was there. Thank God I always used my anonymous phone to call them, not the smart phone you've got, Boris, because then you could have been in trouble.'

'What are you going to do? You have to let me know.' Boris sounded uncharacteristically worried, far from his usual staunch approach. 'Do you want me to come up?'

Unexpectedly Sam laughed, the last thing I would have expected. 'Only if you bring your hunting rifle – but no, don't do that. I'll go and hide somewhere else and leave these two big guys to tackle whoever comes and asks questions.'

Jasper looked at me and shook his head. 'Not good enough!' he said decisively. 'Don't worry, Boris. She's coming home with me right now. I came over in a taxi, so I could have a few drinks - we'll just grab some of her stuff and walk. We can keep each other informed via phone calls, so everyone knows what's going on. No texting and no emails, though. And no calls to or from Sam's burner phone. We'll take the SIM card out right now.'

I got a sports bag out for Sam to pack some clothes and toiletries into while my mind spun with theories and plans. As soon as she had disappeared into her bedroom, Jasper said quietly, 'Listen, mate – God knows what those bastards will do, but say they turn up here with a search warrant on some trumped-up charge. You've got to get rid of all her clothes and things. There can't be anything of hers here for them to find. We'll chuck her SIM card in a bin and throw her phone into the harbour. And I'll take the laptop and the hard drive and those printouts.'

'OK, good idea. Let's put everything in your computer bag. Safer that you have it all at your place. And I'll put Sam's gear down into the basement, they're very unlikely to find it there – and if they do I'll say it's my sister's stuff.'

'Basement?' Sam was back in the living room already with the bag in her hand. 'You haven't got a basement, do you?'

'It's not a normal basement, just a storage space under this end where the house rests on that shelf on the hill, under my bedroom. It's between the concrete pillars that the I-beams rest on, long and narrow, no windows. I don't think they'll find it if the come to search the place. The wall is built of concrete blocks, same as the pillars, so it looks like a retaining wall.'

At the front door Sam hugged me, and I held her close for a moment before she put her jacket on. Jasper picked up her bag and his computer case and they set off into the chilly evening, leaving me to clear the house of any traces of Sam. I did it systematically, so I wouldn't miss anything, started in my bedroom and scanned every surface and continued to her bedroom with the few things I had found. I got the big plastic courier bags her new clothes had come in and the satchel she had carried after she left her backpack at McDonald's, stuffed everything in and had a good look in her bathroom.

Instead of going outside and down around the bottom flat to get to the so-called basement, I opened the trap door in the balcony floor, which is marked on the plans of the house as a fire escape, climbed the ladder twice with all the bags and locked them into the basement room where I kept my bike and a couple of old surfboards.

Being alone in the house felt strange. I locked the balcony doors and did another round to check that nothing of Sam's was left, and then I didn't know what to do with myself. At quarter to twelve Jasper called. 'We're safely here now. It took a bit of time – we did a couple of long detours to avoid areas with CCTV, and Sam's busy unpacking her little bag in the spare room. Not as luxurious as yours, but it will do.'

'Don't be silly, Jasper,' said Sam, who must have turned up beside him while we were talking. 'Remember where I lived for over a year? It's great! And Thomas, there's some washing of mine in the machine. Please hide that as well.'

'Oh, I forgot to say, I got the photo Bess took of the man who asked about me. He's only medium height and a bit stocky, so definitely not Brown. Probably someone based down there who's been asked to do it and report back.'

I got Sam's things out of the washing machine and took them down to the basement, and went to bed.

35

Nothing happened the next day. In the evening we had a phone meeting to discuss how to make the documentary script perfect before Japer got the narration done and loaded it on the seven USBs to mail on his way to work the next day.

'I can't believe it how well that final meeting to edit the script went,' he said when he called from work in his lunchbreak. 'Sam and I agreed on everything, no endless debates, and you mostly stayed out of it as usual. And now they're in the mail! I did a circuit this morning on my way to work – only two in each mail box.'

The following evening a guy in balaclava turned up at the house just after dark; a bit of a surprise, as nothing more threatening than Jasper and some courier drivers had set off the alert signal on my phone since we got back from the South Island.

I was standing in front of the freezer thinking of what to have for dinner when my phone gave out the little wolf whistle it does when the sensors pick up someone approaching the house. There were no blinds or curtains pulled, so I went to the bathroom where I couldn't be seen and checked my phone. The camera view from the front door showed a man in a balaclava walking diagonally across the front yard from the street. He opened the gate to the steps to the flat under the house. Next he appeared on the camera mounted under the balcony and stood for a couple of minutes in a listening stance before he walked slowly along the terrace close to the wall, pausing at each window and peering inside the flat. At the sliding doors he shook the handle quite hard, then he turned and disappeared around the corner. On the camera at the top corner I watched him climb the stairs and blessed the American for having such a great security system installed, three cameras and a large capacity hard drive to archive recordings.

While I stood there watching him on my phone in the semi-dark bathroom I considered a range of options and discarded most, but now I must do something. In my head I went through various scenarios of how to deflect an attack, and what I could do without weapons if he was armed. He could have something tucked in his belt or in a pocket that I couldn't see. On the front camera I watched as he stood in his stand-and-listen stance again, presumably trying to hear where someone was moving around inside, then he cautiously walked along the wall. While he stood still for a moment and bent sideways to look in the first window, I came out of the bathroom with the phone in one hand and my electric razor in the other and went to stand right up against the front door where he wouldn't be able to see me through the windows.

When I swung the door open and stepped out, with the phone in one pocket and the razor in the other, so I had both hands free, he was right there in front of me, totally unprepared. He took a stumbling step back and I followed with a step forward, swung a right handed punch and managed to catch him nicely on his left cheekbone. His head snapped back, and he nearly fell. I grabbed his arm, swung him around and pulled his hand up behind his back, right up to where it would immobilise him with pain. With the other hand I pushed the electric razor into his side just under the ribcage and he grunted something I couldn't hear through the balaclava that covered his mouth.

'Inside!' I shook him hard. 'Let's have a chat.'

He tried to resist, but a bit more upward pressure on his arm persuaded him to do what he was told. We walked slowly into the hall, and I pulled the door shut behind us; another visitor would have been hard to cope with just then. In the living room I let him go after pushing the razor into my pocket before I stripped the balaclava off his head. He was young, maybe eighteen or twenty with a shaved head covered with tattoos.

'What were you looking for?'

His right hand moved suddenly, so I grabbed his wrist and hauled his arm straight up, nearly lifted him off the floor. 'Don't even try! Now keep still!'

I patted his pockets and found a flick-knife, which I put it my own back pocket, but that was all he had. 'Now tell me why you were snooping around the house.'

'Don't be so fucking violent, man! I was just looking for some shit worth taking,' he said, full of bravado, but scared at the same time. 'I need the money.'

'You looked in the windows downstairs, but you didn't break in even though there's clearly nobody at home. And then you came back up and started checking what you could see through the windows along the front where lights are on. What are you really doing?'

'Nothing,' he said sulkily, and refused to meet my eyes. 'I was just checking the place out.'

I had to report him. I was sure he'd been hired to check if Sam was here, so not reporting him would seem strange if I was an innocent citizen. Still with a firm grip on his wrist forcing him to stand on tiptoes, I got my phone out of my front pocket and called 111 and asked for police, while my captive groaned with pain. I was surprised he didn't try to take a swing at me, but he seemed to have given up.

'A guy wearing a balaclava was snooping around the house peering in the windows, but I've got him. He had a knife, which I've taken off him. Could you please get someone to pick him up?' It took a few minutes to give them all the details of where I lived and who I was, but their assurance that a car was on the way was all I needed.

'For fuck's sake,' groaned my captive between clenched teeth when I finished the call. 'Can you let my arm down just a bit? It's hurting like shit.'

'Good! That's just what we want.' But I did relent and let his arm down slightly, but I kept my grip on his wrist, so if he tried something I could immobilise him again. I walked him back to the front hall and ten minutes later we watched a police car pulling up outside. The two cops coming towards the front door saw us through the big window beside the door, standing there with the light on, patiently waiting and one of them shook his head and said something to the other, who grinned.

Five minutes later we had covered the basics, my intruder was sitting handcuffed in the back of the police car with the door open, and we stood on the front step while I showed them the footage of his activities on my phone.

'Good!' said one of them. 'Keep that in case we want to use it. Didn't you tell the operator he had a knife?'

'Sorry, I forgot about the knife. Here it is.' I fished it out of my pocket and gave it to him, and the intruder shouted loudly from the car, 'He's got a gun, he had a gun pushed into my back!'

Now they were interested in me rather than him. 'Do you have a gun licence?'

'No, and I've never owned a gun in my life, legal or otherwise. I didn't poke a pistol into his ribs, I used this.' I pulled the razor out of my pocket and laughed. 'I was in the bathroom when the security alert came up on my phone, so I watched him walking around the house and decided to take the razor – you know, just something that might feel like a gun. And it worked.'

They looked at each other and then at the guy sitting in the car. 'Did you hear that, kid?' called one of the cops. 'You got held up with an electric razor!' To me he said, 'That footage of you grabbing him by the front door – very well done. You've done martial arts?'

'Years of it as a teenager, but I've never used it in a real situation before.'

As soon as they left I called Jasper and told him and Sam; Iknew Jasper would enjoy hearing how accurate his prediction had been.

'Great stuff, action man! Let's hope that's got you out of the loop. And don't delete that footage. I want to see it when we can come over, sounds amazing.' He stopped talking and I heard Sam say, 'Can I have a chat to Thomas, please?'

'Hi, it's me. I'm really worried now. Remember I said right at the start I didn't want you involved? God, I hope this has convinced them you have no connection to me, or I'll never forgive myself.'

'Are you sleeping OK? Or are you still having nightmares?' I needed to get her away from the subject of my safety and her guilt complex, anything would do, but I did want to know she was all right, too.

'Mostly OK,' she said, 'but I use your trick if I wake up after a dream.'

'You hold on to your own foot?'

She laughed. 'No, but I think of you doing it, very comforting even if it's just a thought.'

I put a pie in the air fryer and thought of those padded envelopes now on their way to their destinations. I imagined the Police Commissioner plugging in a USB and watching the documentary, checking the names against some official record of police personnel and slowly setting in motion the machinery that would tear the cabal apart. And I thought of Box down there in Southland, hearing about this from one of those involved, or maybe not finding out until it appeared in the news. He would get rid of his burner phone and hope they would never get to him.

36

A couple of days later I was talking to Jasper on the phone when he interrupted himself in the middle of a sentence. 'Sam's yelling something, hold on.'

'Hi, listen,' said Sam a moment later, 'I was just reading on the RNZ website about a rumour that TV One will screen something they call 'of utmost importance' on the news tonight. I bet it's our documentary.'

We watched the TV news together, Jasper and Sam in his flat and me at home, but equally tense, hoping it would look and sound OK, on my part with a slight sense of unreality. To hear the political pundits and crime experts discussing it made it all the more impactful.

Sam called as soon as it ended, very excited. 'Imagine how Box feels right now! The poor guy, he'll be sweating and wondering if someone in the cabal actually knows who he is. He's probably getting rid of his Box phone as we speak. And then it will hit him like a blow from behind when we expose him, however we do that.'

'We need to make a decision soon about how and when we reveal who he is.' Jasper had taken over the phone. 'Why don't you come for dinner tomorrow? It's not as if you and I haven't already got history - both at your place and here, so even if they're watching you it wouldn't seem suspicious. Because you're not out of the woods yet, there might be others who're not on that list, not to mention that Box himself might organise another attempt. Maybe he was the one who sent your intruder.'

The impact was a greater than I had expected, with extensive cover in the media the next morning. The two major newspapers led with it: headlines in large font and screenshots of the contents. The authorities were caught on the hop, but trying to stop the details spreading was useless, the TV news had already got in first of and those names were out there already. All articles were densely populated with the word "alleged", as we had expected, but they were basically print versions of last night's TV news. Political commentators and academics commented, there were promises of investigations from the Minister of Police and the Commissioner, and rampant excitement on social media.

'I'm exhausted already,' said Jasper and handed me a beer when I arrived at his place for dinner. 'I think I've read and listened to every scrap of news about it, and everyone at work is wondering how this happened, and I take part in the discussions, of course – very funny. Did you see that those files are all on YouTube? That blogger I said would do a great job surpassed himself. If you haven't read his blog yet, you should. Hey, you look damp, did you walk?'

'Of course, I walked. Over Mt Vic and then around town a bit before I got here, made a loop around the Basin reserve just for the hell of it, in case they're watching me. I don't trust anyone or anything now, present company excepted. It's drizzling, but not very cold.'

'I called Boris from Jasper's phone just before you arrived.' Sam was pleased and excited. 'He's so happy it's all out in public now. He can't wait to see the video of your intruder. I told him what had happened and that you were coming tonight, and Jasper says he can download it from your phone and send it to him, without you sending it from your phone, just to avoid any complications.'

'That's what I was going to do right now. I've brought my phone cable so I can transfer the files from my security camera to a laptop here. I really enjoy thinking of how it worked out, very satisfying.'

'Action man in action,' said Jasper. 'I can't wait to see it either, so let's get it on my laptop before we eat. Sam sent me off to the supermarket after the news last night with a list and she's cooked a lamb casserole with ginger and stuff. She told me to buy some particular wine, too, something you like. Gourmet dinner, never happened here before.'

Sam and Jasper sat in front of the laptop right away and went through everything we downloaded from my phone, then after a pause for comments, a second time.

'You did that really well, action man.' Jasper turned to look at me after studying the video clip from when I got the guy a third time, very slowly. 'And he had a knife?'

'Yeah, I took it off him once we were inside, after I scared the shit out of him with the electric razor. I saw that little twitch in his right hand when he thought of getting it out. A flick-knife, the cops have it now. I'd never seen one before, I think they're illegal. And don't you love that bit of him shouting from the car that I had him at gunpoint? And then finding out it was a razor, poor guy, he must feel cheated. What a great thing that American I bought the house from had audio function on the security cameras, or you wouldn't have been able to hear that. So funny - he thought he'd get me into trouble.'

'Why do you keep calling him action man? Did you know he could do that kind of thing, like when he grabbed the intruder?' Sam looked suspiciously at Jasper. 'Is there something you haven't told me? Something he did before?'

'Oh, nothing too bad. I knew he'd done a lot of hands-only fight training when he was younger, so I offered to have a go at him once when we had a drink at his place. I'm so heavy - I thought I'd be able to take him down. You know, just bulldoze him to the floor.'

'What happened?'

'He had me face down on the floor with my arm nearly out of joint up my back in about three seconds. I've no idea how it happened, it was that quick.'

He and I looked at each other and laughed, and Sam rolled her eyes.

After a sometimes quite heated debate about how to release the identity of Box for best effect and without endangering Sam, we agreed to discuss it a bit later, because nothing constructive was going to come out of this any time soon.

'Let's face it,' she said and reached for the chocolate bar I had brought for her, dark chocolate with almonds. 'There's no hurry, is there? We can park it for now. It's not as if Box will leave the country. He doesn't even know his alias and phone number were on that list, so though he's probably furious, he won't be too worried about himself. I bet that whoever put it on the list won't tell anyone either.'

'They might,' said Jasper who had been very vocal about the idea that Box should be exposed right away, which seemed to have taken root in his head since the last time we discussed it. 'Someone might think it will lessen the impact on themselves if they can hand over the phone number of the person who started this, the organiser. I think waiting is a mistake we might regret. What if he takes off for Brazil with his Bitcoin hoard?'

He hadn't let go of the idea that it was important to expose Box as soon as possible. I thought there must be something more behind it, but I couldn't ask in front of Sam or their endless debate would start up again.

'Let's discuss it again in a few days or a couple of weeks. Just to make absolutely sure there's no risk for Sam involved,' I said, not knowing if her own safety was the reason she resisted, but to keep her calm I would back her up on this.

37

But of course that wasn't the end of it. I had known from the time Boris told us about the cabal tracking me that they would try everything they could lay their hands on to find me, and via me, Sam. The combination of the mysterious woman who walked away into the hills after shopping in the village, me turning up and then leaving suddenly after more than a week in the bush when I'd hired the cottage for much longer; it told a story. It must have ticked all the boxes and made them determined to use their resources to find out if I had found Sam.

Nothing in the documentary had mentioned the man in the garage, but it was a huge threat to Brown and at least one other in the Auckland cabal. Sam could identify Brown, tell the world about the man who died and how they took him away in a truck. Getting their hands on Sam would be crucial now, before she could reveal all she knew.

We knew what had enabled this pursuit; the calls from Sam's phone and the pattern of those calls to her sister, and to Jill and Sasha, followed by my actions in the South Island. Not anything that could have been easily predicted, but once the puzzle pieces fell into place it was obvious. So when the police turned up on my doorstep late one afternoon I wasn't surprised.

'Hi,' I said when I opened the door and tried to sound casual and friendly. 'Have you come for that video clip? I've got it saved.'

I managed to get all that out before they could interrupt me, but it was a close call. The woman officer had to visibly restrain herself from interrupting, such was her focus.

'We have a search warrant for this property,' she said and held up a few pages stapled together. 'We have reasonable grounds to suspect you distribute illegal drugs from this address.'

In my head, the options I had worked on since the day Jasper suggested they might try exactly this, were lined up in a row like a list. A trumped-up warrant, he'd said, and I had tried to reason my way through how that could be done. I had read the entire section of law relating to police searches and warrants and a few useful things had come up, so now I knew how I myself would fake a search warrant if I had the resources the police have. And if they had used the same idea I knew what to look for.

'No way!' I said indignantly like any respectable and innocent citizen would. 'That's ridiculous, I've never had anything to do with drugs. Someone's trying to con you. Can I see that?' I reached out and took the papers out of her hand and walked back into the living room and they followed, of course.

'Have a seat while I read this.' I gestured at the chairs around the dining table, but they preferred to stand, said nothing and just looked at each other. With the papers on the table I fished my phone out of my back pocket and snapped a shot of each page as I turned them. At the first click the male officer made a sudden move as if to stop me, so I looked hard at him. 'I'm in my rights to take photos of this document to send to my lawyer, I think. I'm not going to tear it up or anything, there's no need to panic.'

I could see he would have liked to say I couldn't, but he resisted the urge and waited; he knew my rights as well as I did. I read the last page and took a photo of that one too, put the phone back in my pocket and looked up again.

'I see on the first page that this warrant is valid for ten days. Is that right? I suppose that was agreed by police and the judge who signed it?'

'Normal procedure,' said the woman briskly. 'Not that we're going to leave now without searching, not now that you know about the warrant, but it means we can search more than once within that ten day period, and we can deny you access until we've finished.'

She seemed calm and focused now that I wasn't making a fuss, and I noticed her hand reaching for the papers, so I picked them up before she could.

'This warrant is useless.' I held it high, out of her reach. 'Let me guess how you did this. You detached that last page with the judge's signature from some old warrant or copied it, and then you stapled it to a new form with my details on the first page, right? The date of the judge's signature is March 14, several months ago, so those ten days are long gone.'

They looked at each other and the guy snatched the form out of my hand and flicked to the last page. 'What the fuck!'

I saw them out and managed to resist making any sarcastic comments, but I made sure they knew I took photos both of them and the number plate of their car, before I closed the front door. Tension and trying to keep cool had taken their toll, and now I felt as if I'd been in a fight. I sat down and called my lawyer, who had a hard time remembering who I was. I hadn't needed her services since I bought the house.

She found the fake warrant very puzzling. 'But why?' she kept repeating. 'What's behind it? It seems mad, and they must have known they'd be in serious trouble if you noticed it was out of date. Mind you, they probably banked on most people not checking properly or even reading it. Have you been involved in anything risky lately? Do you have friends who use drugs and visit your place?'

I smiled to myself. 'No, nothing like that at all. As I said to someone a few weeks ago, I'm so damn boring it defies description. I tend to keep to myself, work from home, never go out clubbing and drinking. I usually only hang out with my few close friends or my family.'

'Well, send me the photos of the warrant, please, and I'll ask a few questions and lodge a formal complaint.'

'And I've got photos of those cops and their car, too. I'll send those too. It was just a sudden inspiration when they were leaving. You know, trying to figure out why they had done this and then wondering if they were real police, because I hadn't asked to see their ID or anything.'

I hoped this would sound normal enough to be convincing. My planning had included all kinds of contingencies, and those photos were part of it, provided I could manage it, and if not I would still have them on the security camera.

Now there was every possibility that I was closely monitored, and I didn't dare send the photos to Jasper either by email or message. I got them off to my lawyer and called Jasper, who had just got home from work, and told him and Sam the story.

'I was right then,' he said. 'I didn't really think they'd do it, but how satisfying to get it spot on, eh?'

As we expected there was nothing initially from the authorities apart from bland media statements expressing concern and promising investigations, the Prime Minister managed once again to speak for several minutes without saying anything in particular, and the parliamentary opposition leader blamed it on the government. The Commissioner of Police issued a statement saying that all the officers on that list had been stood down with immediate effect, and we knew we would hear no details ·for weeks or months, with everyone saying they couldn't comment until the formal investigation was concluded. The same infuriating delaying tactics they always use.

38

Early in the morning a week later I was drying myself after a shower and thinking of another visit to Jasper's place, hoping to get the Box issue settled once and for all, when he called.

'Sorry this is bad news, and please don't come over here and throw me to the floor, but I had no idea this would happen. Sam's just now been picked up by someone whose name I don't know, and they're driving back to Auckland as we speak. She recorded a message for you on my laptop which I'll play now. I promised not to listen to it, so I'll just set it going and let it run.'

To say I was stunned doesn't even come close to how I felt. Sam's quite brief message said that she was going back to Auckland "to sort things out" and she needed time by herself to work out if she really loved me or if it was something called saviour syndrome, which she explained is when someone feels so connected to the person who saved them that they confuse it with love. She added that she'd always be grateful for everything I had done for her, and that she would be safely hidden and helped by friends in Auckland.

The call came to an end when the recording had played, but I called Jasper right back. 'I can't believe it!' I said and heard my voice sound very unlike myself. 'How the hell did you agree to let her do this? Who picked her up and where is she going to stay? It's crazy!'

'I couldn't stop her, mate. She didn't tell me in advance - I was taken totally by surprise. She must have organised it with that new burner phone I got her when she came to stay here. Calling her friends and setting the whole thing up.' He sighed. 'So just after six she woke me up and said she was leaving that very minute. Someone was waiting in a car outside, she was all packed and organised. And that was it. She walked out the front door with a bag in her hand and left me standing there speechless wearing only boxer shorts.'

'She would! The master planner, always one step ahead. Fuck it, Jasper! What can I do?'

'Nothing – you can't do anything. She left that phone behind, so we can't even call her. If you pursue her about this, it will go wrong for sure. I know she let you push her to leave that damn cave and come to Wellington with you, but this is different. And don't use the phone numbers to those best friends of hers on your phone – just don't! I remember she said she called them from your phone instead of using the old burner phone, so please don't call them. You'll risk turning into a stalker, mate! Can I call in for a drink after work?'

'Of course she's coming back,' said Jasper that evening, bringing it up for the third time in twenty minutes. 'She just needs a bit of time. Anyone could see she loves you, just the way she looks at you sometimes, it's as clear as daylight.'

I shook my head. 'There's no need to try to cheer me up, but thanks for the thought. I think I've come to terms with it now – from her side it isn't love, it's just gratitude and relief that someone else was taking responsibility. Helped along by the contrast between what her life had been for so long and this sudden normality I forced her into.'

The look Jasper gave me was one of mild disgust. 'For Christ's sake, Thomas, you're a fucking idiot sometimes. I suppose it's that action-man persona of yours clouding your thinking. But never mind, I'm not going to argue the point, but I'll bet you a hundred she comes back, no, I'll bet you a thousand.'

'No bets – and I'm not discussing this again.'

There was something in the way he looked at me, as if he was going to start another wave of comfort talk, but this had gone far enough, and I couldn't take any more sympathy. It was like a repeat of my chat to Boris that afternoon when he called after he got a similar message from Sam late the night before from her burner phone.

'Jasper!' I was exasperated now and about to lose my temper. 'If you don't stop this bloody nonsense this very minute you can leave. I've had enough!'

'Keep your shirt on, mate, I wasn't about to start again. I just wondered if you'd like to invite me over when Boris comes. I want to meet him. Or has he cancelled now Sam's not here?'

I went back to the table and poured myself another glass of wine. 'No, he's coming, he's taken next week off. He can't believe she's done this, but he'd already planned to come and visit us, so he's coming anyway. Let's go out for dinner one night when he's here. He's a fabulous cook, so it's got to be somewhere special, he'll enjoy that.'

And that's how we left it, but two days later I got a text message from a number I'd never seen before. "Things are going well, and I promise I'll be in touch in a while. I'm not starting a conversation, just wanted to say I've not totally disappeared over the horizon. S."

I couldn't make up my mind what this meant. Was it reassurance to calm me down? Had she been in touch with Jasper, and had he told her how upset I was? Or was it a further step in a plan to distance herself by sounding like a friend, nothing more? I called Jasper at work, something I'd never done before, and got a "this number is unavailable" message, so I left a voice mail.

He called me in his lunch hour. 'All personal phones are turned off and left in reception, we keep everything locked down tight here. What did she say in that text?'

When he heard the short message he actually chuckled, and I nearly ended the call there and then. 'She hasn't been in touch with me, but she's clearly worrying about you, mate. Can't you tell? She's dying to talk to you and couldn't resist one little message to keep in touch. Just hang in there.'

I had a strong impression he was going to say something more, but he bit it back, so I told him Boris had cancelled his visit after twisting his ankle badly when he jumped out of his forklift the day before. 'He said he'd rather come when he can walk again, so he can do some sightseeing and check out what's changed. He hasn't been in Wellington for twenty years, so he wants to spend some time walking around. I'll let you know when he's OK to come.'

39

A couple of days later I had just got home after an early evening run on Mt Victoria when I got another text message from Sam. "TV One at 8 tonight." Nothing more. I didn't dare respond, just left it, checked the programming online and decided it must be a mistake because no way would she tell me to watch a cooking show. Not unless she was encouraging me to learn to cook. I tried Jasper's phone, but it was on DND, so he was probably working late. When I had finished dinner I turned the TV on and sat down to see what was coming.

'Tonight's episode of Cooking with Laura will screen next week, due to the unique interview opportunity we have been offered,' said the woman on the screen. 'And we apologise, but there is a chance that the next programme will be starting a few minutes late, at this moment we can't say exactly how late.'

I knew who she was, one of the most incisive interviewers currently active on New Zealand TV. A woman who frequently and nearly unnoticeably maneuvered those she interviewed into a corner and left them unable to explain away something or fudge an evasive reply.

'Tonight we are privileged to present to you an interview of a kind we have never done before. We don't know who the person being interviewed is, and we don't know where she was when this was recorded. What you will see is the screen divided into two halves with me on the left side and the unknown woman on the right. I also need to explain that when we recorded this I couldn't see what you see on the right hand side of your screen, I just heard the voice. They sent us the right hand side recording afterwards.'

She paused for effect. 'And we have a promise from the person who set this up and then sent us the finished product, that before the screening comes to an end they will forward a second, shorter recording without me in it, which contains further revelations about the police corruption currently in the news.'

I sat as if turned to stone while my mind tried to work out how this had been done. This must be Sam, but how had she engineered this, and who had helped her? Had she gone back to Auckland to get this set up? How many knew about this and worst of all, would this expose her to renewed danger? Helpless to do anything to mitigate the downstream damage I clenched my teeth and waited.

In the left half of the bisected screen appeared Mary Blackwood, the interviewer, sitting in an armchair and to the right, a strange configuration, an old-fashioned wing-back chair with its back to the camera, but on a slight angle, nothing else. The wall behind it was white with no details, it could be anywhere. The only part of the occupant that was visible was her lower arm on the left armrest. Definitely Sam! I knew the way she half curled her fingers with her thumb slowly rubbing the tip of her forefinger when she was thinking or listening to something, concentrated but relaxed.

'Tell us how this started,' said Mary. 'The notes your ... let's call it producer sent us had very little detail, so perhaps you could fill the viewers and myself in now? How did it start?'

'One evening about fifteen months ago a man appeared at my front door, a frightened and exhausted man on the run.' She was speaking quite casually, as if she was telling a friend about something. 'And I let him into the garage, which is attached to the house, told him to sit in my car – he was ready to buckle at the knees – and went back into the house and locked the connecting door.' Her voice had been subtly altered to sound a bit deeper. I sat as if frozen, I couldn't believe she had decided to tell this story publicly. This wasn't just about Box, this was the whole drama, with all the details.

'That was an extraordinary thing to do, wouldn't you agree?' said Mary. 'He could have been violent, maybe he'd committed a crime. What made you do it?'

'I don't know. I just believed him. I said I would call III, but he said not to. It was dangerous, someone was chasing him to kill him. Someone from what he called a cabal of corruption.'

And so the story continued with the police coming and how they found him dead on the garage floor, then on to how Brown took her into the kitchen and told her about the undercover drug investigation.

'But he isn't called Brown and that investigation didn't exist, it was just a ploy to make me what he called "one of the team" so I would keep it quiet and promise not to tell anyone what had happened that night. He's one of the names in the list that was sent out with all the other files about the corruption cabal, but I don't know which one he is. Tall, thin and with a receding hair line, is all I can tell you, probably mid to late forties. But what I heard those cops say about searching for something that man must have had with him, that was alarming.'

She continued with the details of what she heard through the bathroom window, the discussion about where the man could have concealed the evidence they knew he had with him, and how they loaded his body on the back of a utility truck.

'Not what you would expect, I don't think,' said Mary gently. 'You must have been shocked.'

'Shocked and suspicious, mostly suspicious because of the way they came already equipped with a body bag - not that they knew they'd find him dead. To me it proved they had planned to kill him, like he'd already told me.' Sam sounded calm and decisive. 'And then a couple of days later my house was broken into and very thoroughly searched, turned over by a team of experts.'

'And do you know if they found what they were looking for?'

'No, they found nothing, because just before that search I'd found a little external hard drive in the tub of laundry powder beside the washing machine, which is in the garage. And I'd seen what was on it, which is the material you were sent on a USB stick recently. The hard drive was well hidden in my garden shed, which they didn't search - and even if they had they wouldn't have found it. So I asked a friend, who had contacts in media, to find someone who could publish all the evidence without exposing me or himself, and he did. He talked extensively to Liz McCarroll, whom you probably knew or at least knew about, and they made a date for him to deliver a USB with the information to her at her house.'

There was a sharp intake of breath from Mary, who visibly resisted the urge to exclaim, 'What!?' You could see her mouth forming the word before she stopped herself. I had to admit that the way this had been set up was very clever. Mary must have been given the basic questions to ask, but she had obviously not known the full answers and in some cases probably nothing at all.

Sam carried on. 'My friend's car was pushed off the road after he left her house, but he managed to call someone while he was driving very fast, and he just had time to say what was happening before the call was cut short - when they rammed him off the road, and he died.'

'And then,' said Mary and her voice was trembling, she had trouble controlling herself, 'then Liz, who I knew well, was found stabbed to death.'

Sam replied, brief and to the point. 'Yes, she probably asked too many dangerous questions after that first phone call from my friend, maybe she asked someone who had contacts in the police, and this alerted the cabal. Which triggered what happened to my friend and to Liz. And the rest, as they say, is history.'

'And nobody came after you, nobody realised that you had given your friend the evidence they were both killed for?'

'There was nothing to link us. They had searched my house and presumably decided that the hard drive had never been there, that the man in the garage had put it somewhere else when he ran from that crashed taxi, so I was kind of out of the picture – for the moment. I also supposed that they had found the USB my friend had taken to give to Liz, so they had that. I hoped that would be the end of it.'

'What does that mean, "for the moment"? Something alerted you to a threat now coming your way?'

They inserted a break there, probably to let people pour themselves a drink, which is exactly what I was doing. I tried Jasper's phone again, but he was still unavailable. And then they were back, each one in their half of the screen, and they replayed Mary's question. 'Something alerted you to a threat now coming your way?'

'Brown came back to my house on a pretend errand after the search, and he asked some strange questions. The more I thought about it the more I believed that he knew exactly which files the man in the garage had taken and saved on that hard drive. So, I if they had found my friend's USB in Liz's house they would know it wasn't the original the man in the garage had. You see, when I copied things on the USB for my friend I left out two of the regional spreadsheets. Which would tell them, presumably Brown, that Liz's USB was just a partial copy.'

She stopped talking for a minute, as if she was thinking. 'And I took for granted that my friend's wrecked car would be examined, so they'd know he didn't have the original with him. They could have broken into his house and searched it like they did mine, but they didn't.'

Her hand clenched into a fist on the armrest and her voice got harder. 'And I think I know why they didn't do that – because before they had time to organise it, they worked out the link between him and me, so I was next on the list. Once they knew about that connection, the facts they had made perfect sense – a man died in my garage, another man, who was a close friend of mine, told Liz he had damning evidence about the corruption, she then started asking questions, which spread. They knew when he was going to her place, so it's likely that Liz had told people about him coming and probably when. Then all they needed to do was wait for him to leave and follow him. I didn't know anything for sure, apart from one thing – that having made the connection they would kill me too.'

'Good Lord,' said Mary quietly, as if to herself. 'I wonder why they didn't do it right away. You have a theory?'

'I don't know anything for sure. Maybe they thought that too much activity close together involving my friend and myself would invite scrutiny. Or maybe what I read on the internet about how long it takes to take apart a crushed vehicle was right, and it took them a couple of weeks to dissect it, so the speak. To find that my friend didn't have the original evidence in the car, I mean the dead man's hard drive with all the files. And *then* they'd go to the next probable person, which was me. But of course, all this is just how I've tried to piece it together afterwards, like making a jigsaw puzzle without knowing what the picture is.'

'You must have been so very frightened while you waited to see what would happen next.'

'Terrified, scared out my mind, call it what you will. Too paranoid to sleep, making plans, making lists – you have no idea! I made up my mind to leave, straight after Liz was found dead, which as you know wasn't until several days after she was murdered. I dismantled my entire life in three days - resigned from my job, sold my car and went underground, managed to not get caught on CCTV anywhere and disappeared. And every moment of those three days I expected them to come for me.'

'How did you do that in only three days? It sounds like an impossible achievement.'

Sam told her how she had done it, the meticulous planning and the step by step execution of her plan until she got to the South Island. 'I knew, you see, that not only have the police got access to all these cameras the country's covered in, but they can also upload a photo of a face and get alerted if it turns up on a CCTV camera and then track you from there. And I had to get away before they realised that the man they pushed off to road and killed was a friend of mine. Knowing I was next on the list was a strong motivator to make me move very fast.'

The story continued with Sam's life in the hills, how she found the cave and how she lived, but without any mention of exactly where this was. 'The decision to live in the cave was an overreaction, a drastic mistake based on the idea in my head that because of the resources they have access to they'd be able to find me wherever I was. Because once I was living there I was locked in place with no options, no way to deal with the situation, to make it safe to come out into the world again. But eventually I was found, not because the man who found me knew anything about this, it was just chance - and he saved me from that ghastly isolation, from a year and a bit of no real human contact, a very restricted life full of hardship and loneliness. When I felt as if I'd been left to one side of life with no hope of ever getting back.'

'How did he save you?'

'He wouldn't give up. He persuaded me he would keep me safe and help me expose the cabal, that nothing would happen to me while I was under his protection. I needed help very badly, I was mentally exhausted, and I knew through infrequent calls I made from a burner phone, that they were still asking people about me, they had never stopped.'

Another break and I sat there, my mind in overdrive, trying to imagine how the last part of this would turn out. When I once again called Jasper and got the same DND answer, I knew something was up. He would have been told about this, and he must know I would call him, so he was definitely involved, and he had turned his phone off to keep me at bay. Somehow or other he and Sam had set this up between them and left me out of the planning, which made me furious and feeling more conflicted than ever.

40

When the programme started up again, Mary returned to the question of how I had rescued Sam, and how I got her away from where she had been without being spotted, but she declined to answer.

'It's not important in this context,' she said in that decisive way she sometimes had. 'What's important is to acknowledge that he saved me, refused to let me say no, just sat there on a rock and acted like a rock, stubborn and immovable. I sent him away and he just tramped back in, several hours from the nearest road and continued talking. He's my hero forever, there's nobody I'm more grateful to, he gave me my life back.'

'Thank you!' said Mary. 'And that's where the pre-recorded part of this interview ends. My producer has just confirmed that the promised final part, which I have had no part in, has arrived and is ready to play now.'

I held my breath, so intent on what as to come that I felt slightly sick. I was certain she was going to reveal who Box was, but how would it end? Would he send someone to try to find her before the authorities could get to him? Was he already in hiding? I couldn't remember being so nervous since I was a child.

It started with a now full-screen view of the armchair with Sam's arm on the armrest. After a moment of silence she started talking. 'There is one piece of data we didn't include when we sent out the USBs to the authorities and to media. In the list of names, which was an Excel document, there was originally a hidden row. Row seventeen had been concealed, or folded in, the way you can in Excel, and I want to tell you what was typed into that row. The word Box and a cell phone number.'

'Those of you who have watched the videos of the meetings will have noticed that there was always a phone lying in the centre of the table. That was the cabal mastermind taking part anonymously, the man who called himself Box. He probably never knew that whoever compiled that list had included him, and we removed row seventeen before we copied that file, so you couldn't even see that one had been hidden.' She paused, whether from nerves or for effect I didn't know. Her hand still seemed relaxed on the armrest, so maybe it was deliberate.

'I am going to play some voice clips from the voice on that phone on the table, and immediately after each one I'll play someone saying the same thing in another context. And also some quite unusual phrases, especially one of them. Please pay attention to the Southland way of sounding the R as in the word hard or the word agree. Here they are.'

First an image from the one of the cabal meetings with the voice emanating from the phone on the table saying "of course it's hard to decide" immediately followed by a clip of man standing beside a car talking to someone with a microphone and saying exactly that and sounding the R. Then another sound bite from the phone on the table with the voice saying "let's agree to agree" followed by the same man as before on the stage at a public meeting and saying the same thing, both times with the R emphasised.

'And now one where the R sound isn't important, it's more that the phrase is so idiomatic and not one I had ever heard before. Listen to this,'

She played the phone voice saying, "it's too late, the clock has struck" and then a clip of the man on the same stage saying exactly that.

'Now, what do you think?' asked Sam as if she was talking to one particular viewer. 'Could it be the same man? The man in the video clips from what is a political meeting is called Carton, a very unusual name, so maybe he was called Box at school. He is pretty high up in the police in Southland, grew up there and never lived for long anywhere else, so his Southland R is still strong, and he's standing for Parliament in the next election. And interestingly, he says he is very against gangs and the drug trade.' Another pause, this one definitely for effect, before her final sentence. 'And just so you know, the police were sent this final interview segment just after this broadcast started, so they're probably arresting him as we speak.'

Next we were back to Mary on a full screen. 'Truly the most astonishing thing I've ever been involved in, stunning! Good night, everyone – we now return to the scheduled programme.'

And that was it. Boris called within seconds. 'Hi Thomas,' he said quickly. 'Let me tell you something right away before you burst your boiler. Jasper and Sam have both called tonight and asked me to tell you about that interview we just watched. They both said they weren't going to let you have a go at them before you understand how this came about, OK?'

I tried to sound normal. 'Tell me what?'

'They both said that it was totally Sam's idea, she blackmailed Jasper into agreeing. She told him that if he didn't agree she would just go off and find someone else to record it, and then she'd negotiate with the TV people herself and have them broadcast it, but if he wanted her to be safe, then he would do it with her.'

'And I had to be left out of this?'

Boris chuckled. 'This is the best bit, she told Jasper that she wouldn't tell you because you'd go into full bodyguard mode, and she was afraid you would talk her out of it. Which both Jasper and I thought was very likely. I know you're upset but just wait and let this whole drama come to an end. I'm sure she'll come back.'

'OK, thanks.'

'And I nearly forgot – she said she had to reveal who that Box guy is, or you would never be safe.'

And neither would she, of course, but I didn't have the energy to discuss it, so I just thanked him and sat down to finish a report I was writing. Sam's thinking was coloured by her unreasonable sense of guilt about Dave and Liz getting murdered, which now extended to being terrified about putting me at risk. And maybe she would never get free of that shackle of guilt. I thought I could help her with that, but now I would probably never get the chance. I had to admit what Sam had said about me was true, and I would probably have tried to prevent it, but it was done, she was gone, and it was over. I must accustom myself to my old way of living, not a lot of interaction with others, and from now on a lot of running to keep my mind off things.

An hour later I was sitting in front of my laptop looking at the text on the screen without taking in the words, still sideswiped by the call from Boris. Concentration was beyond me, so I decided to give up on finishing the report and go for a nighttime run through the centre of the city, which I sometimes do as a change from running along the waterfront or on Mt Victoria. I was putting on my running shoes when my phone buzzed with a call from Jasper.

'You've got to get out of the house!' He sounded frantic. 'And turn all the lights off, right now while we're talking! The police just called Sam five minutes ago to warn her that they went to Carton's house and his wife said he took off a couple days ago. He told her he was going hunting and took his deer hunting rifle with the scope, she saw him put it in the car.'

'And?' I turned off the bedroom light and went into the living area to do the same there.

'Apparently he's never gone off suddenly like this before, without planning it in advance and never once on his own. And she didn't know which area he was going to - he didn't tell her. Plus she'd heard him cancel several meetings the day before he left, so the police think he found out somehow that the interview was going to be screened and realised he might be in danger. They told Sam to make sure she was in a secure place just 'in case he was coming for her.'

'And they think he might come here?' I was on my way to the hall now to turn the last light off.

'Are you turning the lights off?' he asked instead of replying. 'OK, then. They think he might do one of those insane things that cornered people do sometimes, kill someone as revenge for something and then they kill themselves. Or commit suicide by police as the Americans call it.'

'Right, the whole house is dark now and I'm in the bathroom. How did this happen? Did someone in the TV team let it out, some kind of hint of what the interview was about? It wasn't advertised with any details about the content, I hope. But how the hell would Carton have found out?'

My mind was working on several things simultaneously; was Sam safe, how did Carton find out in advance, and how could I protect myself if he came looking for Sam at my place armed with a rifle with a scope.

'Oh, for God's sake, it doesn't matter right now,' said Jasper impatiently. 'I don't think there's a chance he found out about the interview. Far more likely that he's been stewing over this ever since that list of names and the other files were made public. Perhaps he thought it was inevitable that something would be discovered about his part. But it's not important. And don't take this maniac on, please don't do anything stupid! He's armed and you're not, he can get you in his sights from a distance without you ever setting eyes on him.'

I didn't reply, just went straight to what was most important. 'Where is Sam?'

'She's at Sasha's cousin's place, because he lives on the eighth floor in a high-rise in central Auckland. The police offered to take her wherever she wanted to go, but she said no, for obvious reasons. She's still convinced there are cops out there who weren't on the original list, and they might think there's more names to come, like she's holding more stuff back to be revealed later.'

'OK, I'll work out what to do.'

'I think you should come here, don't take the car, just walk or run. The police are looking at ferry bookings and trying to track him by camera sightings as we speak - they told Sam. But you've got to get out of the house, right now.'

'OK, I'll run to your place. I've already got my running gear on anyway. See you soon!'

I put the phone on DND and started planning. Of course Carton would come to my place, the cabal knew my connection to Sam, or they thought they did, so they might think she was at my house based on what they'd found out in the village. They'd sent the snooper and organised the fake search warrant, and I took for granted that Carton knew that, or maybe he had organised it himself.

In the dark house with only the ambient light from the city below I grabbed my black running top with inside pockets and pulled it over my head, picked up my keys and the phone and headed for the front door, stopped halfway and changed my mind. If that maniac was already out there, maybe at the top of my short driveway, then leaving by the front door would make me a perfect target walking towards him. Instead I silently opened the sliding door to the balcony just enough to step out, folded the lever down so it would lock when I closed it from outside and moved along the wall to the so-called fire escape ladder. It seemed unlikely that he would be somewhere on the steep slope below the house, but I wasn't taking any chances.

The trapdoor in the balcony floor opened silently, and I rested it gently against the wall and went down the ladder fast. At the bottom I stood for a moment listening, but all I heard were the night noises filtering up from below and the light wind in the trees. I crossed in a crouch to the space I call my basement. However unlikely it was that he was watching this side, if he was somewhere below the house I didn't want the light from my phone to reveal where I was, and I needed to reset the alarm system.

With the door shut behind me I turned my phone on and set the sensor zones to the maximum distance from the house, so I'd get plenty of warning if he approached. Then I played the last hour of saved video on fast forward to check I hadn't missed an alert earlier in the evening, knowing that I sometimes miss the wolf whistle or the vibration when I'm concentrating on something else. But nobody had been near the house from either direction. The question now was how to proceed, how to leave the property in the safest way possible. I could take the wooden stairs down in front of the house and make my way down to Oriental Bay or Evan's Bay, but it might be noisy moving down that steep slope covered in trees and scrubby bush growth. It was bound to be full of trip hazards, the perfect place to break an ankle. I had never gone further than the little flat area at the bottom of the wooden steps and didn't know the best way down from there.

As I stood there in the total darkness of the storage room planning my next move, the phone vibrated in my hand and the screen lit up. The front sensor had picked something up, but at first I couldn't see what had triggered it. I stared at the screen looking for movement and suddenly saw a dark shape on the slight incline to the left of the driveway, barely visible as he moved slowly among the trees. Mesmerised I watched until he disappeared out of view, and in the back of my mind images popped up, like snapshots of the day I spotted Sam climbing that hill to recharge her batteries. How she had moved just inside the tree line, like Carton was doing now, though not for the same reason, and how she disappeared into the deeper shadow, like how Carton was now lost to sight under the trees.

There was no doubt in my mind. The coincidence of Carton having turned up just then, mere minutes after Jasper's call, was incredible, but it couldn't be anyone else. He couldn't send someone else; he was on his own now.

On that side of the driveway was an area of untouched nature, a wide belt of trees and dense undergrowth angling steeply downhill. Further on, houses lined the street, but if he found a vantage point at the higher end between my house and the next one he could wait me out, concealed by the trees. He had a scope on his rifle, and he was sure to have one with night vision. He would have seen that the house was in darkness, but he had all the time in the world, so he would wait, hidden and ready. I was certain that he was hoping to kill both Sam and me, it was the only explanation. He thought she was with me, and if he had driven right up through the South Island and crossed on the ferry just to find me, then he'd be prepared to wait. The fact that it was too late to save himself, and that killing us would serve no purpose, would be irrelevant to him. He knew he was doomed, and he was determined to get his revenge, and then possibly kill himself. So now I had to work out how to deal with this.

42

I was at a huge disadvantage, up against an armed man who could see far better through his rifle scope than I could in the dark. I had no weapon, so I needed something to defend myself with if it came to a close confrontation, provided I could get close enough to take him by surprise. There were no windows in the storage room, but to be extra safe I didn't turn on the light, in case it showed under the door but moved around by the light from the phone screen to see what I could find. The first thing that might be useful was the tether I use to attach the surfboard to my ankle to make it easy to retrieve it in heavy surf. I detached it and coiled it up, and with that in one hand and the phone in the other I moved on to study what was on the shelves at the far end. I found nothing that could be used as a weapon and decided that the strap and my hands would have to do. But then I spotted the perfectly round rock I'd picked up on a beach somewhere a couple of years ago. One of those unlikely looking rocks created by natural forces, so perfectly smooth that it looked manmade, nearly polished, nicely fist sized. I put the phone down and picked it up and it felt good, very good. My fingers closed a bit more than halfway around it, and with that weight in my hand a punch would have a bigger impact. I hung the coiled strap over my shoulder, tucked the phone into the inside pocket and left with the rock still in my hand.

Careful not to make any noise, I made my way along to the downstairs flat and then up the steps on that side and felt the phone vibrate inside my top when the sensors picked me up. The only way to take Carton by surprise was to work my way over to the place next to mine on the far side from where he presumably was, then along the street and down on his side. At some point the plan to run to Japer's place had been replaced by determination to not let this evil guy get away with anything. No more killings and no revenge. Suicide was too easy a way out, and he didn't deserve it. I wanted to get him and hand him in. He had a gun, but if I could take him by surprise and get him on the ground I could probably do it.

In my mind I pictured him in a courtroom or trying to hide from cameras as he was led handcuffed into a police station. He deserved to be disgraced and shamed as revenge for what he set up, and for what Sam had to do to save her life. At the time I wasn't even thinking of the cabal, it was all about Carton.

The wind had died down and the night air was completely still, only vague sounds of traffic from far below, muted and distant. The moon was half full, just rising above the crest of Mt Victoria. Getting on to the neighbour's property would be tricky. Their fence was very close to the edge that separated their higher side garden from mine and climbing it would probably make a noise and alert them.

Hesitating I tried to picture their place as seen from my balcony, what the far side of their land looked like, and realised that like me they didn't have a fence across their land below the house. So I followed the fence line downhill and went up the slope inside their fence, past the house and around the corner to their driveway. Once on the street I stopped and looked past my own driveway and realised my plan had a flaw. If I simply walked along the road he might see me from wherever he was, I would be too exposed, so instead I went in the other direction and up the track Sam had approached from and did a long detour.

Knowing that Jasper might start to wonder where I was if this took too long, I stopped and sent him a message saying I was on my way, checked that my phone was on DND and tucked it back in the inside pocket. A few minutes later I was back to on my street a couple of hundred meters from where I had left for my detour. I walked fast and silent in my running shoes, kept on the darker side and stopped where that slanting belt of natural vegetation separated my place from the one on this side. I mentally tried to reconstruct what it looked like, and gradually an image formed in my mind. From my balcony I could see it sloping quite steeply down away from my place, but just below the level of my house there was a knoll that stuck out which might attract Carton as a vantage point. A bump, a bit higher than the surrounding area, a great position for a sniper. He would be able to see part of my front yard and the big window in my bedroom, not to mention the balcony and probably a wedge of the living room.

Careful where I put my feet I stepped off the edge of the side-walk and made my way slowly in under the trees. While I moved slowly forward I debated with myself which hand should hold the rock. I deliver a good punch with either hand, but I didn't think I would be able to do anything constructive with the surfboard strap with my left hand. Not that I knew what I could do with it anyway, apart from perhaps sling it around his neck from behind or tie him with it, if I could get him on the ground without being shot. I moved the rock from hand to hand while I thought about it and decided to go for the right handed punch if I got a chance to get close to him. Then another idea appeared from nowhere, something I'd heard or read a long time ago, about someone who misled a pursuer very cleverly by throwing something off to one side. I felt around on the ground here and there as I moved cautiously forward, tried to find something I could throw, something reasonably solid. In the end I settled for a straight piece of branch about the length of my lower arm and tucked it in my armpit under the coiled strap.

Now I had to find that knoll, which wouldn't be easy in the dark when my sense of direction depended on vague visual memory and instinct, not a good combination. I moved at a snail's pace to avoid making noise, and luck was on my side. After agonisingly slow progress, stepping over and around things I could barely make out even after my eyes had adjusted, I came across a little track. I stopped in surprise, studied the narrow strip of well-trodden ground in the dim light and remembered seeing three people on that knoll last summer flying a drome. Maybe locals took visitors to the knoll as a lookout spot. I tried to imagine what would happen if Carton returned for some reason, maybe to find another sniper position, closer to the house, and we met? If he didn't see me until I was right in front of him I could probably tackle him before he had time to raise the rifle, if not he could shoot me at close range. I decided caution was called for and took three steps to one side of the track and continued slowly alongside it, keeping an eye on it as well as I could.

And suddenly the knoll was right in front of me. Instead of the trees showing as dark shapes against a darker background, they were now silhouetted against the ambient light that filtered up from below, and I could see the outline of a man sitting on what might be a large bag. He was facing left, towards my house, with his rifle leaning against his thigh. And just then, as I shifted my weight, ready to rush him something snapped under my foot with a sharp, little noise. He leapt to his feet, rifle in hand, and swung around. For a split second I was frozen, then I acted nearly on instinct. I turned, moved the rock to my left hand, grabbed the stick with my right and threw it at head hight to the right hoping the movement of my arm hadn't alerted him. His head swivelled to where the branch landed. He stood perfectly still for a second, then he raised the rifle and looked through the scope in that direction. He stood like that for what seemed like minutes, panning slowly back and forth, while I stood equally still, ready to fight or flee.

Finally he lowered the rifle and turned to look back towards my house, and as he stood there I ran up fast. He had time to swing halfway towards me before I reached him, but I managed to grab his arm holding the rifle. Then he took one stumbling step back and dislodged my hand, so I followed, and now we were face to face, very close and the rifle was useless. I hit him hard and fast with a right uppercut starting with my hand level with my middle, straight up under the jaw and the rock made the impact horrendous. A cracking noise, his head snapped back, and the rifle dropped to the ground. He took a couple of out-of-balance steps backwards and disappeared without a sound, followed by a couple of hard thumps from below, then nothing.

Slowly I went up to the edge I hadn't realised was there and looked down. Not only was it a sharp edge, which I'd never noticed from my balcony due to the trees that grew up from far below, but the drop-off was virtually vertical. There was no sign of Carton. I got down on my front with only my head over the edge to avoid showing up in silhouette and scanned what I could see of the ground directly below, but I saw nothing apart from some houses a bit out from where I thought he would have landed. Then a light came on at the back of one house, a woman shouted something, another outside light came on next door and raised voices could be heard, though I couldn't make out what they were saying. I stayed there for a few more minutes. More voices, more lights being turned on. Someone climbed over a fence and the beam of a flashlight swung wildly, then steadied, swung back and forth in arc and stopped, another shout. Carton had been found.

I left the rifle untouched beside the sports bag where Carton had dropped it and made my way back along the little track to the street. There was nobody to be seen in either direction, so I ran to the steps up to Mt Victoria and continued running. A few minutes later I stopped to catch my breath and called Jasper.

'No time to talk,' I said briefly. 'I'm fine, but I got delayed leaving. I'm on my way now. I'm doing a little detour, but I should be with you in half an hour or so.' I ended the call and ran on, still with the strap coiled over my shoulder and the rock in my hand.

43

When Jasper opened his front door he looked me up and down with a slightly confused expression. 'For fuck's sake, Thomas – is that for us to defend ourselves with?'

I followed him inside, put the strap and the rock on the floor in his living room and sank into an armchair, suddenly exhausted. 'Can you pour me something alcoholic, please? The stronger the better. I think I've killed Carton.'

'What?! Please don't tell me you strangled him!'

'Of course I didn't strangle him! He fell down a steep slope just beside my house and hit something very hard, way down.'

He stopped halfway to the kitchen and gave me a penetrating look. 'Did you throw him? In front of your place? Are you mad?'

'Stop!' I held up my hand like someone directing traffic, palm out. 'Shut up and give me a drink and I'll tell you what happened, blow by blow, but I need that drink first.'

We sat there with only one light on and a bottle of cognac between us on the coffee table, and I told him the story. 'But listen, it might mean trouble for me,' I said when I reached the end. 'He might not have died, and he might say I pushed him, which I didn't need to do because my punch unbalanced him – he took a wobbly step backwards, kind of on a lean, and gravity did the rest. I'll have to wait and see what happens tomorrow, it might be on the news.'

'Hang on, we should be able to find out right now.' Jasper got up and headed for his IT cave. 'Let's see what we can find.'

I made no comment and asked no questions. Whether he was going to hack into some system or whether he was just going to check the online news, I wasn't going to ask. He sat down at his big computer screen instead of one of his laptops, and I leaned against the door jamb and waited while his big fingers moved quickly over the keyboard. 'Ha! Here it is, he's dead. Come and have a look.'

He was in some database that belonged to the emergency services or the police, and there was a minimal entry with the date and time. "White male, middle-aged, no ID. Extensive injuries. Appears to have fallen from height where he was found."

When I had called for a taxi and was ready to leave Jasper looked at the rope and the rock, which for some crazy reason I hadn't dropped in the first rubbish bin I saw. 'You can't take those, the driver will think you're a homicidal maniac. I'll bring them over next time I come if you want to keep them.' He took the rock out of my hand. 'Heavier than it looks, much heavier. You're right, it would have added a lot of impact to that punch. No wonder he went backwards over the edge.'

'I didn't know there was an edge there instead of a slope. I was hoping I'd knock him down - or knock him out and then tie him up. As I said before, I wanted to hand him in alive to punish him, have him named and shamed, as much humiliation as possible.'

But in the back of my mind I wondered if that upper-cut with the rock in my hand had snapped his neck. Maybe those stumbling couple of steps that took him over the edge was gravity pulling him backwards, perhaps he was already dead. On the ride home another thing occurred to me, and I wondered if there would be a visible mark where I punched him. How long does it take for a bruise to develop? Would they do an autopsy and discover he had a broken jaw? But one thing was certain, they would work out where he'd fallen from and find the bag and the rifle, and what they would make of that was anyone's guess.

I slept well that night despite my thoughts on the way home. Somehow the fact that Carton was dead seemed to have removed a layer of threat. There might be others out there thirsting for revenge, but few would be as obsessed as Carton had been. I tried to imagine what his state of mind had been as he drove right up the length of the South Island, waited for the ferry and then slept in his car or in a motel until dark, before he came up my street. An extraordinarily long time to remain focused on revenge and killing. Had his mind snapped, was he deranged or just furious?

When Boris called late the next evening he sounded unusually excited. 'Did you hear that Carton's dead? I've been on the evening shift at the mill, so I just heard about it in the car on the way home. He was found down a steep slope in Wellington, and they've found his bag and a rifle way above, at the place he fell from. Anything you want to tell me?'

'Not right now, if you don't mind,' I said and tried to think of a good reason not to tell him what had happened. 'I knew he might be coming for me and Sam, and the cops told Sam to be careful, but you might already know that. I'm sure she told you that they warned her when they found out he'd taken off.'

'Oh, I knew that bit, but I thought there might be more to it.'

'There is, and I'll tell you when you're here. I don't want to do it over the phone.'

'OK, that's fine. But did you hear what his wife told a reporter on the evening news tonight? Incredible interview – the played it straight after mentioning how Carton died. Sounds like she didn't like him much or she'd never had said what she did.'

We ended the call, and I went straight to my laptop to find the interview, which was, as Boris had said, incredible.

'Oh yes, of course I'll tell you,' Mrs Carton said calmly in reply to a reporter's question about her husband's state of mind. 'I knew he was up to something. He'd been furiously angry about something, he'd barely spoken to me for a few days, ground his teeth in his sleep, very annoying. I stayed out of his way as much as I could. And when I overheard him on the phone telling multiple people lies about why meetings had to be cancelled, I knew something was up. So when he put the hunting rifle in the car I asked where he was going, because it seemed unusual.'

'What did he say?'

'Oh, he just told me to shut up. And then he left.'

'Did you think maybe you should have warned the authorities?' asked the reporter, and she said, 'No, why would I? I didn't know where he was off to, or what he was going to do, so I just waited. And then a couple of days later I saw that interview on TV, but before I had time to call them there were three police cars lined up on the drive.'

I called Boris right back. 'You're right – incredible is the only word for it. She practically interviewed herself. Jasper sent a text message while I was listening to it and told me to check it out. How is your ankle?'

We agreed to discuss a new date for his visit, and I went back to the report I was writing.

A few days later Jasper called in unexpectedly after work with a large pizza box carried flat on one hand and a bottle of wine in the other.

'Dinner,' he said and walked right past me. 'I've got some interesting news for you and leave the door open please. Don't look so damn suspicious, I'll be back in a second.'

He handed me the bottle, put the box on the table and went out to get his computer satchel. 'Let's eat, I'm starving.'

It was a bit early for dinner, but he was hungry and reheated pizza isn't good, so we sat down to eat right away, with Jasper doing something with his phone with one hand and holding a piece of pizza with the other.

'Don't get your hands confused and take a bite out of that phone,' I said after a while. 'What are you looking at anyway?'

'Just checking if anything's out yet about what killed Carton, but it doesn't seem to have been released. I've got my laptop with some very interesting screenshots for you, saved them last night. I'll show you as soon as I've eaten this. I didn't have time to have lunch today.'

As soon as we finished he shoved the pizza box to one side and got his laptop out, the secure that one I recognised by now. 'Now,' he said and looked straight at me. 'Don't get upset, but I think that mega punch of yours killed Carton. Come around to this side.'

He angled the laptop so we could both see the screen. 'I did a bit of sneaky searching, and the autopsy result was posted in the police records yesterday. I'm not sure when this will be made public, but probably not until the inquest, so I had a sneaky look.'

'And? Am I likely to be arrested for manslaughter or murder?'

'Nope. Here's a screenshot of the autopsy report. Read this.' He pointed at a summary at the bottom of a page.

"Extensive external damage to left side of face and head, deep abrasions and crush injury. Fragments in flesh wounds identified as bark and lichen. Mandibular fracture left side. Complete C4 fracture. Broken left tibia."

'So we'll never know. I'm sure it will be classed as an accidental death. The broken jaw was probably due to your punch, which they'll never know, because it could equally well have happened when he his head hit a tree trunk on the way down and so could the broken neck. All that damage to the left side of his face and head must have been from a hard impact. Sounds as if he bounced off a couple of tree trunks at speed. But maybe you broke his neck before he even fell.'

He raised his wineglass in a toast. 'The world is a better place without him. I know you wanted him to rot in prison for years, but this way it saves the taxpayer a lot of money, and he'll never get anywhere near you or Sam. Best outcome from all angles.'

'You're right from one point of view, I suppose. Sam not having to fear him is a good thing, of course, but I'm still worried about how it will affect her when she's called as a witness in a court case against Brown and his companion, which is bound to happen. They can't overlook the fact that those guys took the body away in the back of a truck and she's the only witness. And after that TV interview they know.'

Jasper looked thoughtfully at the screen for a long moment and shook his head. 'I hadn't thought of that. We'll have to wait and see.'

44

On a Saturday morning a couple of weeks later I had just made a late morning cup of coffee when the doorbell rang. Through the window beside the door I saw Sam on the front step looking back at me, and behind her a taxi.

"Hi, can I come in?' She was smiling and sounded relaxed.

Speechless I stood to one side, and she walked in ahead of me. The taxi driver watched us and made no move to drive away. I closed the door and followed her into the living room where she turned to face me.

'Are we still the same? Or have you changed your mind? I just need to know, don't hold back if you've changed your mind.'

I hoped I knew what this meant, but the risk of getting it wrong made me mute for a moment. She tilted her head to one side and studied my face as if she was trying to make up her mind about something. 'Did you see the interview?'

'Of course, and congratulations – it was amazing.'

'Do you remember what I said about you?'

'Yes.'

'Do you want to hear the bit I didn't say?' She sounded very composed, quite casual.

'Please.'

'I could have said, "and I love him". But I didn't dare - in case you'd changed your mind.'

Suddenly my emotional paralysis lifted, and I felt normal for the first time in weeks. I took hold of her shoulders and gave her a little shake before I pulled her close. 'Don't be an idiot! Nothing could change how I feel about you.'

She leaned in for a moment, then she stepped back. 'Great! I'd love to stand here longer, but my car is parked in a no parking zone down by the sea, and I need to pick it up before it gets a ticket. I didn't want you to see it all loaded up in case you'd changed your mind, and I had to go away again. The taxi is waiting outside.'

'Are you staying? For good? Not just a visit?'

'Are we talking exclusively in questions now?' She laughed. 'There's no place on earth I'd rather be than here with you. Let's go and get my car. Coming?'

At the bottom of the hill she paid off the taxi and pointed across the road. 'I bought that a couple of weeks ago – I'll tell you the details when we're back at the house. I have so much to tell you.'

Her car was nearly full; an SUV packed with belongings. As soon as we got in she turned to me and said apologetically, 'I know it looks like a lot, but it's not really. Half your cupboards and wardrobes are empty or nearly empty – this will simply vanish from view. But I still have three pieces of antique furni-ture from my mum's family in storage. The rest is gone, apart from what Emily wants. She'll have to get it shipped over.' Then she grinned. 'I didn't really think you'd turn me away. Jasper and Boris have kept me up to date, but I didn't think it was good manners to turn up with my load and take things for granted.'

'You're welcome to take me for granted any time, you know that.' I studied her profile as she stopped in a turning lane waiting for a bus. 'I like the haircut, very pretty! I've got a lot of questions, but they can wait.'

'I'll tell you everything, every single thing, if I can have a cup of coffee and a couple of biscuits. I'm starving, I didn't have breakfast.'

We unloaded the car, left everything in a pile on the floor in the hall and sat down in the living room with coffee and peanut butter toast, which I decided was a better option than biscuits if she was hungry. 'Tell me why you haven't eaten. You can't have driven from Auckland and got here at eleven.'

'I stopped at Waikanae yesterday and spent the night in a motel. I had hoped to drive all the way in one go, but I got too tired to drive the rest of the way, and this morning I was too nervous to eat.'

'You can't have been nervous of me!'

'It just hit me when me I set out from Auckland, that I was taking you for granted, I mean. And turning up without warning suddenly seemed a bit much. But talking about this without being face to face wouldn't have been any good either.'

'So it wasn't saviour syndrome on your side then?' I tried to sound casual, but this was crucial if things were going to work, and despite her earlier assurance I wanted to hear her say it.

'Oh God no, that was just an excuse.' She sounded quite casual and the way she smiled drove me crazy. 'I'd read about it some-where and it was the perfect diversion, don't you think?'

'What! You used it as an excuse? So why did you leave?'

'For heaven's sake, Thomas! Isn't it obvious? To protect you, of course. To remove you from the whole context of me doing that interview in case it all went wrong. The police told me they would act as soon as they heard the name in that last part of the interview, it was set up just half an hour before the interview screened, but that didn't work, as it turned out – he'd long gone.'

I tried to come to grips with this. 'I found out about that idea of yours about protecting me - either Boris or Jasper told me, I can't remember now. So many second-hand messages. But I thought the saviour syndrome thing was still in place.'

'God no, I've loved you from the word go, right from when we were talking in the cave. Telling you to go away and leave me there was the hardest thing – I thought I'd never see you again. But the sequence of events around the interview could have gone wrong. The screening of the interview and the rest, it was like putting together a jigsaw puzzle, so many moves. But I'll tell you the whole thing if you let me go to the toilet first. I can see you're just about to lift me off the floor and shake it out of me any second now.'

'Right, here it is,' she said a few minutes later and reached for the fresh mug of coffee I had made while I waited, this time with biscuits. 'The agreement we insisted on with the TV people made things quite complicated. It had to be, because I wasn't going to have my moment of glory ruined – anonymous glory but still satisfying, and I think I deserved it. The main part of the interview was recorded with me at Jasper's place and the interviewer in their studio in Auckland, as you could see. Jasper gave them an ultimatum when he arranged it, he did all that, so they'd never hear my normal voice, just in case.'

She thought for a moment, her eyes on the view. 'God, I've missed sitting here with you! Anyway, the rules were that they wouldn't be told where I was or who I was, and he would arrange the voice modification himself. And the best bit, the very final piece from me about who Box was, would be held back, and he'd send it to them while they screened the first part. They had no idea who they were talking to when he set this up.'

She grinned. 'You should have heard the negotiations, hilarious. They came up with everything they could think of to make him send that final segment along with the rest. They said things like, "How will we know you'll really send it?" and "What would we do if it didn't arrive?" Because he'd said the last part would nail the mastermind behind the cabal and they'd be the first to get that information. We decided the best way to get it done the way we wanted was to hold that part back.'

'Explain how this worked, will you? It sounds quite complicated.'

'OK then, this was how we laid it out. First we'd set up the interview via two locations, so we could control that I couldn't be seen, and we'd be in control of the voice modification. We gave them a few facts to base question on to get the interview going, but no details at all, nothing! Then Jasper would record another part with me still in the chair, which by the way he borrowed from the old guy in the apartment next door – they play chess together sometimes. But anyway, in that last segment I would reveal who Box was, and they'd get that later, but they wouldn't know the details in advance. It drove them crazy to think they had no control over it, just didn't fit their world view.' There was that naughty grin again.

'So when the interview was just about to start screening I called the Police Commissioner on his private cell phone, which Jasper got the number to from some list at his work. I called him from yet another burner phone I got in Auckland and said, "watch the very last part of this broadcast, and you'll find out who the leader of that cabal of corruption is, and you'll know who to arrest". He nearly choked, but there was nothing he could do apart from wait for the end of the interview. I had to wait until it was just about to start or the whole effect would be ruined, and the police might have stopped it being screened.'

'Very clever! But what if you hadn't been able to reach the Commissioner? He could have been out for dinner with his phone on mute. Did you have a contingency plan?'

'Of course. After that first call I called Carton's boss in Southland on *his* private number and told him the same thing.'

'And all the time I was moping around here, left out of the action, miserable and alone, thinking I might never see you again.'

She got up and came around my chair and put her arms around my neck from behind. 'I was keeping you safe. I thought if they arrested him straight after the interview, he would be out of action and you'd be safe. So he nearly got you, but you saved yourself.'

She went back to her chair, and I thought for a moment, wondered how much she knew. 'So you heard about that?'

'God yes, Jasper talked to me and Boris at the same time, like a conference call and told us about the drama. He didn't tell us the nitty-gritty details, but I hope you'll do that.'

The look she slanted my way was easy to read; she was expecting the whole story, but she might not get it. I had to think about it first.

'Later,' I said. 'When we've settled down a bit. Let's just enjoy being here together and not feeling threatened by anyone.'

'And now Carton's gone, that strange, vengeful man. Imagine him coming all this way to get revenge when the facts were out there already. But I suppose angry and desperate people do crazy things.'

<h1 style="text-align:center">45</h1>

Over lunch I reverted to the deal with the TV company, because it must have tested their patience to the limit, and I wondered how it had been resolved. 'It was lucky they gave in about your holding on to that last part. Being dictated to probably threw them right out of their comfort zone.'

'God, yes! In the end they had to give in, though, or we could have withheld the whole thing and just put it on YouTube or something. I think the clinching argument was Jasper telling them that the last part was crucial, and they would be the first to reveal what we had found – they couldn't resist. In the end he had to tell them a bit more, that it would reveal the mastermind behind the whole cabal set-up, and until they screened it that guy still thought he was totally anonymous and would get away with it. So we couldn't risk that his identity leaked out in advance – that clinched it.'

She sighed. 'And then, when the police called me and told me to go somewhere safe, because Carton had taken off a couple of days earlier, I realised I'd been wrong. He must have been stewing over the fact that his cabal was in pieces and the risk to himself, ever since we sent out those USBs - that was the trigger that set him off.' She sighed. 'So all my efforts to keep you safe were undone by him jumping the gun, no pun intended, and you could have got killed. I'm sorry!'

I could tell that the guilt complex was taking hold again, so we needed a change of scene. 'Let's go and sit on the sofa so I can give you a hug now and then.'

Once she was on the sofa I laid her down, sat down beside her bare feet and took hold of one, and she laughed. 'God, how I've missed that! A big warm hand holding my foot - best remedy for anything ever. Provided the hand is yours, of course.'

Later that evening we were at the dining table with the remains of dinner pushed to one side and another glass of wine each when Sam suddenly got up. 'Is any of that chocolate left? I'd love some dark chocolate right now.'

'Have a look in the pantry, it's probably where you put it after I bought it. I haven't eaten any since you left - the fun went out of having treats when you weren't here.'

'Yep, two big blocks, one dark and one milk chocolate, hardly touched,' said Sam from the pantry. 'I'd never heard of eating dark chocolate with this kind of red wine before, but Sasha knew. Her dad told her to try and it's delicious.'

We ate dark chocolate and drank more red wine and continued catching up. 'Tell me how you coped in Auckland, where you stayed and how you moved around. It seems incredible that you manged to do all these things, like sell the house in just a few weeks. Boris told me you had, which gave me a tiny sliver of hope. You wouldn't have felt very safe there, I don't think.'

She shook her head. 'Oh no, I didn't feel safe at all. I constantly checked the online media for news, but the frustrating thing was that I have no idea if Brown, or Johnson which he sometimes calls himself, has been arrested. Those that were arrested didn't get bail because they were regarded as flight risks, but no names were published, so I ticked off how many had got caught. There were nineteen names in that list, but I have no way of knowing if one of the two still on the loose is Brown.' She looked at me with the slightly stressed expression I knew well. 'Early on Dave said he'd checked somewhere online when I first gave him the files, and he confirmed all the list names were police, but there were no photos there – if there had been I'd know right away.'

She frowned into her glass, and I realised that she feared Brown far more than I had understood before.

'You were really scared of him then, when he was in the house? Did he do something to you? Did he hurt you that night?'

She made a face and sighed. 'It's probably irrational, but somehow it was really scary how concerned he was about the effect that death had on me, because right from the start I also felt that he was very dangerous. He didn't say or do anything to scare me, he was all concern and kindness, there was just a feeling of menace. I don't think I told you about the conversation in the kitchen that night, did I?'

'You said that he came to talk to you about how important it was that you didn't tell anyone, and the story about the huge drug investigation – and he said you were part of his team.'

'He went further than that, both that time and when he returned after the search of my house. It was creepy, it made me very uneasy. I know my Johanna persona gave him the impression that I would respond to a lot of personal stuff, sympathy and kindness. He told me I was a lovely woman and not to worry too much, and he asked if I was getting enough sleep – and he touched me. At one stage he held my hand in both his for far too long and it made me feel as if he'd threatened me, like a warning. And when he left he put both hands on my shoulders and kind of stroked me.'

I could easily imagine how disturbing this had been. 'It sounds horrible, like he combined kindness and underlying threat to control you. And you were alone in the house. I'm not surprised you need to find out if they've got him.'

'It's the final thing I need to stop constantly wondering if I'm safe, I think.' She smiled, determined not to continue talking about Brown, and I realised I had to do something about it, but for now we needed to change the subject. 'How did you manage to sell the house while you were keeping out of sight at Sasha's place?

'Jill came up with the perfect idea and bought a smartphone for me on a contract in her name. I organised everything from that phone except signing the house sale contract. Jill picked up the paperwork and brought it to me on the excuse that I had two broken ankles and couldn't go anywhere – lies and more lies. And then when the solicitors transferred the house sale money to my bank I went online from the new smart phone and transferred enough money to Jill, and she bought the car for me. It's registered and insured in her name, and I won't transfer the ownership to myself until we know for sure that everything is safe.'

'The perfect planner, as always – very smart. So nobody can track you via the car or the phone. And now only one thing remains - Brown.'

She nodded. 'I still dream about him. And it's no point telling me it's neurotic, I know it is. And let's be honest, I might be totally paranoid forever now, or I might just be the smartest and most security conscious person in the country. It's irrelevant, isn't it? It makes me feel good to make sure I'm safe however irrational my fear might seem to others. And before you think of it and ask how I got to Auckland safely without being picked up on CCTV anywhere – lovely Sasha took a couple of days off and picked me up from Jasper's as soon as that interview was recorded. She's so proud of herself, she'd hardly every driven outside Auckland and never such a distance.'

She grinned. 'I know Jasper told you I took him totally by surprise, the poor guy. He couldn't do a thing to stop me, just stood there at the crack of dawn in his boxer shorts and watched me walk out the door. I have apologised since, don't worry! So I've stayed with Sasha, because there are no kids at her place, who might talk about me, like at Jill's. We had a few evenings with Jill at Sasha's flat, which she's moved back to. It was lovely, nearly like normal life. It was only a few days I had to stay with her cousin - until I knew Carton was dead.'

'And very lucky that the house sold so quickly, too - it seems to have happened nearly instantly.'

'I know, not what I'd expected at all. The first tenants left, so I told Jill, who was the contact person for the rental agency, to say I was going to sell it. This was when I was first at Jasper's place, and I used his phone. The real estate agent said it would probably sell quickly, because it's like a collector's item even though it's quite run down. It needs a whole interior refurbish, but it sold faster than fast and for a surprising amount of money, far more than I would have thought.' She laughed. 'Not that I knew this, but apparently it's desirable because it's mid-century classic, which I gather means it really was designed and built in the early sixties, in that typical minimalist style of that era, it's not just a later copy. Emily and I shared that money of course, so I bought the car and put the rest into an investment account.'

I stood on the balcony in the dark and talked to Jasper, while Sam put her some of her things away. 'Can you find out who's been arrested? Sam is still scared that the one who called himself Brown will turn up one day. She's been counting down as they've arrested people and they're a couple short. And she doesn't know how to find out if they've locked him up yet. She doesn't know his real name or who to ask.'

'Easy!' said Jasper. 'Can I come for dinner tomorrow if Sam isn't too tired from all that driving? She said she was going to do it in one hit.'

'She stopped for the night when she got tired, so she got here this morning. I don't think she's getting enough sleep, probably because of how scared she is of Brown. And she really is, it's as clear as daylight. Come for dinner tomorrow, and could you bring pizza – I don't feel like shopping for Sam to cook something. Or we can have freezer food or pasta, your choice.'

'Pizza,' said Jasper. 'I'll find out about Brown. I bet the cops want to know which one he is too, after he and that mate of his carted that dead guy away. And where did they get rid of the body? I never thought of that before. Lots of facts still to emerge.'

We had just ended the call when Sam joined me on the balcony. 'What are you doing out here in the dark? You're not worrying about anyone watching the house, are you?'

'Just looking at the view and enjoying an evening with no wind. Let's go to bed.'

46

Jasper arrived with two pizzas, a giant one for him and me to share and a very small one for Sam. 'I know what she likes now, anchovies. I fed her on pizza and pasta nearly every day apart from the day you came over and she made that casserole, remember that?

Sam had been pleased to hear that Jasper was coming over, but I didn't tell her what I had asked him to do in case it wasn't possible. Now the look on his face made me think he might have some good news.

'So, here's the latest,' he said casually, carefully balancing a slice of pizza halfway to his mouth. 'They've locked Brown up.'

'Really? How do you know? Which one was he?' Sam was twitching with impatience, but she had to wait for answers while he chewed a giant mouthful.

'I used the names list to check all of them. It's a place I can access, which you can't, so don't try. I looked up all the names from that list one by one and by using your description I found him. The combination of his photo and his height did it in no time. He's real name is Garth Sallow, so then I checked the names of those arrested. Another thing you shouldn't try. Sallow sometimes uses the name Gareth Brown in other contexts, too – Brown was his mother's maiden surname.'

'What does that mean? Does he have a fake identity online or something?' I couldn't understand what he meant by that phrase, "other contexts". 'Is he involved in other illegal activities?'

'I don't know.' He looked thoughtful now. 'He's on a couple of social media sites as Gareth Brown. I've no idea why. Maybe I should make the authorities aware, so they can look into it. I'll do it from work - we sometimes give them bits of information we have access to.'

'Is that legal? Or don't laws apply to this mysterious place where you work?'

'Don't ask!' said Jasper, and I laughed. This is what he always says when I ask anything about his job.

Sam was looking absentmindedly at her plate and had made no comment on Jasper's findings, apart from saying, 'Great!'

Now she looked up and gave me her wicked smile before she turned to Jasper. 'Thomas says he won't tell me the details of what happened the night Carton came, but I'm sure you know more than what you told me over the phone. You'll tell me, won't you?'

'That's not what I said, I only said I'd tell you later, that's all.'

Jasper looked at me and then at Sam and said in disbelief, 'You'll tell her later? What's the point of that? Of course, you have to tell her. Typical action man stuff, she'll love it.'

So that's what we did, between us we told Sam the whole tale with all the details including the autopsy results and nobody ever had a more attentive listener. When we reached the end she had only one question, 'Where is that rock now?'

'On the floor just inside the front door, I think,' I said after a moment's thought. 'I'm sure that's where Jasper put it when he brought it back. I threw the surfboard tether away. I have a better one on the new surfboard I keep in the garage.'

She got up and returned with the round rock. 'What a perfect sphere! And very heavy – no wonder he fell backwards off that ledge. I want to go and see the knoll tomorrow. Have you been there, Jasper?'

'I'm over all this now, and no, I don't want to see it. I'll just have a look from the balcony next time I'm here in daylight.' Then he grinned. 'And Sam, about that rock. I think it should sit some-where prominent in here like an ornament - on that bookshelf perhaps. It will be a memento that only we understand. If anyone asks why you have it on the shelf, you say it's just a nice rock. I don't think it should go back to the basement.'

MANY THANKS

We hope you've enjoyed reading this story and would consider leaving a review on your favourite review site, or with the retailer you purchased from.

These are not only much appreciated, they also help other readers discover new authors.

For more about other titles from this author, please read on.

ALSO BY TINA CLOUGH

THE GIRL WHO LIVED TWICE

 What would you do if you woke up one morning and found that time had rewound exactly a year? Would you revisit your past mistakes and try to do better? Would you try to get revenge on those who had wronged you? Or would you use what you knew to get rich? When Mia finds herself in her own past, she must decide how best to use her pre-knowledge of one year's worth of events and personal issues.

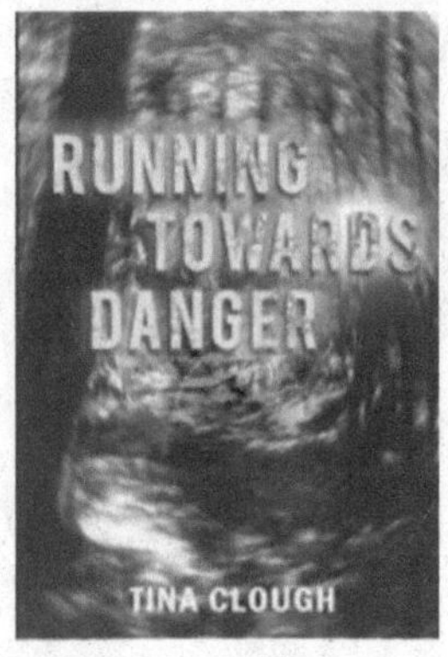

When Karen's flat-mate Nick is gunned down in front of her in the street her life is turned upside-down. Everything she thought she knew about him turns out to be a lie. She becomes a suspect in the police investigation and drug bosses think she knows where Nick has hidden a large sum of money. When her life is threatened, she decides to leave town and disappear.

Karen becomes Cara and creates an anonymous existence, severs all links to her past and adopts a cash-based way of life that leaves no electronic traces. But despite her careful planning danger still stalks her and she is forced to make dramatic choices in the face of threats and brutal violence.

Can she trust the man she is attracted to, or has he been sent by the killers to gain her confidence and find the money they believe she has?

THE CHINESE PROVERB

Book 1 - Hunter Grant Series

Army veteran Hunter Grant thought he had left war behind in Afghanistan – a conflict that left him with physical and psychological scars.

But finding an unconscious girl in the Northland bush and gradually untangling her story involves him in warfare of a different kind in his own country.

Hunter sets out to find and punish the man Dao calls Master, but he soon finds there is more to this story than enslavement. Before long he himself is being hunted by the overlord of a drug empire whose sole objective is to kill Dao because she knows too much.

Protecting her and waging war while trying to keep the police from stifling his enterprise takes all Hunter's ingenuity and determination and puts him in deadly jeopardy.

ONE SINGLE THING

Book 2 - Hunter Grant Series

Journalist Hope Barber disappears two weeks after returning to New Zealand from an assignment in Pakistan, leaving her front door open and her bag and phone inside. The police are tight-lipped about their reluctance to act, and Hunter Grant and Dao agree to help Hope's brother Noah find her. Details about Hope's time in Pakistan gradually emerge but only raise more questions.

Was Hope under surveillance?

Was she linked to terrorists?

And who is the man Hope called 'my stalker'?

FOLDED

Book 3 - Hunter Grant Series

First notes asking for help and folded into tiny origami shapes are found outside a city apartment building, then a physics textbook with tiny writing between the lines and then the woman who found them abruptly resigns and disappears. Are the notes asking for help real or is it a game? Hunter Grant, ex-army and with a pragmatic view of justice, reluctantly agrees to help find the missing woman.

Things get complicated when a high-powered lawyer arrives form the US, and shortly after his meeting with Hunter and Dao, a "cease and desist" letter arrives from the Cayman Islands. Inspector Bakker - a woman, who in Hunter's words "looks as if she would be useful in a brawl, provided she was on your side" - takes instant exception to his involvement and threatens to arrest him for interfering in an investigation.

Dao sets out alone on a dangerous mission, driven by a compulsive need to find out what has happened to the girl who wrote the notes, and Hunter looks death in the face when he decides to risk everything to put an end to the Darknet forces that threaten their lives.

THE SHADOW BROKER

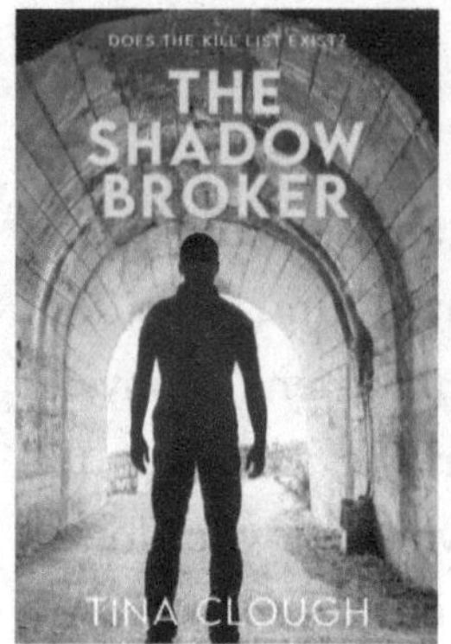

It is 2026 and individual freedoms are severely curtailed, with state surveillance everywhere. State Security has a Watch List, and being on it means that nothing you do or say escapes the authorities, but does the Kill List really exist? And if it does, how would you know if you were on it?

Coded messages on a found burner phone, top-level government corruption and a shadowy mastermind who calls himself The Broker. In this climate of state control, three unlikely friends start quietly looking for connections and set in motion a deadly game of hide and seek that will change their lives forever.

Trying to uncover the truth means risking your life, and nothing is more dangerous than searching for evidence of government corruption.

LETTERS FROM THE PAST

Letters from the Past is a series of stand-alone novels where a letter from or about the past reveals something that changes a woman's perceptions of herself or of her family, and that affects her outlook on life.

These books are such fun to write, and I am always working on the next title in this series. I hope you will enjoy reading them as much as I enjoy writing them!

Tina

Having had nobody in her life since her husband died, Lara unexpectedly finds herself involved with three men. One is planning to use her, one she plans to use for her own ends, and one becomes a "friend-with-benefits" with surprising results. Sometimes a quiet schoolteacher is not all she seems at first glance.

Callista experiences an event of apparent ESP at the Okehampton Castle ruins and becomes a media sensation, but the effect it has on her life is dramatic. How do two people, one calm. one seriously claustrophobic, who feel they are poles apart, cope for an hour and a half in total darkness in a stalled lift? And can they handle the consequences?

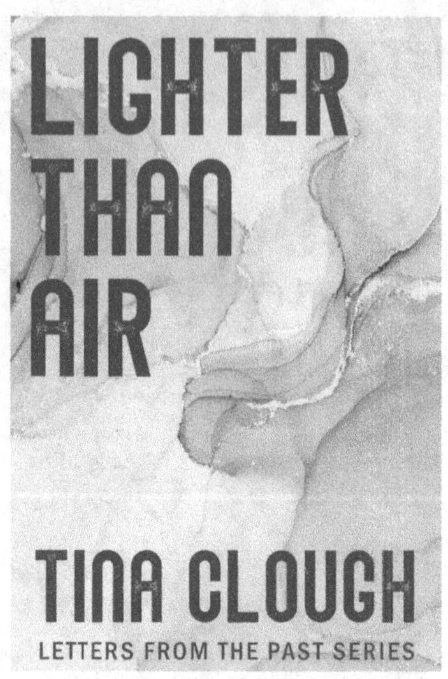

Sofia's life is in turmoil: a difficult diva mother, a letter with a confession about a family killing and having to accept help from a man she loathes when she is injured. Can reluctant attraction turn into love?

Who is the stranger living in the empty house Miranda inherited from her grandmother? Why is he living like a secretive recluse in someone else's house? Reckless Miranda decides to confront him, and what she discovers prompts her to set out on a fearless quest to bring justice to a man who has given up hope. But is the gamble too great or a risk worth taking?

When Emma finds an old letter in a library book she is instantly intrigued, but by researching the origin of the letter she unwittingly opens the door to danger and becomes the target for threats and harassment. Nearly desperate, she takes a leap of blind faith into the unknown and accepts an offer of help from a stranger - but can she trust him?

Jamie, an ardent protester against the gigantic Vista Resort development and Leo Masters, the high-powered developer, seem unlikely to ever agree on anything. But unexpected coincidences and chance brings them together in a fragile state of mutual respect. Will courage and kindness resolve the situation, or do they need help?

After a bizarre accident with ESP overtones, the media haunt Arapera. But can she trust an offer of help from a man she has only met once? Or will she regret it for the rest of her life if she doesn't take the chance? Sometimes life is a knife-edge balance between staying safe and taking risks, and there is no way of predicting if the gamble is worth it.

When crime-writer Saskia finds an unconscious stranger, she has a strange and strong emotional connection. Pretending to be his cousin and with no thought for the consequences, she spends weeks at his hospital bedside. But what will happen when he wakes and discovers she has invaded his life, breached his privacy and made crucial decisions on his behalf?

ABOUT THE AUTHOR

Tina Clough grew up in Sweden and now lives in New Zealand; dividing her time between writing fiction and translating and editing medical research papers.

Between working and writing she looks after an acre of fruit trees, vegetable gardens and roaming hens.

Apart from reading her interests include photography, wine, growing organic vegetables, making jam and kayaking.

https://lightpoolpublishing.com

9 781738 627264